THE Hot BLOOD SERIES

KISS AND KILL

The Original Erotic Horror Anthology
Edited by Jeff Gelb and Michael Garrett

$5.99 U.S.
$7.99 CAN.

COLLECT ALL THE BOOKS IN THE *HOT BLOOD* SERIES

HOT BLOOD

HOTTER BLOOD

HOTTEST BLOOD

DEADLY AFTER DARK

SEEDS OF FEAR

STRANGER BY NIGHT

FEAR THE FEVER

KISS AND KILL

Available from Pocket Books

Books Edited by Jeff Gelb and Michael Garrett

Hotter Blood*
Hottest Blood*
The Hot Blood Series: Deadly After Dark*
The Hot Blood Series: Seeds of Fear*
The Hot Blood Series: Stranger by Night*
The Hot Blood Series: Fear the Fever*
The Hot Blood Series: Kiss and Kill*

Books Edited by Jeff Gelb

Hot Blood* *(with Lonn Friend)*
Shock Rock*
Shock Rock II*
Fear Itself

By Jeff Gelb

Specters

By Michael Garrett

Keeper

*Published by POCKET BOOKS

THE Hot BLOOD SERIES

KISS AND KILL

Edited by Jeff Gelb and Michael Garrett

POCKET STAR BOOKS

New York   London   Toronto   Sydney   Tokyo   Singapore

An *Original* Publication of POCKET BOOKS

A Pocket Star Book published by
POCKET BOOKS, a division of Simon & Schuster Inc.
1230 Avenue of the Americas, New York, NY 10020

ISBN: 0-671-53766-0

First Pocket Books printing March 1997

10 9 8 7 6 5 4 3 2 1

POCKET STAR BOOKS and colophon are registered trademarks of Simon & Schuster Inc.

Cover art by Gerber Studio

Printed in the U.S.A.

Copyright Notices

To Claire Zion, a savvy, brave editor who knew a good thing when she read it—with our thanks, respect, and admiration

CONTENTS

CONTENTS

PREFACE

What gets your hot blood boiling?

Discovering that your lover is more dead than alive? A sex partner who needs pain to feel loved? Coveting your best friend's wife until you discover there's more to her than meets the eye?

If so, you'll find it here. And it's only the tip of the iceberg in this eighth edition of the *Hot Blood* series.

Some say eight is enough. But not in this case. We promise there will be more bedtime stories to come as the *Hot Blood* series continues.

Sweet screams.

Jeff Gelb
Michael Garrett

KISS AND KILL

HEROINE

Graham Masterton

*H*e propped his bicycle up against the side of the Dog & Duck and went inside. The old oak-beamed pub was hot and noisy and much more crowded than usual. Bombing operations had been stopped for two weeks to allow the aircrews to rest and the riggers to repair all of the damaged aircraft. Through the haze of cigarette smoke, he could see McClung, his ball-turret gunner, and Marinetti, his navigator, playing darts on the other side of the bar, and one of his waist gunners getting intense with a ruddy-faced girl from Bassingbourn village.

He elbowed his way to the bar. As he did so, he jogged the arm of a girl in a rusty-colored tweed suit and spilled her cider.

"Hey, watch it!" she said, turning around.

He held up both hands in surrender. "I'm sorry, that was clumsy of me. Let me buy you another."

"Oh, don't worry," she said in her clipped BBC accent, brushing down her lapels with her handkerchief. "It wasn't much."

"Well, let me buy you another one anyhow. Just for the sake of the special relationship."

"I can't do that," she teased him. "We haven't been introduced."

He beckoned to Tom, the landlord, a doughy-faced man with a ponderous way of talking who always reminded him of Oliver Hardy. "Tom, do you know this young lady?"

"This young lady here? 'Course I do. Anne Browne. Major Browne's youngest."

He took her hand. "Pleased to make your acquaintance, Miss Browne. My name's Clifford Eager II, but you can call me Cliff."

"I think *Eager* would be more appropriate, don't you?" She smiled.

Cliff ordered a pint of Flowers and another half of cider for Anne. He offered her a Lucky and lit it for her. "Major Browne's youngest, huh?" he asked her. "How many others are there?"

"Four, all told."

"All girls? And all as pretty as you?"

"Now then, Eager."

But the fact was, she was not only pretty, she was *very* pretty, she was showgirl pretty, and she obviously knew it, too. She had a pale, heart-shaped face, with wide gray-blue eyes the color of sky when you see it reflected in a puddle. She had a short, pert nose. Her lips were full and painted glossy red, and they had a permanent pout, as if she had just finished kissing somebody. Her hair was chestnut-brown, shiny and curly, and fastened with two barrettes. She was quite petite, no more than five foot four. Underneath her severe utility suit she wore a soft white sweater which couldn't conceal a bosom that was more than a little too large for a girl so slim.

"You want to sit down?" he asked her. They pushed

their way through the jostling, laughing throng of customers until they found a small table in the corner, underneath a hunting print of the *View Hulloa!* In the public bar, a rowdy group of American pilots were singing "Tramp, tramp, tramp, the boys are marching," with increasingly ribald words.

"What's a respectable girl like you doing in a den of iniquity like this?" Cliff asked her.

"I'm meeting a friend. I'm going away tomorrow, and she was going to lend me one of her dresses."

"You're going away? Anywhere interesting?"

"Torquay, that's all. I've got a job there, in an old people's home."

"I shall miss you."

"Good gracious, you don't even know me."

"That's why I'm going to miss you. I meet the best-looking girl in the whole of East Anglia, and what happens? She leaves me and goes off to Torquay."

"Well, I expect you'll be busy again soon."

Cliff put his finger to his lips. "Shh, mustn't talk about it. But, sure. They're giving us a break after Blitz Week. Then it's going to be back to the old routine. Get up, fly to Germany, drop bombs, come back again, wash your teeth, go to bed."

She drew sharply at her cigarette, her eyes watching him through the smoke. He was handsome in a big, undisciplined way. He had a broad face and strong cheekbones, and deep-set, slightly hooded eyes. He was wearing a leather flying jacket with a lamb's-wool collar. She couldn't imagine him in a suit.

"Where do you come from?" she asked him. "Is it the South? You have a very drawly kind of accent."

"I come from Memphis. Well, close to Memphis. A little place called Ellendale. It has a store and a church and a movie theater, and that's just about the sum total."

"I'll bet you can't wait to get back there."

"Soon as we've done what we came here to do."

She paused. Then, unexpectedly, she took hold of his hand. "Are you afraid of dying?" she asked him. "I think I am."

He grinned at her. "Hey, you don't have to be afraid of dying. You're going to be okay, down there looking after those old folks."

"Well, of course. I just wondered, that's all." But still she didn't take her hand away.

Cliff waited for a moment, and then he said, "Listen—I'm *always* afraid of dying, if you must know. I can never sleep the night before we fly, and I spend the whole time saying my prayers. When you're up there, you don't have too much time to worry about it. You're too busy getting yourself there and getting yourself back again, and trying not to bump into the other airplanes all around you. But there was one time when we were hit by flak over Emden, and we lost the whole of our nose section. How we managed to fly that baby back to Bassingbourn I shall never know. See this gray hair, right on the side here? I looked in the mirror after that mission, and there it was."

Anne crushed out her cigarette in the big Guinness ashtray. "If I ask you something," she said, "will you answer yes or no, nothing else; and if the answer's no, will you say no more about it, and pretend that I didn't say a word?"

Cliff started to smile, but then he realized that whatever she was going to say, she was utterly serious about it. "All right," he agreed. "I think I can manage that."

"Tonight, will you sleep with me?"

He opened his mouth, and then he closed it again. He looked around to see if anybody else had heard her, but they obviously hadn't. They were singing

"Run, Rabbit, Run" and stamping their feet. He looked back at Anne, and she still had the same intense expression on her face, and she was grasping his hand so tightly that her nails were digging into his skin.

"Are you sure that's what you want to do?" he asked her.

She nodded.

"Don't you have a boyfriend or anything? What's he going to say?"

"Nothing. We're only chums."

"Well, I don't know, Anne, you're a beautiful girl, but—"

"You're too religious, is that it? You're a Southern Baptist or something?"

"Anne, I don't know what to say."

"All you have to say is yes or no. Is that too difficult?"

Cliff took a deep breath. Then he said, "Okay, then. Yes. I may be stupid, but I'm not *that* stupid."

Tom had three rooms upstairs at the Dog & Duck. Two of them were occupied, one by a man who was traveling in laxatives and the other by a wiry elderly couple on a hiking holiday. Cliff had seen them in the saloon bar, poring over prewar Ordnance Survey maps and arguing with each other in tense, sibilant hisses. "No, we *can't* go through Little Eversden, it'll take us *miles* out of our way."

The third room was the smallest, overlooking the pub's backyard, where all the barrels were stacked and the dog was kenneled. It was wallpapered with faded brown flowers and furnished with a cheap varnished chest of drawers and a single bed covered by a pink, exhausted quilt with a tea stain on it in the shape of Ireland. On the wall above the bed hung a print of a First World War soldier saying good-bye to his wounded horse—*Good-bye, Old Pal.*

"Cheerful," said Cliff, nodding toward the picture.

Anne gave a nervous little laugh. She sat on the edge of the bed with her hands folded and looked up at him with an expression that he couldn't read at all. It wasn't demure, but on the other hand it wasn't the expression he would have expected to see on the face of a girl who had just invited a total stranger to bed.

"I hope you don't think that I've ever done this before," she said. Her hair shone in the light from the bedside lamp. The lamp had a pretense parchment shade, scorched on one side, with a picture of a galleon on it.

"I don't know what I think," said Cliff. "All I know is that you're a very pretty girl and I'm a very lucky guy."

He took off his steel-bracelet wristwatch and laid it on top of the nightstand.

"It's funny, that, isn't it?" said Anne. "The first thing that people do before they make love is take their watches off . . . as if time doesn't matter anymore."

Cliff took off his flying jacket and hung it on the hook on the back of the door. "Do you want to switch the light off?" he asked her.

"No." she mouthed.

He sat down on the bed next to her. "I feel kind of strange," he admitted. "We haven't even kissed yet."

"Well, then, let's kiss."

He put his arm around her and drew her closer. He looked directly into her eyes, as if it would help him to understand her, but all he could see was the blue-gray rainwater color of her irises, and his own reflection. He kissed her very softly on the lips, scarcely brushed her, but that was enough. They kissed again, much more urgently this time, and her tongue found its way into his mouth and licked at his palate and his tongue. He kissed her cheeks and her nose and her eyes and her neck, and he felt his penis begin to rise inside his shorts.

He took hold of her fluffy white sweater and lifted it over her head. For a moment, with her arms raised and her eyes covered, she looked as if she were in a position of bondage. But then she emerged, her face flushed and smiling. "Here . . . stand up," he said, and lifted her onto her feet. Without her high heels, she stood no taller than his second shirt button.

He unbuttoned her red tweed skirt and tugged down the zipper. Then he slid the thin straps of her satin slip off her shoulders, so that it slithered to the floor. She held him around the neck and kissed him again, dressed in nothing but her brassiere, her satin step-ins, her garter belt, and her sheer tan nylons. Her brassiere was slightly too small for her, so that her breasts bulged out on either side. In her deep, soft cleavage nestled a silver medallion on a fine silver chain.

Cliff's hands were broad and big-fingered, and he had difficulty unfastening her brassiere, especially since it was too tight. "Shoot—this is worse than trying to unwrap chewing gum with your flying gloves on." Anne laughed and kissed him on the nose, and reached behind with both hands to unfasten it for him. Her bare breasts came out of the cups like two warm, white milk puddings, with wide aureolas of the palest pink. He cupped one breast with his hand and gently circled the ball of his thumb around her nipple, so that it stiffened and knurled.

He trailed the fingers of his other hand all the way down the curve of her back, and around the cheeks of her bottom. She shivered and came in closer. When his fingers stroked her between the thighs, he found that her step-ins were already slippery and wet. He took hold of the thin elastic and drew them down her thighs. Then he picked her up in his arms and laid her on the quilt. Her breasts spread sideways, and he took them in his hands and kissed them, sucking her nipples and flicking them with the tip of his tongue.

While he did so, she reached down and started to unbutton his shirt.

"You're beautiful," she said, in the same way he had said it to her.

He stripped off his shirt, dragged off his socks, and unbuckled his belt. In a few seconds he was completely naked, kneeling between her glossy nylon-sheathed knees. His body was white-skinned but very muscular, with a cross of dark hair between his nipples. There was a white scar on his left shoulder where he had been hit by shrapnel over Emden. His stomach was so flat that it made his stiffened penis look even bigger than it was, with its purple helmet and its thick, veined shaft.

She reached out and gently touched it with her pink-painted fingernails. Cliff couldn't take his eyes off her, and he quivered when she drew her nail all the way down the underside of his erection and lightly scratched his tightly wrinkled testes. A single drop of clear, sparkling fluid appeared at the opening of his penis, and she collected it with her finger as if she were collecting dew from a mushroom, and tasted it.

As she did so, she opened her thighs, and within the dark fur of her pubic hair, her vaginal lips opened with a soft but audible click, revealing a crimson opening that was brimming with juice.

And then he thought: *Holy shit—no rubber.*

She took hold of his shoulders and drew him toward her. For a moment he hesitated, and she felt his hesitation. "What's wrong?" she whispered. "Don't tell me you don't want to do it."

"Listen—I don't have any rubbers. Well, I do, but they're back at the base. Maybe I could go down and ask one of the guys if he—"

She smiled and shook her head. At the same time, she grasped his penis and luxuriously rubbed it up and down. "I don't want you to use a rubber. I want to feel your naked cock inside me."

"But come on now . . . what if you get pregnant?"

"Then all the better. That will give me one more reason to stay alive."

With her other hand, she reached between her legs and parted her wavelike lips even wider, and guided his penis so that the head of it was nestling between them. He looked down at her, and he thought that he was probably as close to heaven as he ever would be. Then, she dug her fingernails into his buttocks and pulled him into her, and he wasn't even close, he was there.

They made love all night, and she didn't want to stop. The stained-oak headboard knocked against the wallpaper so persistently that Tom came and told them to move the bed away from the wall. "You can shag all you like, but the rest of us don't want to hear it."

When Cliff was exhausted, Anne knelt between his legs to suck and lick at his softened penis. She succeeded in cramming him all into her mouth at once, balls and everything. Then she sat astride his face so that his own semen dripped out of her vagina and onto his forehead. "I anoint you," she said.

Toward dawn, she fell asleep against his back, with one of her fingers deeply inserted into his anus. He slept, too, and because of the blackout curtains, neither of them realized it was morning until they heard the thunderous banging of beer kegs being dropped into the yard outside. They sat up simultaneously and stared at each other.

"Jesus, it's eight-thirty. I have a briefing at nine."

"And I've got a train to catch."

They climbed out of bed, and Cliff pulled the curtains open. It was a bright morning, and he had to lift his hand to shield his eyes. His face was puffy and pale, and his back and thighs were covered in red scratches. Anne's lips were swollen, and there were chafe marks on the white flesh just above her stocking tops, from Cliff's stubble.

She came up to him and put her arms around him. Her breasts swung, and her nipples grazed his stomach. "If I never meet you ever again, I want to say thank you," she said.

"Oh, come on, we'll meet again," he chided her, and then realized what he had said. "Don't know where, don't know when . . ."

"Well, perhaps," she said.

"What do you mean, 'perhaps'? Give me your address in Torquay. I have three days' furlough coming up soon. I could visit you."

"I don't know the address yet. It's called Sunnybank, but I don't know which road."

"You're not going to vanish and not give me any way of getting in touch with you? Not after last night?"

"I wasn't looking for any kind of attachment."

"Oh, really? I thought we were pretty attached. Most of the time, anyhow."

She kissed him and curled herself into him in a way that no girl had ever done to him before, almost as if she wanted to be a part of him. "Eager . . . that wasn't the reason I wanted to do it."

"So, what reason?"

"Please, Eager. Don't ask me. I don't want either of us ever to find out."

They stood close together by the window, and outside the huge white cumulus clouds sailed through the morning air, fully rigged to cross the North Sea to Holland, and to Germany, and even beyond. Cliff watched them and couldn't bear to think that he and Anne were going to be parted, that he might never touch her again, not even once. During the night, their intimacy had become complete, as if they had crawled through each other's bodies like potholers down some dark, wet sluice. They had done almost everything that two lovers are capable of doing to each other, and more.

Eventually, however, Anne touched his lips with her fingertips and said, "I have to go. There's a train from Royston at nine-fifteen."

"Do you have time for breakfast?" Cliff asked her. "When he can get the bacon, Tom does a great bacon and eggs, when he can get the eggs."

She shook her head. "Honestly, I'll be late."

"Then do you mind if I do?"

He picked her up in his arms and carried her back to the bed. He laid her on the twisted sheets and opened her legs. Then he licked her, very slowly and sensually, all around her clitoris. He probed the tip of his tongue into her urethra and finally plunged it as deeply as he could into her vagina. She lay motionless while he did it, one hand resting very lightly on his shoulder, staring at the ceiling.

They parted outside the pub. Although the day was bright, there was a stiff wind blowing, and her scarf flapped.

"Cheerio then," she said.

"Cheerio."

She took hold of his hand and momentarily covered

it with hers. When she took it away again, he found that he was holding the silver medallion that she had worn around her neck. On the other side of the road, a gaggle of geese were honking loudly as a postwoman cycled past. "What's this for?" asked Cliff.

"Well." She shrugged. "Keepsake."

He held it up, and it flashed in the sunlight. "What is it?"

"St. Catherine. She's my guardian saint."

"Wasn't she broken on a wheel or something?"

"That's right. But no matter how much she suffered, she never denied her faith. She was a heroine."

A bus appeared in the distance, a toytown bus, cream-and-white. It came closer and closer across the wide, flat countryside, and all the time Anne said nothing, but smiled as if she were going into Royston for an hour or two to do some shopping, instead of disappearing out of Cliff's life forever.

It was only after she had boarded the bus, and he saw her sitting at the back with her hand half-covering her mouth, that he realized tears were streaming down her face.

For the remaining four days of the rest-and-recuperation period that had followed Blitz Week, Cliff immersed himself in planning, organizing, and flying practice. He worked almost as hard as he had during the weeks when the Eighth Air Force had been bombing deep into Germany every single day. His ground crew took to calling him Cliff Hangar, because he was always hanging around the hangars.

He was doing everything he could to keep himself busy, and not to think about Anne. But he couldn't get her out of his mind: the way she had felt when she was lying in his arms, the way she tasted, the way she laughed. What haunted him most of all was the way she had been so demanding and yet so lacking in guile. She had only been going to Torquay to nurse some old folk, and surely there were plenty of men in Torquay. Why had she acted as if she wanted to live through a whole lifetime of sexual experience in just one night?

Everywhere he went, he carried her St. Catherine medallion. It dangled from the switches above his head when the 379th Bombardment Group resumed attacks on the shipyards at Kiel, the Heinkel aircraft factory at Warnemünde, and the Focke-Wulf factory at Oschersleben, only ninety miles southwest of Berlin. He didn't know whether the medallion brought him good luck, but after eleven daylight missions to the Ruhr, the worst damage his Fort had sustained was a flak-riddled starboard elevator.

In October, the weather closed in, and for days on end the East Anglian countryside was swept with rain and muffled with dirty, low-flying clouds. Three missions were attempted, and each time most of them were called back, because the cloud over Germany was even worse—sometimes rising up from ground zero to thirty thousand feet. They managed another light raid on Oschersleben, but they spent most of their time waiting for the weather to clear, with rain dripping off the plexiglass noses of their grounded Forts.

One dark Thursday lunchtime, Cliff finished his twice-weekly letters to his mother and his brother Paul, handed them over to the censor, and then cycled to the Dog & Duck for something to eat. The cloud was so low that he was actually cycling through it, actually breathing it in. The countryside all around him was almost invisible, so that he felt as if he were cycling through a bone-chilling dream. The grass on the roadside was a vivid, unnatural green.

He reached the pub and left his bicycle where he always did, propped against the wall. He walked in, and the saloon bar was almost empty, except for a ruddy-cheeked old farmer who grew potatoes and curly kale thereabouts and a foxy-faced British squaddie who was smoking roll-ups as if he had only fifteen minutes left to live.

Tom came up to the bar and asked him, "What'll it be?" as if he were asking Stan Laurel about his prospects with his sister-in-law.

"Pint of Flowers, please, Tom. And what have you got to eat?"

"Cottage pie. More cottage than pie, though." He meant that there was far more potato than meat.

"How about a cheese sandwich?"

He sat at the bar drinking his beer and eating his mousetrap sandwich, listening to "Music While You Work" on the wireless, turned up just loud enough to be irritating and not loud enough to be enjoyable.

He had almost finished when the door at the back of the pub swung open, and he saw somebody standing in the stairwell. The day was so dark that all he could see was a silhouette, limned by grayish light, but there was something about the figure's hair that gave him a cold sliding feeling all the way down his back.

"Anne?" he said. "Anne, is that you?"

The figure remained where it was for a moment or two and then turned without a word and climbed up the stairs. The wireless was playing, "Sally, Sally, pride of our alley . . . and more than the whole world to me . . ." Cliff climbed off his barstool and made his way to the back of the pub. Tom didn't pay him any attention—the access to the toilets was through the same door. Cliff reached the foot of the stairs just in time to hear the latch of one of the upstairs bedrooms closing. He hesitated, listening, and he was sure that he could hear someone walking across the creaky floorboards of the back bedroom and sitting on the bed with a bronchial groaning of bedsprings. He grasped the banister and mounted the stairs two at a time, as quietly as he could, until he reached the landing.

He listened again, but all he could hear was the wireless, and in the distance the harsh, lonely droning of a B-17's engine being tested.

He approached the back bedroom door and tapped on it. "Anne?" he called. After all, if it wasn't Anne, all he had to do was apologize. But supposing she didn't answer?

"Anne, it's Cliff."

He waited almost a minute more. He was about to go back downstairs, but then he thought: *Damn it, what am I scared of?* He opened the latch and pushed the door halfway open, giving a loud, false cough as he did so. "Hullo there? Anybody there?"

Although the curtains were drawn back, the room was almost impenetrably gloomy. All Cliff could see through the window was fog. It looked just the same as it had before, with its dull brown wallpaper and its cheap varnished bureau. *Good-bye, Old Pal* was still hanging on the wall above the bed. And *on* the bed lay Anne, completely naked, with her hands held behind her head.

"Anne?" he said, closing the door and sitting down next to her. "Why didn't you answer me? I nearly gave it up."

She gave him a faint, tired smile. "I knew you'd come," she told him. She took one of the hands out from behind her head as if his appearance had freed it for her. He leaned forward and kissed her, and she ran her fingers into his hair. "I knew you wouldn't let me down."

He reached for the bedside lamp with its galleon shade, but Anne held his wrist and said, "Don't . . .

15

not this time. I'm not really looking my best." And she was right. As Cliff's eyes grew gradually accustomed to the gloom, he could see that she was desperately pale. The only color she had was in two plum-colored circles under her eyes and two hectic spots of crimson on her cheekbones. They looked more like bruises than rouge.

"Honey, what's been happening to you?" Cliff asked her. "Are you all right? You look like somebody beat up on you."

She lifted her head to kiss him again, and as she did so she winced in obvious pain. "I'm all right, really I am. I'm just pleased to see you."

"I want to know who did this. It wasn't that old boyfriend of yours, was it? The one you were 'just chums' with? I'll have his ass in a sling."

"Sh-sh-sh!" Anne quietened him, her finger pressed to her lips. "It was an accident, that's all. A car, in the blackout. It was all my own fault. I don't want you to be angry, darling. I just want you to stay here and make love to me."

Cliff glanced toward the door. "I don't know . . . have you told Tom that you're here?"

"It doesn't matter. All you have to do is lock the door."

Cliff kissed her again, and then again. "Do you know what?" he said. "I think you're amazing. And this time I happen to have some rubbers with me."

"You don't have to bother about those."

"Well, if you're sure . . ."

He stripped off his flying jacket and his gray cable-knit sweater. It was so cold in the bedroom that his breath smoked, and he wondered how Anne could stand to lie there on the quilt with nothing on at all. He pulled off his pants, and already his cock was rising. "Come on, let's get under the covers."

"I want to look at you first."

He knelt on the bed between her legs. She ran her fingers around his shoulders and down his chest. She sat up, wincing again, and kissed his nipples. She bit them, too, and he said, *"Ouch!"*

"Why don't you do that to me?" she asked him. Those rainwater eyes were unusually dark, the pupils widely dilated.

"You mean, *bite* you?"

She held up her left breast in her hand, offering it to him. He looked at her for a moment, very unsure of what she really wanted him to do. Then he tentatively kissed her nipple, and sat up straight again, smiling. In return, however, she gripped his penis so hard that her nails dug right into it.

"Hey, ouch, Jesus," he said, trying to pull away, but she gripped him even harder.

"Why don't you bite me?" she repeated. "You're not frightened, are you? I'm only a stupid tart with no morals at all! What does it matter if you bite me? What does it matter what you do to me?"

Still Cliff hesitated, but then Anne took hold of his balls and caught the skin with her fingernails, pulling it upward. It hurt, but in a strange way he was beginning to find it exciting, too, and his penis swelled even harder. He bent forward and took her nipple between his lips. He could feel it stiffen against his tongue. She clutched his balls even more painfully, so he nipped her nipple between his front teeth.

"Harder," she demanded. "You can bite it right off if you want."

He bit it harder, and she gasped, and lifted her hips.

"Hey, look. I'm sorry, I didn't mean to do it so doggone hard."

"Harder," she panted. "For God's sake, darling, do it harder!"

17

He took a deep breath and then bit her nipple so hard that he tasted blood. She let out a high, strangled yelp and bucked up and down on the bed so that the springs scrunched. Cliff bit her again and again, first one breast and then the other, biting them until he could almost feel his incisors closing together, and then chewing them with his molars. All the time she gasped and shivered, and there was a thin slide of blood coming out of the side of her mouth where she had bitten her tongue. Cliff lifted his head and said, "Anne—Anne, listen to me—I can't hurt you anymore—I'm just not—"

But Anne opened her legs wide and said, "Fuck me, Eager. Fuck me just as hard as you can."

"Anne, I—"

"Fuck me, you bastard, if you care for me at all!"

He took his penis in his fist and guided it into her wide-open vulva. He had never known a girl so wet. Her upper thighs were smothered in juice, and even the quilt was soaking. He thrust himself into her as hard as he could, but even that didn't seem to be enough for her. She rolled him over and sat on top of him, straight upright, so that he penetrated her as deeply as he could. With every thrust he could feel the neck of her womb touching the head of his cock, and with every thrust she shuddered and wept.

She reached behind him and tried to force two or three sharp-nailed fingers into his anus, and it was then that his muscles tightened and he climaxed, far too soon, but he simply couldn't help it.

Anne literally hissed with rage and disappointment. "You bastard! You complete bastard! How could you do that to me?" She pummeled his shoulders with her fists and then started to tear at his chest hair.

"For Christ's sake, Anne—"

But she climbed off him and worked her way up

until she was kneeling over his face. "Now bite me some more. Bite me *there.*"

"Anne, forget it, honey. I'm not going to do it. I'm not that kind of guy."

In a sudden and explosive rage, she seized hold of his hair and sat down on his face with all of her weight, so that her vulva was forced right into his mouth. She dragged her hips from side to side so that her lips were scraped against his teeth, and her pubic bone bruised his nose. All he could taste was salty blood and starchy semen.

This time, he took hold of her wrists, gripped them tight, and bodily twisted her away. She hit her head against the wall, but he rolled off the bed and stood up, panting for breath.

"What the hell?" he asked her. He wiped his mouth with the back of his hand.

She stayed where she was, with her back turned to him, shivering, saying nothing.

"Come on, Anne, what the hell is this all about? I can't hurt you. I love you, if you must know. You can't expect me to— Jesus, I don't know."

"You love me?" she asked, without looking around. "You really love me?"

"What do you think, goddammit?"

With her fingertip, she traced the pattern of one of the brown flowers on the wallpaper. "If you really love me, then you'll do what I ask."

Cliff stood on the threadbare rug beside the bed, wondering what to do. In the end, he felt so cold that he pulled on his clothes. "Listen," he repeated, "I love you."

Still she said nothing. He looked at his watch and realized that he should have been back on base more than twenty minutes ago. He bent over and kissed her shoulder, but she didn't respond. Her fingertip kept on tracing the pattern of the flower, over and over, as if she were trying to memorize it.

"Major Browne?" he asked, one hand clamped against his ear to suppress the deafening drone of a taxiing Fort.

"That's correct. How can I help you?"

"I'm not too sure. My name's Captain Cliff Eager. I'm stationed at Bassingbourn."

"American, by the sound of it."

"Yes, sir. That's right. Well, the truth of it is, I met your daughter Anne just before she left for Torquay."

"Oh, you did, did you?"

"Yes, sir. We sort of struck up a friendship. But I saw her this afternoon, and I have to tell you that she didn't look too good. I'm worried about her."

There was a lengthy pause. Then, "You say you saw her this afternoon?"

"Yes, sir. Anything wrong with that?"

"Well, nothing. Except that she's still in Torquay."

"She couldn't have come back to see you? I mean, maybe she's on her way now."

"Impossible, I'm afraid. Her contract won't allow it. You must have made a mistake."

"A mistake? What kind of mistake?"

"Well, you know, mistaken identity. One young English rose looks very much like another, don't you know?"

"You're trying to tell me that I didn't meet Anne, I met some other girl who just happened to look like her?"

"It's the only feasible explanation, old man."

"Major Browne, I hate to contradict you, and I hate to shock you, too, but Anne and I were more than just good chums. And we were more than just good chums this afternoon."

Another pause. Then, "Look here, Captain Eagle or

whatever your name is, what you are describing is not only impossible but scurrilous. I seriously recommend that you forget all about Anne and get back to the business that your government sent you here for. Otherwise I shall have to have strong words with your commanding officer."

"But, you listen here, Major—"

"No, Captain, you listen to me. Anne has gone to Torquay, and she has not yet returned. And if you know what's good for you, you'll believe that, too. For her good, if not for your own."

Cliff hung up and sat for a long time staring at the telephone as if it were going to ring, and it would be Anne.

A week and a half later, it did, and it was.

Cliff had just returned from a mission over Brunswick and Halberstadt, and he and his crew were so tired that they were hallucinating. Everything had gone wrong. Unexpected easterly winds had slowed them down on their way to the target, and the three-stream bomber force had failed to rendezvous with its fighter escorts as they crossed the Dutch border. Altogether the U.S. Eighth Air Force had lost sixty-five aircraft that night, six hundred fifty men, and Cliff had lost so many friends that he couldn't even count them.

When the phone rang and he heard her saying, "Eager? Eager, is that you?" he couldn't believe it at first.

"Anne? Is that really you? Where are you calling from?"

"The Dog & Duck, where else? Aren't you coming to see me?"

"Your father said you were still in Torquay."

"Well, let's put it this way. I am, and I'm not."

"You sound tired," he told her.

"Well, my darling, I haven't been getting much sleep. The people here keep me awake most of the time. They're very demanding."

Cliff smeared his eyes with his hand. He was still trembling from six hours of battling with the Fort's controls. "Listen . . . how long are you going to be there? I just finished debriefing. I need to take a shower. I've been flying all day, and I stink like a polecat's armpit."

"Don't worry about a shower. I need to see you now."

"Anne, honey, can't it wait until tomorrow morning?"

"I need to see you now. I *have* to see you now. If you don't come to see me now, I'll never forgive you."

"Listen," he said, "why don't we—" but he heard the click as Anne put down her receiver, and then the endless purring of the dialing tone.

"Oh, shoot," he said.

At that moment, McClung came past and said, "Problems, Captain?"

He had a sudden apocalyptic vision of all the Forts he had seen this afternoon, plunging down through the clouds with blazing young men on board. He wondered what they were thinking about as they fell to earth twenty-three thousand feet below. Did they pray? Did they think of their mothers? Or did they calmly accept that their lives were over?

And McClung was asking if *he* had problems?

It was already dark by the time he reached the Dog & Duck—windy and very cold, but dry. It was a real bomber's sky, eight-tenths cloud, with just enough breaks to see the stars. Across the road, in Poulter's Farm, a dog was barking.

There was a darts fixture tonight, and the pub was

crowded. He asked for a Scotch, paid for it, and tipped it back in one. Tom said, "All back safe?" but Cliff shook his head. There was a roar from the crowd as somebody scored a double top.

When Tom had his back turned, Cliff went through to the back of the pub and climbed the stairs. It was so dark that he barked his shin on the top step. He cautiously made his way to the back room door and opened it. He had never realized before how much it creaked.

Inside, the blackout curtains were drawn tight, and he couldn't see anything at all.

"Anne?" he said. "Can't you switch on the light?"

"Not yet," she replied. Her voice sounded oddly clogged, as if she had a bad sore throat. "Come in, darling. I'm here on the bed."

He groped his way into the room and closed the door behind him.

"Lock it," said Anne. "Now come over here and sit on the bed."

Cliff did as he was told. Immediately, she sat up and put her arms around him and kissed him. She was naked, and she was very cold, as if she had been lying there uncovered for hours.

"You're freezing," he said. "Come on, get under the blankets. You'll catch your death."

But she ignored him, and kept on kissing him and kissing him. It was while she was kissing him that he realized how swollen and puffy her lips were. He fumbled for the bedside lamp.

"No!" she said. "Please don't! You won't understand!"

But he did, and when the light abruptly flooded the room, he couldn't believe what he saw. Anne's body was covered in weals and bruises. Both of her eyes were swollen up, so that they looked like scarlet plums. Her lips had been split, and the sides of her mouth were crusted in scabs. Whole hanks of her hair had been pulled out, revealing patches of raw scalp. There were criss-cross marks across her thighs, and her pubic hair was shriveled, as if it had been burned.

"For Christ's sake," said Cliff. He was shaking with shock. "Who did this to you? What the hell bastard could have—"

She reached out and gripped both of his wrists. "Please, Eager, I'm begging you. Don't be angry."

"How can I not be angry? Look at you! I'm going to call the police!"

She gripped him even more tightly. *"No,"* she pleaded. "Please, Eager, no."

"Then what am I supposed to do? Sit back and allow this lunatic, whoever he is, to beat you to death?"

"Just be loving, Eager, that's all I ask. Just tell me you need me."

Cliff took a pack of Luckys out of his shirt pocket, shook two out, and lit them both with wildly wobbling hands. He passed one to Anne and took a deep, long drag on the other. "You need a doctor," he told her. "For Christ's sake, you need *two* doctors. One for your body and one for your brain. How can you let anybody *do* this to you?"

She stroked his cheek. "I love it, when we're together," she whispered. "It's all I have to live for."

"This has to stop," he insisted.

"Yes," she said, trying to smile. "And I promise you, Eager, it will."

"Promise?"

"There's only one more thing I want you to do for me."

"I'm not biting you again. Forget it."

She took hold of the hand in which he held his lighted cigarette. "I want you to burn your name across my breasts. Then I want you to stub it out inside me. You *must.*"

He pulled his hand away. "Are you kidding me, Anne? What the hell's wrong with you? Come on, I can't take any more of this! You're going to have to see a doctor, and then I'm going to call for a cop!"

"Please, Eager," she begged him. "Please, Eager. I can't bear it unless it's you."

But he stood up, and when she tried to cling to him, he pried her fingers away, and she was too much in pain to be able to follow him. Her head fell back on the pillow, and he dragged the quilt around her to keep her warm. "I won't be long," he told her. "I'm just going to call for a doctor."

She watched him go to the door. Her swollen eyes were crowded with tears. "Please," she whispered, her voice strangled with misery. "Please don't, Eager. Please."

He hesitated for a moment, then he went out and closed the door behind him.

The doctor puffed up the stairs like a GWR locomotive, every puff smelling of whiskey. He wore a bowler hat and pin-striped trousers and carried a brown Gladstone bag.

"I don't know who did this," Cliff told him, opening the door. "I just want you to understand that it wasn't me."

The doctor didn't say anything but looked at him piggy-eyed.

"All right, then," said Cliff, and switched on the light.

The room was empty. The bed was empty. The quilt was smooth and undisturbed. Cliff laid his hand on the pillow, and even the pillow was cold.

"I hope this isn't some kind of a joke," said the doctor, taking off his hat. "I was listening to ITMA."

Cliff lifted the quilt, but even the sheet underneath was chilly. Nobody had been there, not tonight. He stared at the doctor, and he didn't know what to say.

"She's not here, then, your lady friend?" the doctor asked him.

Cliff said something, but what he said was drowned out by the droning of a fully laden Fort taking off southwestward into the prevailing wind.

He let himself into the house and called out, "Babsy! I'm back!"

In the living room, little Pete was sitting cross-legged in front of the television, solemnly watching Howdy Doody. "Hi, son! Howdy-do to you!"

He hung up his hat on the hall stand, brushed back his close-cropped hair with both hands, and walked through to the kitchen, where the late-afternoon sun was shining. Babsy was rolling out pastry on the kitchen counter, her blond hair tied up in a scarf. But she wasn't alone. A lean, tall, white-haired man in an inappropriately wintry suit was sitting at the breakfast table, with a stack of papers in front of him. He stood up as Cliff came in, and Cliff looked at Babsy in surprise.

"You didn't say we were expecting visitors."

"You weren't, Captain," said the white-haired man in a rather faded British accent. "I'm afraid to say that I arrived unannounced. Your good lady was kind enough to allow me to wait for you."

Cliff walked around the counter, put his arm around Babsy, and gave her a kiss. "Is something wrong?" he wanted to know.

The white-haired man shook his head. "Quite the opposite. You might just say that I'm laying a ghost to rest. My name is Gerald Browne—Major Gerald Browne. You and I once talked on the telephone, several years ago."

Cliff said, in disbelief, "You're *Anne's* father?"

"Perhaps this is something you'd rather talk about in private."

"No, no—I—" Cliff began, but Babsy laid a hand on his arm and said, "Why don't you take Major Browne into the yard? I have to give little Pete his supper now, anyhow."

They went out into the small backyard and sat on the white-painted swing. It was a treacly Memphis evening, and the sky was gold. Cliff offered Major Browne a Lucky, but Major Browne declined.

"Anne told you that she was going to Torquay, but in reality she was doing nothing of the sort. She was being flown into France to make contact with the Resistance and to set up a communications system."

"She was *what?* Anne? But she was only just a kid!"

"I think you forget, Captain Eager, that in those days you were all just 'kids.' Anne was an SOE wireless operator, very highly trained."

"But I saw her, after she left. She came back, and I saw her twice."

Major Browne's eyes brimmed with sadness. They were rainwater eyes, just like Anne's. "Well, Captain, I didn't believe you then, but now I think I do. Although she was very brave, Anne was terrified of being captured and executed. She felt that she hadn't lived her life to the full. She hadn't even had a proper lover. That was why—well, when you met her for the first time that evening, she was so forward. She felt she had to cram a lifetime of experience into just a few hours."

"How do you know that?"

"Because six weeks ago, the French authorities returned her diary to me, the diary she kept both before and after she was caught and imprisoned by the Gestapo. Your name comes up again and again. When they tortured her, she always tried to imagine that it was you who was torturing her, instead of them. She felt that she could bear the pain if it was inflicted with passion, and with love. And she did bear pain—much more than you or I could ever imagine.

"It was thinking of you that helped her to endure her suffering. In her mind, she says, she wasn't in Amiens prison, but in your arms. And, by the way, she never gave away any of her codes or any of her comrades, not till the last."

Cliff found that he had to wipe his eyes. "I saw her. I held her. I don't understand it. The last time she came—she was so badly hurt, I couldn't bear it. I left her and went to call for a doctor. When I came back . . . the bed was empty. She was gone. I thought she'd just—"

"Do you remember what date that was?"

"For sure. It was the day we lost sixty-five Flying Fortresses over Germany, all in one day. October 16, 1943."

Major Browne nodded. "That was the same day that Anne was tortured for the last time by the Gestapo. According to the French, they did unspeakable things to her with cigarettes and burned a swastika on her chest. When she still refused to speak, they shot her."

Major Browne handed Cliff the small brown diary with its stained, creased cover. "Here, Captain, I think this is yours, more than anybody's"

That night, while Babsy quietly breathed, Cliff stood by the bedroom window staring out at the moonlight. Between finger and thumb he twirled the St. Catherine medallion that Anne had given him. St. Catherine, broken on the wheel.

He was about to go back to bed when he was aware

of a figure standing in the deep shadows on the far side of the room. Or maybe it wasn't a figure. Maybe it was nothing more than Babsy's wrap, hanging on the back of the door.

"Is anybody there?" he said, very softly.

Then, "Anne, is that you?"

PLAYERS

Deidra Cox

Candles flicker. Black haze, the scent of smoke. The heat, alive and pulsating. It coats the small room in a humid layer of moist growth. Dark, leafy plants around us.

And the flowers. Eternal spring. A diverse mixture of loud odors and clinging vines. Lazy ivy climbs up the mottled wall. A visual reminder of the long-dead past. This pleases me.

"I need him to love me," the woman says quietly, her voice timid as the new moon. Slight frame, painfully thin. Her face resembles nothing more than a ravaged skull. Bones slicing through meat and gristle. A glaze of fresh tears fills her sunken eyes, and her manner is reverent, head bowed, hands clasped in a neat shape.

A tear slides down her hollow cheek and falls to her neck. I watch its descent hungrily, yet knowing the flavor would be bland. Sighing, I relax, prepare to wait.

How odd we must appear. Maria, the bereaved and

loyal spouse, and myself. Despite my eccentricities, I hold no vanity concerning my chosen state.

Ancient beyond comprehension, huddled in my black robes. My withered flesh is cool, blood thin and weak. Cells dry, deficient. Dying, but I have a hope for the future. In Maria.

Her tale is a familiar one. Infidelity laced with the promise of a bright cruelty. Oh, the easy path a faithless man does trod. Never once pausing to weigh the consequences.

"Perhaps," I begin, "your loss is a blessing, no?"

The look of panic is expected. A timeless response. Escape the tiger? Unthinkable. Let us offer our throat and belly to the fangs, as well.

"I have two children," Maria says. "They need a father." She twists the hem of her frayed skirt. Her knuckles are swollen and knotted with disease. Soon the rest of her body will yield to the arthritis drain.

I lick my lips and exhale slowly. "Yes," I agree. "Children do require guidance. But maybe someone else might prove more suitable."

Maria feigns a bitter smile, and I wonder at her sudden mood swing. With an unforeseen grace, she lifts her faded blouse, and a maze of crusted scars blooms across her chest and shoulders. The breasts are especially colorful, the nipples mutilated and healing badly. The brutal display bears witness to a special talent, and I study the artwork carefully.

"No other man will have me," Maria tells me. "Carlos has made sure of that."

A shudder passes through me as I test the mangled flesh. A ripple of anticipation nestles in the pit of my stomach. "Where did you hear of me?"

"My grandmother, Magdalene. She came to you with a similar problem."

I examine Maria's face closely, following the pattern of bone lying taut. Lifting my nose to the air, I sniff and catch her scent. To my amusement, the woman is disturbed by my actions and quickly makes the sign of the cross.

Ah, yes, I remember the Spaniards and their Cristo. Wooden statues and women of stone. Why didn't poor Maria and all the others like her visit their priest? Seek counsel in their piteous churches rather than plead with me?

Because I am the Filth-Eater.

The answer satisfies me, and I savor the fear issuing from the young woman. Yes, I can see Magdalene, find remnants of her line. Flesh melted in a trial by fire. Unfortunately, Magdalene's weakness is manifest in her granddaughter, continuing the fine tradition of abuse. A loathsome trait, yet a useful one.

"Did you bring the tribute?" I ask, eager to begin.

Maria reaches for the bag by her feet. Inside are the offerings I desire, and she places them on the table. Three separate collections. A lock of black hair, sleek and crisp. Tiny shards of clipped nails. A vial of saliva. Each precious and highly binding.

I run a gnarled finger across the items and feel the strength emanating from them. The subject is enticing, excessively so. Unable to prolong the moment any further, I snatch the pieces in my hands, hair and nails mixed together in a jumbled wad, and gulp them down. Nourishment. My blood sings within my veins, the potency, the power of this man. Remarkable.

The vial. My eyes latch upon the clear fluid inside. Ignoring Maria's quiet revulsion, I drink the sweet sap. Golden honey, flowing down my throat. Oh, yes, Señor Carlos Mantega will do nicely. He will serve me well.

The purity of the gifts brings about the change. Atrophied muscles smooth into flexible tissue. The wizened shell begins to blossom. Nothing elaborate.

Nothing dramatic, yet the power is mine to call upon when needed.

The hunger burns brightly, and I cast my gaze toward the faithful Maria. I can read her thoughts plainly as if spoken. The uneasy doubts. The suggestion of terror clouding her senses.

Despite this, she pulls away and searches in her bag. A tattered picture wavers in her trembling hands. "You'll want this."

I smile widely, fully aware of the terrible effect my mirth has on the poor human. Nevertheless, she persists. Her need of him greater than her fear. "But he doesn't always go to the same place."

"I do not require these aids," I say, my tongue feeling thick and heavy. "Your husband belongs to me now. I will find him."

Maria drops her head, unable to withstand the tremendous longing reflected in my burning gaze. In spite of the sticky heat, she shivers. "You won't hurt him, will you?"

Once again, I smile. Oh, foolish mortal. Redemption can never be bought without the exquisite froth of pain.

After Maria's abrupt departure, I retreat into an inner sanctum. Behind these secret panels, the old ways reign eternal. The altar never dries. Honey mixes with flesh and amaranth seeds, shaped into the image of the Precious Hummingbird. Sprinkled with blood and broken into edible pieces.

The weight of the ages presses around me, and I lift my hands in supplication, calling upon my holy brethren. Smoking Mirror, for strength and courage. Serpent Skirt, for the fertility and subtle beauty of Mother Earth.

I feel their spirit embrace me, merge with my own troubled reserves. The combined force of the ancients sweeps through me, carries my essence back to the lush jungles and jeweled cities. The memory of drums vibrates in each heartbeat, and the sacrificial knife glows just before the blade drives home . . .

When my prayers are finished, I arise to wash and dress for the evening. Red silk. The fabric caresses my skin. Lustrous, firm breasts, begging to be touched, stroked with desire. Silk brushes against my thighs, gliding sensuously.

I check my appearance in the mirror. Yes, my kindred have woven an alluring web for the fly. Long black waves melt to my waist, mounds of fluid satin waiting to be parted. Perfection. And all this I owe to Maria's treacherous husband.

Carlos Mantega. A thread connects us. A velvet cord drawing me near. I follow his path across the city, stepping boldly. The crowds do not interest me, although their bounty could prove just as vital. I am promised to another. We are one. Bound by his sins.

His trail is warm, sweet like chocolate, and I thirst to drink from him, lick the fragrant droplets from his salty flesh. I grow restless, quick in my pursuit, and lose sight of my surroundings. The hunger is upon me, and I am like a wild beast, a jaguar snarling in the jungle. I hurry, almost running in my haste.

A dark alley separates me from Carlos. I can feel him calling to me. His essence is tantalizingly close, and I rush into the narrow row. Immediately, they spring from the shadows. A young pack, primed for the kill. They swarm around me. The strongest of them dares to put his hands upon me, cruel fingers biting into my throat.

This barbarian, Chichimec, "Son of the Dog," he dares to touch the sacred vessel, and my rage bubbles to the surface. His threats are as vomit to my ears. Profane, guttural, and filled with vows of further violence.

Dog, I have dealt with your kind since the beginning. Even in the absence of the ritual, my people come to me, seek the services of the Filth-Eater.

While the temptation to toy with the youth is great, my desire for Carlos is an open flame. I carry him in me, and those pieces cry for unity. The need to complete the cycle increases each second I delay.

The strength of my brother, Smoking Mirror, sings in my blood, and I grasp the youth by the head, twist him to face me. A thick spray shoots from my mouth and drenches him with viscous green mucus. Screams, shrill and lovely.

Suddenly, I am released while my would-be captor claws at his eyes. The blindness is temporary, yet more than enough for my purposes. The dogs circle their fallen comrade, uncertain how to proceed, lost children looking for guidance. Watching their feeble attempts at menace, I allow the mask to slip and give them a glimpse of my true nature. Shrieks of madness and the sound of running, swift and fading.

Don't worry, my little ones. I will find you when your harvest is ripe. And then I will relieve you of your malignant fruit.

I find myself alone, the hunger gnawing at the lining of my stomach. The craving pulls me through the maze, and I hurry, dodging the casually strewn garbage along the way.

At the end of the alley, my final destination beckons across the street. Rundown bar. Seedy neighborhood in various stages of urban decay. I enter, ravenous.

Dimly lit interior. Slow hum of a ceiling fan in the center of the room. The crack of the cue ball as it connects with multicolored orbs rolling atop the pool table.

Although I do not see him, Carlos Mantega is here. I feel his presence. Taste the sweat above his upper lip. Follow the curve of his spine, supple and strong. Oh, how deeply I long to touch him.

The bartender sets a dirty glass before me as I slide onto a ragged stool. While I slowly sip the lukewarm beer, he moves in, chest swollen, hips thrust out. Easy smile and a dark heart.

Reaching into the black secrets of lust and pride, I probe the man's ego and after locating the select area, an urgent jab. An ugly grimace splits his face, shock mixing with genuine pain. The amorous barkeep slinks away. Problem solved.

I do not relish this, the inflicting of pointless humiliation. It isn't the proper order of things, yet he is unnecessary, a distraction I cannot permit.

Ah, the vivid shade of red flashes behind my eyes, and cinnamon, the scent teases my senses. My skin flushed, a deep heat rushing through my limbs and collecting in the core.

Oh yes, he is here. I give the stool a lazy push, and there is Carlos seated behind a battered piano. An assortment of chipped and dirty mugs set across the dusty top, liquid contents vibrating slightly. The music he plays is annoying. Ragtime, jazz, a tender sonata. The music of this age does little to ease my tension. The rhythms are flat and unappealing.

I force my irritation aside and focus on Carlos. A handsome one, my chosen pet. His physical beauty is a pleasant surprise. Long black mane drawn into a silky braid. Eyes that pierce, equally as dark. Proud jaw, regal structure.

Visions of long ago intrude, mingle with the present. I see Carlos on a pyramid, paying homage to the Sun. The skin of a mighty jaguar adorns his head and shoulders, announcing to all his position as a Royal Knight. I see the feathered mantle, lovely turquoise and green plumage swaying softly on a gentle breeze. Vicious claws shredding the feathery layers. Fluffs of emerald down flutter to the cold stone.

A coarse round of laughter shatters the dream, and I

revert to this bland version of reality. A place where the gods starve for attention.

A faded blonde drapes her plump arms around Carlos's neck, but he doesn't rise to the invitation. Slender fingers caress the stained keyboard, wringing a dull melody from the hidden strings. Suddenly, I am envious of the instrument, of his brief talent. Those slender fingers scamper so artfully. How skilled might they prove on warm flesh.

An excruciating spasm racks my belly. A defiant reminder of the importance of my quest. I am hungry. A bottomless pit aching to be filled.

Smoothing the wrinkles from my dress, I stand and wait for his show of respect. I do not have to tarry long. I never do. His reaction is almost instantaneous. The seeds within me bud, stretching to him and seeking. His music halts, a single drawn-out note painfully abandoned.

The light of recognition shines in his dark eyes and a slow smile. New lands to explore and plunder. Yes, come to me, my love. Come to me, and let us speak of dust and remembrance.

The faded blonde lingers, her lips forming a willful pout. She protests ineffectively. Luckily for her, she is forgotten. She is no more for Carlos. He sees nothing except my image seared upon his soul.

His arms entwine around my waist, a seasoned fit. He murmurs false endearments, and I voice the proper responses. My demeanor is soft, alluring, yet not too lenient. A challenge must exist. A savory bait dangled.

Carlos does not disappoint me. He swallows my crumbs, his lust rising as a swollen river after the summer floods. He guides me from the bar into the night. A thousand hearts call to me, their appeals float to the heavens above, but I cannot answer, for I belong to Carlos. Tonight.

His hands envelop mine. Strong and cool. Smooth and limber. No hint of a callus anywhere on my lover's palms. Not an honest man, my Carlos.

The scent of him is maddening. It wafts beneath my nostrils, the heady aroma. My insides quake from his nearness. Soon, I vow. Soon.

His abode is a place of misery. Rich tapestries. Plush carpets to cushion my feet. Beautiful flowers adorning the altar. Carlos has not bowed to any of these sensual trappings. Bare walls, the plaster cracked and peeling. Cold wood floors, a thick layer of dirt and grime spread everywhere.

Confident of his charms, Carlos leads me to the bed. Those swift, clinging hands mold my body as the blind reading braille. As he kisses my neck, I stare at the filthy mattress where we will lie. The odors that drift upward. Sweat, dried semen, and urine. Unwashed bodies melting in a mix of unbridled lust. Yes, this will make a fitting altar for the act.

His mouth, hot and tasting of peppers, claims mine. Our tongues dance, exchange strokes in a simulation of sex. Excitement builds as my hunger threatens to explode. I cannot wait any longer. I do not want to.

Abruptly, I end the embrace, leaving him bewildered and more than a little angry. Large smile as I lean forward, snapping the buttons from his shirt with my teeth. At the edge of the fabric, bare skin peeks through, and I give his taut stomach a light nip. Not much, just slightly drawing blood, but oh, the exquisite flavor on my tongue.

Inflamed by my ardor, Carlos pulls me to him, ripping my dress. Red silk and denim fall around our ankles as we writhe like snakes mating upon stone. His sex stabs my belly, and his lips ravage my flesh. His mouth suckles at my breast, and I am reminded of poor Maria, the scars she must wear, and I smile.

I firmly lift his head from his place of worship and

place his fingers in my mouth, licking each digit ever so slowly. Carlos maneuvers to the bed, lying flat, and I swing my leg astride him while he plunges into me. The sensation is glorious, my shriveled canal stretching to accept his member.

Rocking my hips, I sink over his chest, black hair falling like tears. A gentle kiss by the corner of his mouth while my fingers probe the base of his skull. My nails dig sharply in the appropriate area, and he stiffens. Surprise devouring his mind, and then, sleep. A sleep only I can stir.

Lost in the land of dreams, Carlos seems as innocent as a newborn babe. Yet I know how foul is the foundation that lies underneath his veil of purity. The dark and wicked things that fester and brood into private sins.

His organ remains erect, rigid within my oily sheath, and I tighten the damp walls around him, giving myself a brief moment of pleasure before the purging.

Where to begin? How to determine the root of Carlos's grievous ways? With some, it is the eyes. The sin of coveting. Once blinded, the temptation is gone. Others, the troublesome tepuli, the male rod surging toward the wellspring of life like a thirsty beast.

I could render Carlos impotent, never to penetrate a hapless woman again. But somehow I doubt that this course will resolve Maria's pain. Her grief. No, Carlos requires a harsher measure.

I close my eyes and softly chant the prayer of purification. My hands caress the dense fur atop his torso. Deft fingers ruffle the humid curls.

Then, while my lips form the ancient sound, nails slice through skin and muscle, bone shreds easily at my command. A red fountain spurts a king's tribute, and I lap as much as possible.

An anguished cry escapes from Carlos as the nightmare tries to interrupt his sleep. Pausing in my work, I run a bloody paw across his fevered brow, and peace, once more, reigns in his dreams.

I watch my fallen prince with a wet smile. His life fluids seep around us, soaking the mattress, yet he sleeps as I have wished. And there, the prize. I gaze upon the apple, ever so tainted by the most vicious of worms, and I cannot deny myself. A savage shout, and I rip the still-pulsing heart from his chest and feed.

Oh, the sweetness, the blessed nourishment his wickedness does provide. The evil of his crimes races through me, and I sob joyful tears as my orgasm quakes. Grinding my hips till the last spasm is spent, the need sated, and I am totally filled.

And then, as always, the bitter taste of my meal emerges, builds in my throat. Nausea, ripe and bloated, churns the bile until I veer over the ragged cavity and empty the decayed remnants. Acid chunks spew forth, cleave together, forming a perfect, chaste heart. A new beginning.

With a loving touch, I fondle the mutilated tissue, helping the puckered skin to mesh. The healing process is rapid, fueled by the regenerative energy radiating from my fingertips. Soon, no hint of deformity remains.

Soft, pink skin. Handsome chest, free from blemish. My Carlos sleeps, a new creature. His face, smooth and unlined. Gone is the cruel curve to his lips. Innocence shines on that serene visage.

Unable to resist, my attention strays to his unruly mane, rogue locks pulled free from the tired braid. I give those strands a playful tug, just enough to cause a slight frown, as from a small boy losing a favored toy.

"It is finished," I breathe, the words solemn and complete. Maria will have her husband by her side. For a time. Although his past has been erased, men like Carlos follow a predictable pattern. A set course. I expect to see him again.

Tenderly, I brush his mouth with a kiss, tongue darting wetly. The dreamer sleeps on, unfettered by conscience or past. I turn to leave, my work concluded. But the connection between us still binds. This man has moved me as no one else. Not since the days of smoke and sacrifice.

A token. A remembrance of me. Yes. I must leave him that.

I sit beside him, bed sagging underneath my weight, his semen leaking down my thigh. He rests so easily. Gentle sigh, and his slumber continues.

Taking his hand in mine, the strains of a dim melody play in my head. I bring his hand to my lips. Licking the flesh, savoring his scent. Soft flicker of tongue against the knuckles.

Then I spread my jaws and neatly sever his fingers from the palm. Hot splash of blood hitting the back of my throat. Meat and bone, the satisfying crunch echoing in my ears.

And the music of screams as Carlos awakens.

THE 121ST DAY OF SODOM

Brian Hodge

It was thin and delicate enough to be female, but because there were no breasts I had to assume otherwise. It stood before us without moving because it hadn't been told to do anything else, and while it had arms and legs and stood on two feet, the leather hood over its submissively bowed head made something of it a rung or two below human. This was obviously the intention.

"See how compliant it is," Drake told us. "Oh, it'll stand like that for hours if I don't give it something to do."

That leather hood: black, naturally, and tight as burnt skin. It could see from inside, but the visible eyes were hard flat buttons that held everything back. The nose was no more than the hint of a bump, the mouth a three-inch gash of open zipper through which we caught an occasional glimpse of lip or flicker of tongue.

"Can it breathe with the zipper shut?" Aimee asked.

Of course Drake would know, but he gave a practiced shrug of ignorance. "Maybe we'd better find out, don't you think?"

He told the slave to step up to the edge of the table, and it did. Told it to bend forward at the waist and lay the side of its head on the tabletop, and it did this, too. One, two teeth at a time, Drake ratcheted the zipper halfway shut, then paused to study the hood and the nameless and faceless entity inside.

"You don't need air tonight, do you?" he murmured.

"I need only to——"

Drake went suddenly livid, pale face flushing from contoured jawline to the widow's peak of midnight-dyed hair, receded just enough to lend him a touch of faux aristocracy in his haughtier moments, and these were frequent. He slapped a chastising hand down upon the hood. Aimee and I watched taut muscles flinch and squirm across the slave's naked back, like watching the trembling of a puppy newly learning the brute power of its master's wrath.

"Who told you you could speak?" Drake shouted, then waited to see if it would take this bait and slip up again. When it did not, Drake nodded, satisfied. "So you're not afraid of suffocation? You may speak now."

"No, master," it said, genderless and muffled. "I fear only disappointing you again."

"Don't you all," he said, then with a casual flick of his hand shut the zipper the rest of the way. "And stand up straight, for God's sake, somebody may want to set a drink down."

We watched it then, standing before our table like a waiter who had forgotten why he'd come. No one else in the club paid any attention, immersed in their own tableaux and their rigidly prescribed rites of seduction, surrender, and will.

Its stomach began to convulse first, with quickening

attempts at stealing breath. The suggestion of a mouth, open and straining, formed behind the opaque skin, a circle of leather dimpling in ever so slightly. The head would sag, then snap upright, as if fighting sleep. Finally, the slave collapsed to its knees, falling forward and banging its head on the edge of the table.

Drake relented, opening the zipper, and the leather sphincter stretched as the slave drew reedy gulps of air. He pulled it toward his lap, cradling the head with peculiar tenderness as it knelt and seemed blissfully content to be stroked like a pet.

"Looks like they might have a little trouble when it's shut," Drake said, finally answering Aimee. "Any more questions?"

She would have a thousand, I knew, and if Drake answered each one, she would have a thousand more. The trouble was knowing where to begin. I was having this problem myself.

Drake smiled at the confused interplay of repulsion and longing on our faces. He stroked the head with fingers long and slender, patient as a spider, gazing fondly at the two buttons that were the only other facial features apart from that zippered mouth.

"Oh, they're a responsibility, all right," he said, "but how can you resist them when they look up at you with those eyes?"

Drake had owned the club for more than three years, so he told us, but it had become what it now was by accident only within the last nine months. He gave us the original name, something so clever and vapid that I forgot it immediately. Business was good almost from the very beginning, but Fetish Night—instituted to invigorate the ordinarily dead Monday scene—proved so insatiably popular that it soon cannibalized the other six as well. There's no way of knowing how significant a deviation from the norm exists out there until someone gives them all a place to go. This Drake did, and thus was born Club Kinque.

He gave us a swift tour before the doors opened that night at nine, showing the layout of this building he'd found in a part of the city where blight was high and property values comparatively low. The first floor was unused except for storage and access, the clientele entering through a closed-off bay to pay their cover and find their way up a stairwell where urban primitivists had slashed paint on the walls to glow beneath the bruised nostalgic violet of black lights. The second floor was cavernous, with dance space and lights and screens and a booth for a DJ who was always busy except for the nights when a live band had been booked, often notorious acts that few other venues, if any, would dare handle, such as the Genitorturers and Crash Worship. The third floor was barred to all under twenty-one, with tables and booths and a warren of mood-lit nooks more intimate still, where practitioners would gather for piercings and brandings and whippings and so on. Like the Christian heaven, it was insulated from the chaos below, except for the more intense bass thuds, and while speakers continually played ambient industrial music from Sweden's Cold Meat Industry label, and other sources obscure enough to suit Drake's aesthetics, the volume was never so loud that you could not hear the crack of a lash across bare buttocks tightened in sweet dread.

It wasn't until later that I learned how important that quiet really was, but by then . . . well, you can guess the rest, I'm sure.

We'd seen enough our first night there, Aimee and I, to stoke us amply when we got home very late. We'd had just enough to drink to fuel desire without sapping performance, neither of us giving much thought to the morning's obligations. I commuted to *Chez Noir Monthly* via fax and modem, and since we'd moved back to the city, Aimee was doing radio promo again, spending more time out of the office than in.

Undressed and tall, she was radiant in her heat and need, and she knelt upon the bed, hinged at the waist with her rump high in the air, dark hair slung across the pillow as she awaited the fall of the belt. It was looped double in my fist, and I on my knees above her, trying to muster nerve enough to swing. I swatted her with a soft wet smack of leather on skin, and tried once again when my arm faltered, the same as when I tried to talk dirty and the words would clench in my throat because I found it such an unnatural act—not wrong, just beyond my nature.

"Harder," Aimee whispered, desperate and feverish.

I managed another swing but no more, and she turned on me in disappointment until I forced the belt into her hand and lay flat out, asking her to use it across the plain of my stomach. She cringed as she brought the belt down; it barely tingled. At least I could share in her frustration, wanting the hot cherry glow of flogged skin and being denied.

In Drake's world, there were two kinds of people: those who topped and those who bottomed. With standard-issue consummation, Aimee and I could meet each other halfway easily enough, and had been happily doing so for four years. But when the theater of the boudoir turned to dominance and submission, we'd both been cast in the same role. Two Juliets, as it were, and no Romeo.

We tossed the belt to the floor, and when Aimee threw a long, tapered leg over me to straddle my hips and ride me hard, I know we both were better for it, if still plagued by how conventional it felt. We could at least laugh about it, about our limitations.

Four years. They say the itch doesn't come until the seventh, but with the pace of life on an exponential increase, I suppose it's inevitable that we look beyond the horizons of our marriages sooner than our parents did, and in places they never even dreamed existed.

"I wonder," she said, "if it feels claustrophobic inside one of those hoods."

Even our very first night at Club Kinque, Aimee was hardly a stranger to Drake, and when we returned the next night, he seemed to have expected it all along, if nowhere near as triumphantly gloating as I might've expected. Then again, I'd always imagined him as the type who had spent too much time cultivating his jaded nonchalance to gloat over anything. It took effort, maintaining that much lassitude, and I suppose I did envy his control.

Aimee had dated him years ago, breaking it off because he was too unapologetically self-absorbed and always would be, something she tried not to be judgmental about, just regarded it as a matter of fact. Drake congratulated her on her perception and offered to pay for the cobalt laser treatment to erase the padlock-and-thorns tattoo he'd had put near her pubis. He was no sore loser because, she guessed, he saw himself as naturally dominant over ninety-nine percent of everything else that particular day.

Or maybe he just had the advantage of incredible foresight. *You'll be back someday,* former boyfriends are prone to believing, but in this case it was the truth.

She never used him as a weapon against me, but I always knew he was there, an indelible piece of Aimee's past, what dead comic Sam Kinison once called "the darkest chapter in her sexual diary." An unabashed erotic explorer, Drake supposedly had fucked his way through the *Kama Sutra* by his nineteenth birthday. From there, he'd graduated to various rites of sex magick as described by Aleister Crowley, made pilgrimages to legendary Eastern brothels, and when fleshly sensation became saturated, finally, turned to the epic panorama of deviant psychology mapped out in the surviving works of Donatien Alphonse François, the Marquis de Sade. Contemptibly familiar acts can become fresh again when put into a new context.

"He just didn't know the meaning of the word *love*," Aimee told me. "The closest he could get was *adoration*."

When they met again, by chance, it was through her job. Some luncheon gathering of the city's music business types, promoters and radio personnel like Aimee, and venue owners. Undoubtedly, Drake relished his status as a wicked and unsettling pariah, Club Kinque going strong for the better part of a year and beholden to no one and nothing but human appetites for its success.

Their reunion was warm and cordial, leading to the inevitable what-are-you-doing-now inquiries. Drake gave her a business card with only an address and, along one edge, a riding crop. We later joked about it, imagining polo players and blue-blooded equestrian snobs showing up, to get the shock of their lives.

"Bring . . . whoever," he said, although he knew damn well she was married, and to whom. "You might even like it."

When Aimee brought it up after a week during which I could tell something was eating away at her, I felt more intrigue than threat. This surprised us both. *How understanding, how open-minded,* some might say on learning that not only was I willing to suffer an evening there for Aimee's sake but that I actually felt drawn to go. *How secure in his relationship he must be.*

I'd have to laugh in their faces, for this would obviously be coming from people who didn't even know me.

So we came. We saw.

He conquered.

We were VIPs, on the short list of those whose cover charges were waived, but night after night he kept us on the periphery of it all, like UN observers or anthropologists who, while prized guests, were still expected to remain ceremonial exiles.

On the one hand, I suppose it truly was for our edification, so that we'd learn the protocol of the S&M world. On the other, it was pure calculated manipulation, feeding our heightened senses a nightly diet of eroticism but denying us any chance to participate until such time as Drake would decide we could.

To challenge him in this was unthinkable.

One frustrating night, as we sat sidelined, a female dom approached us. Asymmetrical ebony hair stuck to her sweaty throat, and alabaster skin showed through innumerable slits in her black latex outfit, making her as sleek as a carnivorous zebra. She regarded us with painted Egyptian eyes.

"May I borrow him awhile?" she asked Aimee. Submissives could be loaned and traded, as long as permission was granted, although she'd apparently mistaken Aimee for my keeper. "I promise to return him in good condition."

Something in me longed to go with her, submit to her pointed fingernails and whatever else she had in mind. Never would I know her name—never would I *deserve* to know her name, for she was clearly a more highly evolved creature than I. Her will overruling my own, there would be something monumentally secure in giving in, knowing I was free of all responsibility but to endure, or perform on command. She might pull apart slitted latex, then the muscled globes of her ass, and my only purpose would then be to lick. It would not be adultery—we'd discussed this. It would be taking our places in the natural order, among those who knew how to treat our inferiorities much better than we could treat them in each other.

But asked for permission to borrow me, Aimee didn't know how to respond. If anything, this stark latex mistress had every right to commandeer us both.

Assuming Drake would've allowed it.

"You're grazing the wrong field, my lovely. This one's still being seeded," he told her. I'd not even known he was nearby. He levered the handle of a whip beneath her chin and pushed up, then pinched her one displayed pink nipple, rolling it like a hardened pebble. She tensed against him, obviously unaccustomed to being put in this position yet aware his word was law. "Now run along and find something not quite so tender, why don't you, while I'm still in a forgiving mood."

When released, she did not look back.

"Sorry about that," Drake said, joining us. "It's only been recently that I've broken Cleo of the habit of hitting first and asking questions later. Where would we be without the rules? This isn't a place for anarchists, you know."

"It seems plenty rife with arch-capitalists," I said, and did wonder how rich this place had made him. If money had subsumed his every motive. "Starting at the very top."

Drake smiled, in his way. His was no natural smile—a mild upturning of the corners of his mouth that never touched his eyes, as if he feared the crinkles would set and mar him. He would be near forty, seven or eight years older than I, but his face was so scrupulously unlined that he didn't look it, except for the subtle receding of his hair.

"Only until closing time, then." He shrugged, showing more interest in the whip handle than anything. He tapped a finger on a shiny wet spot, then dabbed it to his tongue. "Oh, look. Cleo left her sweat behind. I think this has *your* name on it?"

He pushed the reversed whip at my mouth, touching the pommel to my lips until they parted. He worked it in an inch, another, then held it there until my eyes shut and I tongued Cleo's sweat from the end, tasting salt and leather, and feeling all of what I was outside these walls melt suddenly away, leaving only the core that wanted to serve.

"That's good, oh, that's *very* good," Drake said. "For the first time, I'm actually convinced you're sincere about this." He pulled the handle away, and I felt bereft as an infant yanked from its mother's breast with milk yet to be drawn. "Because, really, you've no idea where that whip has been."

Aimee was eyeing it, too—long, studded, phallic. "Where?"

"I used to tell people it was a gift from Robert Mapplethorpe and they might've seen it in that rear-view self-portrait of his. But I don't think anyone believed me, so I quit wasting my breath on them after a time. You can believe whatever you wish."

He traced the handle's wet pommel along Aimee's nose, and she misunderstood, opening her mouth, tongue creeping forward as if to receive a communion wafer. When her eyes shut, Drake cracked her so sharply across the bridge of her nose that both shocked eyes brimmed with tears.

"And *you*," he said. "That's the very last time I'll

tolerate an unauthorized question from you. You will not speak to me again unless I've told you to do so. And if you ever entertained any sad little thoughts that we were in any way equals? *Get over them.*"

After he left us, I dabbed at the trickles of blood from my wife's nose. The part of me that should have been outraged and murderous was small, getting smaller, might disappear altogether. Aimee and I hugged each other, for some test had been passed, our commitment assured, and when I looked into the quietly suffering depths of her eyes, I knew that we loved enough to each hand the other over to the care and keeping of someone else, who could take us farther than we could ever take ourselves, and this seemed a rare and wonderful love indeed.

What Drake had hinted about closing time being the end of all capitalist pursuits became clearer once he began demanding that we stay after hours. Doors were locked, the second floor flushed of dancers, and the third cleared of slumming pretenders to leave only those whose commitment to the lifestyle remained sacrosanct, Club Kinque becoming Drake's personal fiefdom until long past dawn most mornings. It drew people I'd never seen during regular hours, and the age restriction that shackled Drake in business was given the disdainful boot from his personal life.

Three nights running, Aimee was given by him into the service of a girl ten years younger, eighteen at most, who would sprawl in a rattan chair, fingering for slow hours the moist tangle between her thighs as she dangled each petite and high-arched foot before Aimee's hooded face. The zipper was open, stripping from her the status of person, consigning her to that of orifice. I could see the lips that had for years kissed mine now slide exquisitely over each small toe, sucking it in its turn, Aimee's tongue caressing and bathing the cleft between before moving on to the next.

My own task was more passive, and generalized, a receptacle of pain for whoever wished to inflict it. Hooded as well, wrists cuffed in thick leather and chained overhead, I was a fixture made available for the supple rawhide lashes of a twenty-inch flogger. Wielded by hands whose skill ranged from novice to expert, it sent stinging jolts through me, amassing into a raw heat that burned me loose of all that parents and school and church had indoctrinated into me that I should strive for, while constantly reminding me that I would never be good enough at any of it for genuine approval.

So they hit me and I endured, and a few would warm their cool hands on my fevered skin, even their faces, my hard-earned sweat to some like wine. Two women and a man lowered me exhausted to the floor one night, spread upon my striped back a banquet of fruit, and ate it all while around us unfolded dozens of other scenarios limited only by the imaginations of those who put them into play and the physical limits of those upon whom they were enacted. They coupled in constantly changing configurations and numbers, mouths and genitals and hands furiously busy. Semen oozed down thighs and throats, and blood was let from willing limbs and torsos. An ancient marble tub large enough for three sat imperially in one corner for the enjoyment of water sport enthusiasts. On any given night, a ferocious dom in rough trade leathers might be seen oiling a muscled forearm, flexing in anticipation. A single woman might exhaust a dozen partners, or punish half as many into insensibility, before she was done for the night. A single man might milk his glands until they scraped painfully dry. From every quarter and every corner, cries of ecstasy rang indivisible from cries of pain, as Drake lorded over all like a satyr.

"Something, isn't it?" he said one night, kneeling beside me where I lay chained to the floor, awaiting . . . something. "Like the ocean: always the same, always in flux. Ho hum."

I had turned to the side to look his way, anonymous and safe within my hood, eyes inscrutable behind tiny holes drilled in the center of the buttons. I dared say nothing, for nothing was asked.

"De Sade was the inspiration. Ever read *120 Days of Sodom?*"

I shook my head; he patted it to reward my obedience to the law of silence. This was why I never feared losing Aimee to him; he showed equal interest in me.

"Lovely story. If you were to start out summarizing, it would sound like the beginning of a bad joke: A duke, a bishop, a judge, and a banker lock themselves in a remote castle in the Alps. They want to remove themselves from society after they've exhausted the passions they can gratify around Paris. So the duke conceives the idea of their establishing a School for Libertinage at the edge of the world. Four months devoted to nothing but limitless hedonism."

I became aware that Drake was holding something in his hand but could not yet see what it was.

"They assemble around themselves an entourage of wives—they marry each other's daughters—and retired old Parisienne madames, and a squad of horny fellows with names like Towercock and Volcano and Asschopper—who, if they were around today, would be video superstars—and, finally, an assortment of beautiful pubescent boys and girls to gratify their each and every whim, nabbed from across the countryside, and hideous old whores to chaperone them. Not the least among the laws imposed is that calling upon God for help or deliverance is punishable by death. And so, in that castle, they all stay for four unimaginable months."

Drake brought his hand up from alongside his thigh, and the object he held he turned over and over, inspecting it casually.

"Except de Sade *was* able to imagine it. Part of their nightly entertainment was hearing stories told by the four madames, each woman assigned to a different degree of passions: the simple, the complex, the criminal, and the murderous. One hundred and fifty scenarios exemplifying each, six hundred in all. And de Sade lists every single one of them. It's the most astounding collection of eroticism, perversity, degradation, blasphemy, and atrocity that anyone's ever imagined, or ever will. The first time I read it, I closed the book, and I said to myself, 'Now *there's* ambition.'"

What Drake held was a tapered iron bulb, the size of a skinny egg. From the narrower end emerged a threaded shaft, topped with an ornate head, like that of a skeleton key.

"Of course, I can't conduct wholesale slaughter, but I believe I still might've done de Sade one better, in my humble way. I've never needed to kidnap a single soul. So many walking around today have been twisted into such Gordian knots that, whatever I or anyone else here has an appetite to do, there's somebody eager to let us do it to them. I built it . . . and you came." He ran a hand along the leather contours of my skull. "Never think I don't appreciate how pathetically dependable you are in that respect."

He held the iron bulb up for my inspection. It wasn't all of a single-cast piece—I could see fine cracks running the length of it, between segments.

"Do you know what this is?"

I shook my head no.

"It's called a rectal pear. They come in oral and vaginal models, too, but it's primarily the use that dictates the name. A lesser-known example of Renaissance-era technology. Can you imagine being the one who first *thought* of such a contraption?"

Drake turned the screw and the bulb slowly split apart, three segments opening like a lotus, wider and wider still.

"Heretical preachers got them in the mouth. Women judged guilty of fucking the devil got them in the cunt, and queers in the ass—*that's* ironic, considering. The original models had sharp prongs, too, but don't worry, I'm not interested in ripping you apart inside. We just need to loosen you up a bit."

He turned the screw again, counterclockwise this time, and the segments drew back together.

"Some of the lads have their eye on you, and I'm sure it's not escaped your attention that a few of them are what the *Kama Sutra* calls 'horse men.' For their needs, you're what's called a 'deer woman.' The inequality requires some correction. Take it like a good boy, and this year, for the first day of Christmas, maybe I'll give you a partridge in a rectal pear tree."

Drake oiled the cold iron, and I was silent, even in the pain, silent through it all, and when by the tilt of Aimee's head I saw she had noticed this new ordeal, I liked the idea that I could not see her true eyes, nor she mine. We could be feeling anything. She watched as long as she dared. And then she turned away.

Life lived for another can become an end in itself that rearranges everything else to fit, and so it was with Drake and the world that had coalesced around him. Club Kinque became the mold into which

Aimee and I had been poured, and it shaped us in its own image.

Our lives away weren't lived so much as tolerated, counting the hours until we would be allowed back to take our place among the lowly and the servile. While there we were nothing, but away we were even less— we were purposeless, cursed with too much time and nothing worth devoting it to.

When Aimee lost her job, it was a relief to her, because she no longer had to pretend. And I let the messages accumulate on the answering machine, the fax paper spool onto the floor, and soon *Chez Noir Monthly* got the idea. There was no longer any point to me writing lifestyle articles. I'd found one.

When Drake informed us one night that we wouldn't be allowed in the next, or the next, ad infinitum, we had no idea what to do and might even have killed ourselves if we'd not clung to the hope that maybe he would change his mind. Drake was not above admitting mistakes, when it suited his purpose.

"It's just like when my father walked out when I was twelve," Aimee said, beyond tears. "All you can do is wonder what you did wrong."

But we hadn't. Break the rules—silence, obedience—and the punishment was swift, its reason clear. Our week of exile seemed like something else altogether.

And when it ended, Drake coming to us personally to invite us back without explanation, I suppose a part of me recognized that it was only more manipulation, engineered to break down the last fibers of our being before taking us over altogether. I knew this. Maybe Aimee knew it, too. But it didn't matter. We were so grateful to have our place defined for us again that it *couldn't* matter.

Because Drake knew best.

And when, three nights later, he told us that we

shouldn't count on going back home anytime in the foreseeable future, I for one welcomed the news like a revelation from the one true god.

The new hood fit me all the better since Drake had shaved my head. He said we would do this periodically, until there had been collected enough clippings with which to weave a hair shirt, like those worn by monastic penitents. Although as far as Drake was concerned, I had nothing to repent, unless you count being born.

This new hood, a variation on the old one I'd grown so fond of, had no buttons for eyes, had no eyes at all. Blind, breathing behind a closed zipper through tiny perforated airholes, I waited otherwise naked for hours in a small room until he came for me and clipped a leash to a ring at the back of the hood's neck.

"On all fours should do just fine," said Drake, somewhere in the dark. He tugged on the leash to get me moving, and I found the proper pace at his side.

"We have a number of voyeurs present tonight, so I've had to stage quite the theater of the arabesque. You're star attraction number thirteen. Don't worry—you'll know what to do when you get there."

One corridor, then another, through doorways, the old wooden flooring hard beneath my hands and knees. At last, he led me into what I knew instinctively to be Club Kinque's main room. I sensed around me the great restless stirring of bodies and expectations, and my entrance was greeted by a smattering of ironic applause.

Another ten feet, fifteen—I halted when I felt a sudden yank on the leash, cocking my ears to each small noise. Drake walked a step or two ahead, and it felt as if he turned the leash over to someone new. The pressure resumed, a gentler hand now tugging me forward, and I groped blindly with palms extended, felt a smooth knee on either side of me. Drake had left me between the parted legs of someone who seemed to be reclining on a padded bench. I slid my hands higher, felt supple and hairless thighs. A woman.

"And so the dog sniffs out the bitch in heat," Drake called to the spectators, with some drama, "and nature takes its course."

I felt him unclip the leash, then the unexpected attaching of two new clips to the same ring on the back of my neck. What these would connect with, I couldn't predict.

He opened the zipper across my hood; an instant later, I felt the sole of his boot on the back of my head, pushing me roughly forward and down, until my mouth squashed into the anonymous sex of the stranger before me. She was shaved hairless, her swollen cleft as slick and wet as a peeled plum.

Drake hadn't lied: I knew what to do.

Until we have a cold, we forget how much our sense of taste relies on our sense of smell. As I could smell only leather, I was unable to taste her at first, could only feel the wet velvet folds that parted for my tongue, and beneath them, the hardness of bone as she ground her hips at me.

My hands moved up, around her haunches, atop her lower belly, and my fingertips brushed a familiar pad of shiny scar tissue just as, from within, some reservoir seemed to open and spill thickly across my lips and tongue. My sense of taste wasn't gone, only delayed. And just as I knew the feel of where Aimee's tattoo had been removed, so, too, did I recognize the bitter-salt taste of semen. So much of it, though. It ran down over my leathered chin, dripped to my bare chest, trickled lower.

I gagged, spitting, trying not to retch, and in unanticipated revulsion threw myself back from the soaked V of her thighs until I felt a hard yank at the back of my head. I'd forgotten Drake had clipped me to something else.

The blindness was maddening, as around me erupted both gouts of laughter and sighs of disappointment. I clawed at the lacing on the back of the mask, pulled it apart, and peeled the leather from my shaved skull. I knelt blinking and naked in the sudden glare of light, the mask bunched in my hand, and I saw now that a taut pair of thin, stainless steel chains were clipped to the ring on the back. I followed them up, to a pulley suspended from the ceiling over my head. Followed them to another one over where Aimee lay with her knees bent and parted wide as she leaned wantonly back on both elbows. I followed the chains down again, saw at last where they connected.

The two rings were the diameter of a quarter, pierced through either corner of Aimee's mouth. As I held the chains forgotten and taut, her cheeks were painfully stretched, as if she were a hooked fish. Watery blood seeped from the unhealed piercings, to run down her chin as the semen ran down mine. I realized what I was doing to her and let the mask go; her skin drew back into place.

"I'm sorry," I whispered, in what must've been a moment of weakness.

Aimee's eyes held mine, beseeching, gone somewhere I'd yet to follow and maybe never could. I wasn't sure she was even aware it was me.

"Again," she murmured. She licked her lips. "Pull it again."

Although I suspect I had performed much as I'd been expected to, I still had broken many rules and was treated accordingly. I was taken to the first floor, which I'd always thought was unused except for storage. Perhaps I'm still not wrong.

I was folded inside a small penlike enclosure, hands cuffed behind my back, allowed less than four feet of slack in the chain between my collar and an iron ring embedded in the cement floor. I could squat over an open drain for my toilet, while descending from the ceiling was a flexible feeding tube whose end bent into my mouth, secured to one cheek with cloth medical tape.

Water came down every few hours, and twice daily some thicker concoction, bland and powdery tasting, like a protein shake—but really, Drake might've put anything in it. It pumped from the end of the tube, oozed between my teeth and across my tongue, and I swallowed.

For hours each night, I could hear music from the dance floor overhead, filtered of treble to a framework of thumps. Whenever it ended and silence fell, I knew that closing time had come again . . . and my master's voice was soon to follow, from two floors above.

"From *120 Days of Sodom,* the Complex Passions, entry ninety-seven," he began, then read: "'A man is whipped by three girls, alternately wielding a martinet, a bull's prick, and a cat o' nine tails. A fourth girl kneels beneath him sucking his cock and reaming his ass while she is being sodomized by the man's valet.'"

"Amen," I said around the feeding tube, imagining myself as that anonymous man.

"I've sent for a bull's prick, so perhaps we can give this a whirl," came Drake's voice. It might've been true, or maybe he was just toying with me, making promises he would never keep. "But it may take time. The bulls, you realize, are very attached to them."

His voice echoed hollow along a tarnished brass pipe, running through the ceiling from far above and down into my pen, like a speaking tube on an old ship that linked the captain at his helm with engineers belowdecks. Drake could've afforded something more modern, an intercom, but I believe he enjoyed the sense of human proximity that would've been lost to electronics.

"Entry one thirty-five: 'A girl is bound hand and foot, facing a wall. Between her and the wall is placed a blade of sharp steel adjusted to the height of her stomach. Then she is beaten. Whenever she leans forward to avoid the lash, she is cut.'"

"Amen," I said, and now imagined being the girl.

"We tried this a little earlier," he told me. "She's quite resilient, isn't she? Not that *you* ever tested her limits. Then, she never tested yours, so your relationship really was a complete waste of vows, wasn't it? You may speak."

Whatever I said, my mouth wasn't close enough to the pipe for him to hear me.

"Back to work, then. No . . . rest for the wicked." He sounded so weary I felt mildly concerned for him. "Did you know her bleeding coagulates quicker than anyone else's I've ever known?"

Drake sighed; from somewhere near him came the faint sound of a high, feminine whimper. Or maybe it was laughter. With Aimee, it had sometimes been hard to tell the difference.

"Really," he said, before rattling the brass plate back over the mouthpiece, "between the two of you, you're exhausting me."

Well now, whose fault was that, I wondered, if he wasn't up to the job? I wondered, too, who wielded the real control here. For while Drake was the one who inflicted the pain and degradation, we were the ones inciting him to it in the first place, effortlessly, making him dance to that subtle and needy tune of our own.

He seemed so much less worthy when I thought of it that way.

Two evenings later, another heavy fluid meal found its way down the tube and into my mouth. As the flow was about to stop, I felt a new texture I'd not been fed before, some smooth solid bit catching on my tongue. I chewed at it for a moment and found it too tough, so I leaned over to spit it onto the concrete.

It took me a minute to realize what it was, but this was only a problem of context. Most people aren't accustomed to seeing someone's baby toe anywhere else but still on the foot.

A valuable reminder—still and all, we are but the sum of our parts, and sometimes not even that.

I began to laugh, loudly, laugh until Drake at last came down and opened the door of my pen, as we both knew he would eventually have to do. He glared at me with haggard, dark-rimmed eyes.

"It's not de Sade, but listen to the story anyway," I told him. "We'll start at the end, too, then work our way back over the years. 'One Sunday afternoon, a fifteen-year-old boy is home alone with his father when the man goes into cardiac arrest. He sends his son to the medicine cabinet after his nitroglycerine tablets. But when the boy gets the tin, all he can think of is being a lot smaller, and the first time his father forced a new crayon an inch up into the boy's urethra for wetting the bed. And the things this led to over the next few years. So the fifteen-year-old boy holds those pills just out of reach and watches his father crawl halfway across the family room before the old man finally gives out.'"

I nodded down toward that pitiful toe, rotting on the floor like a pale little nut.

"Is that the best you can do?" I demanded then,

with all the impudence of a runaway slave come back to seize control of the Big House.

Drake said nothing, the sum of his own parts, and turned away to come up with some better method to start prying apart the rest of mine.

COMEBACK

Graham Watkins

*H*is brow deeply furrowed, Tony Andrews stared at the card he himself had written. *This can't be right,* he thought. And yet the numbers on the rundown factory he was standing in front of agreed with those on the card, and he was on Seventeenth Street, he'd already checked that.

With a disgusted snort, he started walking toward the front door even though he knew it was a mistake; this wasn't a movie studio. Either he or the man who'd called him, the supposed movie producer, had screwed things up. Not even the lowest-budget films—not even the most sleazy of porno films— would be made in a rat trap like this.

When he'd gotten the call a few days previously, he'd been more than pleased. It had been his first offer in almost three years. Thinking about it as he walked up to the door, he shook his head. It was incredible how fast things could change in this business. In the mid-'80s his phone had been ringing off the hook, all the time. Back then, every producer of hard-core films wanted Big Tony, heir apparent to the legendary but late Johnny "Wadd" Holmes.

Unfortunately for Tony, he'd never really appreciated that he was only one of several dozen exceptionally endowed men who'd been told that they were Johnny Wadd's heir. After a few years in the business, Tony had gotten a little jaded; the pace—at his peak, he'd been doing as many as six films a week—had gotten to him. A few wrinkles around his eyes and a couple of episodes where neither his costar nor the "fluff" girls could coax an erection out of him had suddenly brought the phone calls to an almost overnight halt. Since then, he'd done a grand total of ten films—ten films in the first seven of the last ten years—and in three of those he'd been playing the role of John Holmes, to whom he bore a certain resemblance. Once the parts were gone, so was most of his money. Tony, like his role model Holmes, had sniffed a great deal of his earnings up his nose and had been reduced to living in a walkup apartment in East L.A. as he fought for a chance to make a comeback.

A chance he believed he'd finally, after dozens of disappointments, gotten. The caller had identified himself as Jerome Tompkins of the Forever Young company, a manufacturer of "adult products." He'd said he had a need for Tony in the production of, as he'd put it, their current line.

And now this, this rundown and apparently abandoned factory. Standing on the landing in front of the door, he reached out for the knob but hesitated; if this wasn't a mistake, then it was going to be a low he'd not yet experienced, he was sure of that.

On the other hand, he told himself, even a job for some super-sleaze producer was better than none. He tried the knob, the door opened, and he walked inside.

The place was not, as it turned out, abandoned. The

front-office area looked to be in near ruins, but a young man in T-shirt and jeans was seated at a desk just inside. He looked up from a magazine when Tony came in.

"Yeah?" the young man asked. "Whatcha want?"

"Uh—my name's Tony Andrews—I'm looking for Jerome Tompkins?"

The kid grinned. "Oh, yeah. Big Tony. Jero said you'd be dropping by." He stood up. When he did, Tony noticed a remarkably obvious handgun stuffed into the waistband of his pants. "Oh, don't worry about this," the boy said, seeing where he was looking. He patted the gun. "You saw how the place looks, we get lotsa bums wandering in here. Some of 'em don't leave just 'cause you tell 'em to."

The boy walked to the door and locked it. "C'mon," he said. "Lemme take you down to Jero. I gotta get back, we're expecting some more folks today." Turning, he walked down a hallway lit only by a few bare bulbs and littered with trash. Tony, though somewhat hesitantly, followed.

"Uh—look," Tony ventured as they walked along. "Uh, what kind of an operation is this, anyhow? I mean—"

"I'll let Jero tell you that." He tossed Tony a grin over his shoulder. "I know what you think—but you're about to get a surprise, Tony!"

He stopped at a door near the end of the hallway, fumbled with keys for a moment, then opened it. On the other side was a stair leading down; it was brightly lit and bore little resemblance to the hallway Tony was standing in.

At the base of the stairs, the difference became even more dramatic. The basement hallway was lushly carpeted, immaculately clean; rows of offices and suites lined both sides. Near the far end was what looked to Tony like the entrance to a soundstage.

"Damn!" Tony muttered. "Surprise ain't the word!"

"Yeah. Jero values his privacy." He stopped at a frosted-glass door. "Here's his office." He opened the door and led Tony in.

At a desk in the back of a spacious suite sat an outrageously beautiful woman. He stared at her; dark-haired but light-skinned, she was more striking than most of the actresses he'd costarred with.

"Big Tony!" she enthused. "We're so glad you came! I'm Mimi Trask, Jero's secretary." Winking and holding up a finger, she picked up her phone. "I'll let him know you're here." She spoke into the phone for a moment, then hung up. "He'll be right out."

"I'll leave him with you, then," said the kid who'd escorted him down. "I gotta get back up to the door."

"'Kay, Zeke," Mimi answered. "See you later." She looked back at Tony and smiled as if she were about to say something else, but just then the inner office door swung open. An athletic-looking sixtyish man in a business suit came out.

"Tony!" he roared heartily. "Glad you came! I'm Jero Tompkins!" He extended a hand.

Tony took it. "Well, I'm glad to be here, Mr. Tompkins, I—"

"Jero, please! Nobody calls me Mr. Tompkins!" He almost beamed at Tony. "Well! I suppose you're curious about our operation here?"

"Well, yes, I am . . . I mean, when I saw the way the place looks from the outside, I thought . . ."

"We're a very exclusive company," Jero told him. "Very exclusive. We do not cater to the mass market here, Tony! No, what we produce is for a very limited, very select audience!"

More than once in the past, Tony'd found himself accused of being perhaps less than brilliant. That something wasn't quite right here, however, was too apparent for even Tony to miss.

"Look," he said. "Look, Mr.—um, Jero. I don't wanna insult you or anything, but look, you aren't into anything—uh—really far out here, are you?"

Jero cocked his head and looked curious. "Far out?"

"Oh, gee, I dunno—like, ah, snuff films or anything? Look, don't take no offense or nothin', I'm just—"

Jero's curious look faded to a tolerant smile. "I'm not taking offense, Tony," he answered. "In point of fact, you aren't the first person to ask that question. It's understandable; there are so many tales about 'snuff film' makers, and, because we've taken the trouble to camouflage our facility, well, it's a conclusion several people have leaped to."

"So you aren't? Making snuff films here, I mean?"

Jero laughed. He put an arm around Tony's shoulders and steered him toward the door. "Tony, there are no makers of snuff films. You were in the business for years. Did you ever know any?"

"Well, no. But there were always people saying somebody they knew knew somebody that—"

"Which is the way rumors always are. Think about it; using the special effects that're available now, we can create an on-screen death so realistic you'd have absolutely no way of telling it didn't happen. We can behead people, disembowel them, whatever. And no one gets hurt. If we can do that, then why actually kill anyone, why take the legal risk? It doesn't make sense, now, does it?"

"I guess not. Uh—you make any of those, um, special effects snuff films?"

"We've done a few," Jero answered offhandedly. "You just met Mimi, she starred in one of those. She

69

was stabbed a dozen times and then beheaded. If I showed you the loop, you'd swear it was real. But you were talking to her just a few minutes ago."

"Oh." Tony hesitated. By that time, they were well out into the hallway outside Tompkins's office. "Uh, Jero, you aren't wanting me to play in a film like that, are you? I mean, I dunno if—"

Jero gave him another curious look. "You'd refuse, Tony? I thought you were eager for a new role. I thought you wanted to make a comeback."

"Oh, I do—I am. But—well—" He paused again, scratched his head hard. "Well—maybe I would—if it was fake and all, maybe—"

"Don't worry, Tony." Jero laughed. "I was just curious about your reaction. We weren't planning to use you in a fake snuff film anyway. As I said, we only do a few of those, mostly by special request. The major part of our business is a little more ordinary, but, I think, just as interesting!" He stopped, looked around. "Ah, yes," he said, pointing at a door. "This is a good example." He turned, opened the door, went inside. Tony followed.

This room seemed to house a light industrial division. Several uniformed technicians looked up as they came in. "Here," he said, pointing out a computer-driven lathe. "We're making ben-wa balls. I'm sure you're familiar with them?"

Tony frowned. "Yeah, sure. But they're pretty damn common—"

Jero picked up a small globe, handed it to Tony. "Like this? These are common?"

Tony examined it. It was a simple perfect sphere, golden metallic, with a tiny perforation passing through its center. "It's nice—"

"The surface is eighteen-karat gold," Jero informed him. "We also do them in platinum. But that's not all. Roll it in your hand."

He did, rolling it gently. To his amazement, it began moving on its own. He opened his hand, cupping it, staring at the golden ball; it swirled around aimlessly on his palm.

Tony looked up at Jero. "How? Does it have a motor in it?"

"It's hollow, Tony. It contains a series of balanced weights and a gyro. It was developed for us by a Swiss clockmaker skilled in old techniques. Just a slight stimulation is sufficient to keep it moving for quite a while. These are quite expensive; we have an economy model that does indeed contain a series of small motors and a rechargeable lithium battery, which is switched on for a preset time by external movement."

"Economy model?"

"Yes. The motorized sets sell for a mere twenty-five thousand per three-ball set. Quite a bargain." He took the ball back from Tony's almost numb hand and directed his attention to an area where a number of technicians were making jewelry. He didn't have to be informed of the value. The diamond-studded nipple rings and the platinum ampallang with emeralds set in both balls spoke for themselves.

"I can see why you don't want attention drawn to this stuff," Tony said. "I can't believe this place isn't crawling with armed guards."

"There are plenty of them around," Jero said offhandedly. "They don't make themselves obvious." He started toward the door. "But come, let's go to the doll shop."

"The doll shop?"

"Yes. You'll find that even more interesting, I'm sure. And it's right next door to the photographic studios—which is, as I'm sure you know, where you'll be performing at least some of your services for us."

"Okay." He followed Jero into the hallway again and down to the area he'd identified earlier as a soundstage. Just before they reached it, Jero stopped at another door and went in.

Here was another machine shop, this one involved with the production of various tiny motors and what Jero informed him were servo mechanisms. Proudly, Jero showed him one and had a technician demonstrate its operation. Puzzled, Tony watched as a series of miniature motors pulled a small elastic band back and forth, a remarkably smooth and almost lifelike movement, but one whose purpose eluded Tony completely.

"Tell him, Mike," he asked the technician. "Explain what it's for."

"Well," the man said, "it's a part for one of our 'love dolls.' It—"

"Love dolls? You mean those inflatable things?" Tony laughed. "You make those here?"

"Yes, we do," Mike, answered, unfazed. "Very special ones. This mechanism, Tony, will be a part of a lower lip. You understand?"

"You make the lips on these things move?" Tony asked. "Really?"

"Yes, indeed," Mike replied. He glanced at Jero. "Shall we show him Janice? She's finished, she's ready to be shipped."

"Surely. Why not? He's interested in our operation."

"Okay." Mike got up from his workbench and led Tony across the room. As he went, he glanced around, seeing that at least twenty or thirty techs were working here. From a shelf on the back wall, Mike took a mahogany case; setting it on a table, he opened it.

Tony stared at the doll inside. Most of the torso was deflated, but the head and a number of other parts— the groin area, the hands and feet, the knees and elbows—were not. The face looked very lifelike, a stunning young woman with reddish hair. Her eyes were closed.

"Now what?" Tony asked as Mike took it out. "You blow her up?"

"Nothing so crude," Mike answered. He showed Tony a small gas cartridge. Fitting it to the doll's navel, he pressed a button. In a matter of a couple of seconds, the doll inflated to life-size.

"Turn her on, Mike," Jero urged.

Grinning, Mike ran his hands up into the doll's red hair in the back; he must've hit a switch there, because her eyes slowly opened.

"Hi, lover," the doll said in a sultry voice. "I'm Janice. I'm ready to satisfy your every desire." As she spoke, her eyes moved; the motion was realistic but aimless.

"Damn," Tony breathed, impressed. He reached out, hesitated; when there was no objection, he touched the doll's breast.

"Oooh, yes," Janice breathed. Her hands moved a little.

"God, it feels like a real tit," Tony muttered. "Doesn't feel like vinyl at all."

"The surface textures," Jero told him, "were a priority." He smiled. "She's fully automatic, Tony. There's a chip in her head controlling her movements. She's limited, she can't get up and walk around, but you'd be surprised at what she can do!"

"Like what?"

"Put your finger in her mouth. Or in her vagina."

With a little hesitation, Tony moved a finger toward the doll's mouth. When he touched her lips, she sighed and her mouth opened, revealing a very authentic-looking tongue. As he pushed his finger inside, she started sucking it, even moving her tongue around the tip of it.

"That's awesome!" Tony enthused. "Man! That feels so goddam real!" He withdrew his finger, put it in her vagina. The opening not only moistened itself immediately, but it tented to fit his finger precisely; at the same time, Janice drew her legs up a little, bending them at the knees, and began to move her hips sensuously.

"She won't do the same thing every time, either," Jero said as Tony stared dumbfounded. "There's a randomizer in her program. She shifts around—though you can set some of the variables yourself."

Tony withdrew his finger. "Incredible," he said. "But Jero—a thing like this—it's got to cost—"

"That model," Jero interrupted, "will sell for three hundred thousand dollars. She's rather bottom-of-the-line."

Tony looked amazed. "But who the hell would pay that kinda bucks for it? It's still a damn doll!"

"You'd be surprised. There're diseases out there these days, Tony. AIDS. There're men for whom half a million isn't much who don't want to take any risks. That's what we provide."

"You must make some hellacious videos, too!"

Jero and Mike exchanged glances. "Ah, well, I suppose you could say we do. Should we proceed to the staging area?"

"Yeah. I wanna see this!"

By comparison with what he'd already seen, the "staging area" was more than a little disappointing for Tony. He'd expected something lavish, something like a major Hollywood studio. Instead, the central part of the staging area consisted of a single low bed with video cameras and lights standing all around it, sticking up under it, hanging down over it. Beyond were tables covered with computers; the floor was hospital tile. On one wall was a large industrial-type sink, on another various devices that looked like they belonged in a hospital.

"I don't get it," Tony said. "No sets?" He pointed. "This is gonna be bad, there's gonna be cameras in all the backgrounds—"

"Now, Tony, that really isn't your concern, is it?" He shrugged.

"But I might as well explain—all of our cameras here are computer-controlled. Nothing ends up on the primary tape except the images of the performers."

"Oh. Sorta like the way they make those space movies, huh?"

"Something like that." Jero looked like he was about to say something else, but at that point a burly man came out of an office off to their left. "Phone for you, Jero," he called. "It's Zeke. He says Cecilia Desmond is here."

"Oh, good. Look, Dave, just tell him to have Mimi bring her down here, okay?" The burly man nodded and disappeared back into the room.

"Cecilia Desmond?" Tony asked. "The one who starred in *G-Spot Goddess?*"

"The same. She's going to be your costar."

"She is? But Jero—hey, don't get me wrong, she's a knockout, she's great, but—didn't she do that exposé on adult films?"

"*An Inside View.* Yes, she did—and a lot of the industry didn't find it flattering, especially since a lot of the things she said—"

"Weren't true," Tony finished for him.

"Right. And yes, she's not been welcome on any adult sets since. But she didn't parlay *An Inside View* into the movie career she'd hoped for. She's been trying to get back in—just as you have—and we thought we'd give her the chance. As you say, she is an exquisitely beautiful woman."

75

"But—I mean, you're all concerned about your secrecy here—aren't you worried she'll—"

"Do an exposé on us? No, Tony. We're not worried about that." As if knowing that it was about time for Mimi and the actress to arrive, he turned toward the door. A moment later, it opened, and Mimi ushered a woman who was, if anything, her superior in appearance into the studio. She was slender, dark-eyed, her hair short and quite black, her legs extraordinarily long; her breasts were quite large, larger than was proportional for a woman her size.

"Cecilia!" Jero gushed. "So glad you came!" He turned to Tony, introduced him. "You know his films?"

She extended a hand. "I haven't seen 'em," she said flatly. "But I've heard of you. A pleasure, Tony."

"You'll be working with Tony," Jero informed her. She glanced at him. "Yeah? Cool."

"So," Jero said, looking from one to the other. "Are you two ready to work?"

"Uh—now?" Tony asked.

"Any time," Cecilia answered promptly.

"You have a problem with now, Tony?" Jero inquired, his brow furrowing with concern.

"Well, no, no, I don't. It just didn't look like you were set up here—"

"As I said, our cameras are computer-controlled." He glanced toward the office. "Dave!" he called. "Come on out here. Bring Jock with you. We're going to shoot some video!"

Dave came out immediately, bringing with him another equally burly man, and the two of them set to checking the equipment. "Okay," Jero said, pointing toward the bed as the lights began coming on. "Let's get undressed, let's get to it."

Tony shrugged. This sort of hurry-up operation

wasn't unfamiliar. It wasn't quite what he'd expected from Jero's company, but it really didn't matter, as long as he was paid. He started unbuttoning his shirt, then realized they hadn't even discussed the pay, hadn't signed a contract. Jero told him reassuringly that he didn't need to worry about the money. When Cecilia took up that line of questions, Jero told them they should perhaps regard this first tape as a tryout.

"We always take care of our employees," Jero insisted. "You can trust or not. I'm sure you've both done tryouts before in any event."

Tony glanced at Cecilia; she shrugged, went on removing her clothes. As he undressed, Tony watched her; the promise her body had offered clothed was surpassed by the reality. Feeling aroused already, he took her by the hand and led her to the bed. Both climbed atop it. As the video cameras began their almost subliminal whirring, Tony kissed her, toyed with her breasts. She moaned and squirmed theatrically; she clearly knew her craft well. Kissing down the front of her body, Tony pushed his head between her legs and began to lick at her genitals.

"Don't bother with that," Jero called. He and Mimi had seated themselves in folding chairs they'd gotten from somewhere. "Come on back up. Cecilia, you want to go down on him?"

"Uh—sure." Following his example, she grazed her tongue over his chest, then fairly quickly moved on down until her head was in his lap. She looked up at him and smiled. "You're huge," she said admiringly, wrapping her hands around the shaft of his by now almost erect penis. "I think you're the biggest one for me." She puckered her lips and began licking his penis; a second later, she slipped as much of it into her mouth as would fit and started moving her head on it.

"Notice the way she pushes the head into her cheek, the way it bulges out," Tony heard Mimi comment. "It's an interesting effect."

"It is," Jero agreed. "Take a note, Dave."

Cecilia shook her head and grinned, but kept sucking his penis for several minutes, until finally Jero called to them to move on to intercourse. "Missionary first," he ordered.

Cecilia stretched out on the bed. She squirmed a little—quite apparently not in pleasure—as he gently slipped the full length of his penis inside her. He moved on her for a while, feeling good about the way things were going. He found it a little annoying when Jero called out for them to shift, for Cecilia to come atop him, but they dutifully shifted positions, her straddling him and impaling herself slowly on him. Jero called out for him to lie still, to let Cecilia move her hips on him; again they complied, Tony contenting himself to caress her full breasts. She was getting used to him now, he could tell, beginning to enjoy herself—and he'd been enjoying himself from the beginning.

"Now, boys," he heard Jero order. He glanced around. Dave was leaning over the table behind Cecilia. He'd grabbed her by her hair and was pushing her head forward. Abruptly, Cecilia went rigid atop him, her eyes wide open. Tony stared, not knowing what was happening.

Then Cecilia began to fall over onto him, and he saw that Dave had driven an icepick-like instrument into the back of her neck, angling it upward so that the tine had to be up inside her brain.

"What the fuck?" Tony screamed. He flailed under her. Dave dragged her off him. The other man, Jock, was standing close, too. Tony felt a pinprick pain in his arm, swiped at it. As Dave dragged Cecilia off him, he lunged to his feet.

"Get her back on the table," Jero commanded. "Come on, boys, you know this has to be done quickly!"

Ignoring Tony, Dave and Jock put Cecilia on the table, face up. Dave had removed the icepick from her neck. She lay twitching, her eyes still open; Tony could not tell if she was dead or alive. Jock apparently wasn't interested in such questions. He pulled up some sort of machine with a tank on it, grabbed a clear vinyl hose with a huge hollow needle on the end of it, and promptly drove the needle deep into Cecilia's navel. He then flipped a foot switch on the machine, and the clear tubing immediately turned red.

"Be careful!" Jero yelled. "Don't damage the skin!"

"You lied to me, you fuck!" Tony cried. "You said you didn't do snuff films!" He took a step toward the older man; then, feeling unsteady on his feet, he grabbed at a nearby table.

Jero laughed. "We don't," he said. "We might not've even gotten Cecilia's demise on tape. It doesn't matter."

"Then why? Why'd you kill her?"

Jero shook his head. "We use only the best materials in our products, Tony. Can you imagine a better covering for a love doll than human skin?"

Tony held the edge of the bed even more tightly. "You mean to tell me—that other one, that Janice—"

"Yes, of course. Another out-of-work actress." He looked over at the now still and somewhat shrunken form of Cecilia. "We'll cast her facial bones and her pelvis. The final product will be very much like Cecilia indeed!" He smiled as the men started spreading a thick brownish cream over the corpse, rubbing it into the skin. "And she'll stay like that indefinitely, too. The chemical treatments we've developed for preserving the skin—I can't take the credit for them, of course, but we're working miracles here. It's just a modification of ordinary tanning, but the way we do it, the skin stays soft and supple—well, as far as we know, forever. Our oldest models aren't showing any degradation at all, and they're over ten years old now. Always young, never changing. Wonderful. Just wonderful."

"But why me?" Tony wiped at his face. He was feeling more than a little sick. "Why me, why this sham of a video?"

"Oh, it wasn't a sham, Tony! When we make our little motors, when we arrange Cecilia's mouth and hips to move, they'll move much as hers did in life. To simulate this, we must have good pictures of this action!" He grinned. "And I want to thank you for providing them!"

"Why me?" Tony asked again. "Why not one of these apes? Why . . ." His tongue felt thick, he lost his balance, he sank to his knees; only then did he notice the empty hypodermic syringe lying on the floor beside the bed.

"Your size made for some very definitive pictures, Tony," Jero explained. "But that isn't why we wanted you here. That was just a side benefit. It wasn't the main reason."

Tony just stared dumbly. Dave and Jock, evidently finished for the moment with Cecilia, picked him up under his arms and pulled him toward the bed.

"We also," he heard Jero saying from behind him, "make a line of dildos, Tony. Very realistic ones, very expensive ones . . ."

RAZORBLADE VALENTINES

Thomas S. Roche

Valery and I came to realize over the years that Kathryn was not going to leave us. She was with us to stay—and, more importantly, we were with her. Sometimes love, or pain, or admiration, becomes its own kind of goddess, or god, to be worshipped rather than experienced. And so it was with Kathryn. The agonies she had imposed on us brought me back repeatedly to suffer with her, and with her other guests, who returned from their respective lives before/beyond the grave to witness the morbid ritual of love and obsession. Kathryn would not be denied.

I suffered from intermittent delusions and/or hallucinations occurring every Valentine's Day. They grew more convincing as the years wore on, until the real world conformed to my delusion, rather than the other way around. Every annum the Day approached with relentless abandon, every day a fragment of Kathryn's cruel laughter, every moment a moment closer to her. I sipped flat champagne and blew soundless horns every New Year's Eve. I looked at the faded black-and-white photographs with alternating anticipation and terror. Kathryn, beautiful in her black dress, never cracking a smile. I could remember that the photographs had once held a smiling Kathryn, but over the years that had gradually changed, and now would never be again. Kathryn's smile had gone.

A week into February, I stood in the parlor looking over the faded pictures in their vaguely postmodern frames. Valery approached, looking over my shoulder. She sighed.

"We can't go this year," she said.

"I know," I answered. "I know we can't. We're going to stay here."

And I turned and embraced her desperately, abandoning myself to the fear, trying to blot the memory of Kathryn out of our minds. I ran my fingers through her long blond hair, tangling myself in it, smelling her scent. We went upstairs and made love violently on the velvet-canopied bed. Valery's taste enveloped me, her scent aroused me, her fingernails carved furrows of desperation in my back. Valery bit me at the moment of our greatest passion, when both of us climaxed whispering fervent wordless prayers to our dark gods. I remembered a particular night with Kathryn . . .

The next morning in the mailbox, I found a pair of plane tickets in an envelope full of cash. Kathryn did not require original receipts. The envelope, tucked in among the catalogs and bills, was addressed to the house in the hills, where I had lived when it happened. But it had somehow made its way here. The Berkeley postmark was Valentine's Day twelve years ago. It had been the same, eleven times. I could recall the words Kathryn used when she came to me in my nightmare that night, and I knew that none of her threats was empty. Fate, or something like it, had conspired to place me at her mercy again, and I knew that I would go, as would Valery, and that the unholy ritual would be reenacted as if it were inscribed on the insides of our skulls with a chisel. The rest of them would be there, too. It would be Valentine's Day. And Kathryn's Valentines would open themselves, one by one.

The limo driver met us at the gate, dressed in a tuxedo. The arrangements had been made by phone, no doubt paid for by household account. He took us to our hotel and told us he would return at the appointed time.

As if to blot out Kathryn's memory, Valery and I came together hungrily once more and made love in the frigid hotel air amid the contemporary sterility and commercialized charm. I lit a cigarette afterward, sprawled among the rumpled sheets, witnessing Kathryn's face in the smoke. Valery took a drag and sighed sadly.

"We can't escape," she told me. "We're being punished, every year, like clockwork. She'll never let us go. But we can't live forever . . . or can we? It was so long ago . . ."

It had been like this every year. Remembering, dreading the moment when we would see Kathryn's ash-gray face and taste her blood-red lips.

I looked at Valery. Her hair, so carefully grown out and styled, so meticulously bleached blond, had begun to become shorter and go dark. It was now a blackened ash-gray color. Her face had become paler, her lips a slightly deeper red. Much as it pained me to admit it, she wore it well. The years had started to melt off her face, like clockwork. I sighed and shook my head.

"It was Valentine's Day," I said. "It was tomorrow."

My tuxedo and Valery's dress were waiting in the hotel room closet. Valery sat at the vanity, staring into the mirror, applying her makeup with a grim, doomed sort of determination. Her hair was now completely black, almost blue-black, and hung in a smooth curtain to her shoulders. I watched as she applied the makeup until her flesh was pale gray and her lips were the color of Kathryn's blood.

The dress was the same, flawless. She had worn it every Valentine's Day since the first one. It came to a point and was clasped with a black lacquered rose between her milk-white breasts. She had grown thinner through the night, her flesh wasting from her bones, until she was thin and pale as a corpse. It was a horror to see her, but the old habits took me over, and I found myself admiring her, admiring her proximity to death. Similar changes had come over me, and my hair hung long and black. As I dressed, I noted my meticulous California tan fading, my well-trimmed beard shedding like the skin of a snake. Fragments of it lay scattered about the white pillow. My cummerbund was red.

The limousine arrived at the appointed time.

The guests had started to arrive. The limousine dropped us off, and we walked slowly, clutching each other, up the long, winding path to the big double door.

Roz was there, and Michael and Lydia and Andrew, Peter and Ian, Alice and Mario. Their hair was, as a group, jet black. They were flawless, pale, corpselike, beautiful. They moved with wispy precision, making strained conversation in hushed tones, floating through the room, flirting vaguely, eating crudités. Kathryn stood on the landing, surveying the room. Her eyes shone black, her lips red, her face expressionless and eternally twenty-three. She wore her black dress, of course, and the rose décolleté. I could still see through her flesh. That would change as midnight approached.

I looked up at her, shook my head. I turned to Valery.

"This can't be happening," said Valery. "It can't be Valentine's Day."

"Oh, but it is," I said grimly, pulling her close. I managed a smile and then started to laugh hysterically.

There were many of us, come to pay respects again. Each of us bore the sad expression of loss, of guilt, of the need for expiation. Each of us tried to avoid looking toward Kathryn's faintly translucent form on the balcony.

She was beginning to solidify. I looked up, grinned at her, and tipped my drink.

Embarrassed, Valery looked away.

Kathryn stared at me, the edges of her blood lips slightly downturned.

"Bitch," I muttered. I had used up all my sympathy for her in the first eleven years following her death.

The grandfather clock struck midnight like the slow chime of a death knell. Kathryn glanced back down at me as she floated up the stairs and disappeared into the master bedroom.

The guests began to file silently up the stairs: boy, girl, boy, girl, boy, girl. I followed Valery at the end of the line.

The clock's chimes completed their cycle. It was Valentine's Day.

It is possible that this series of events was caused by a fully virtual shared hallucination. Such things have been documented in the literature. I cannot believe that Kathryn was able to exert her hold physically from beyond the grave, year after year, on upward of a dozen people. But I also cannot believe that I am mad.

Regardless of the cause, or the method, we all knew we were real. The bedroom was filled with silent, translucent bodies awaiting their turns.

Kathryn stood at the foot of the bed as we crowded around the edges of the big room, keeping a respectful distance.

Her flesh was still translucent. I sadly watched as she lowered herself onto the bed, blinking once. In her right hand gleamed her grandmother's razor blade, smooth and slim and deadly. The white lace bedspread buckled stiffly. The bed was canopied in red velvet. We stood watching helplessly, for Kathryn would not be corporeal until the ritual had been enacted.

I could not help but watch as Kathryn's ghost performed the ritual. As always, it was my inclination to grab her, to make her stop, to save her. But that was not possible. She set the razor on the bed behind her, then unclasped her dress. She shrugged the garment off, letting it fall over her shoulders. She wore a flawless white slip, silk, and beautiful as ever. The black dress dropped to the floor, and she easily stepped out of it, then began to shed her underclothes.

Kathryn climbed onto the bed and prepared herself for suicide.

Disrespectfully, I tossed my head and lit a cigarette. Valery glared at me, horrified, but no one asked me to put it out. Valery's horror grew as I blew smoke toward the bed.

Even I did not dare to speak, however, not until the ritual was completed.

I considered Kathryn. How fascinating she had been in life, how pale, how young, how dangerous. Her sadness had taken us all by storm, and she had become our lover, as a group. The sadness had encompassed all of us, and we were powerless to stop what happened.

Kathryn drew the blade slowly up her wrist.

Her flesh solidified somewhat, becoming more real. But she was untouchable for now—we knew that from experience.

Shaking, Kathryn held the blade in her other hand. She was barely able to make the cut. But once it had been made, she knew that her part of the task was accomplished. The blood drained from her wrists, spreading across the bedspread. If it had not been for her hereditary medical condition, she might not have died like this. She might be alive today, attending concerts . . .

Fuck it. The task had been accomplished again. There's no point in dreaming.

Kathryn's translucent breasts rose and fell gradually, then more slowly, then not at all. Her eyes fluttered closed; then she blinked once, twice, three times. I could still see through her body, faintly. The eyes came shut again. Her lips parted slightly. Kathryn's body quivered, then jerked. It was a long time before her eyes opened again.

I crushed out my cigarette on the floor.

Kathryn's nude body had become solid. She was now a corpse, no longer a ghost. She was still as frail and lovely and waiflike as ever, but she had become real, and our obligation now began. We were, after all, her guests in this demented liturgy.

Roz went first this time. She had been the one who found Kathryn. Slowly, Roz unhitched her dress, and Sharon helped her out of it. I watched as Roz shed her clothes, then crawled naked onto the bed and embraced Kathryn. She removed the razor from between Kathryn's breasts and set it on the oak nightstand. Very gently at first, and then more passionately, Roz brought her lips to Kathryn's, working them farther open. The tongue lazed out of Roz's mouth, and she began to kiss Kathryn with all her dead soul.

Her tongue trailed down Kathryn's throat, tasting the splattered drops of blood. Roz kissed down to Kathryn's breasts, stroked Kathryn's face, affectionately brushed back the jet-black hair. She stroked Kathryn's eyelids, closing them, then moved her way down the body as they opened themselves.

I hated myself for doing it, but I watched with fascination. The unholy liturgy continued.

Roz's face descended, and Roz chanted her requiem into Kathryn's lifeless body.

Gradually, Sharon's hands began to work on her own clothing, and her own shimmering black dress fell away. She joined Roz on the bed, gaining her courage from Roz's ministrations. Sharon twined her body around Kathryn's. Sharon began to kiss Kathryn as Roz continued.

Sharon swung her legs over Kathryn's body, crouching down to kiss her.

Roz lifted her face, weeping softly. She had fulfilled her responsibility to Kathryn's memory. But she lowered her face again, and her head bobbed up and down slowly. Gradually, her body faded, until I could see the skull tattoo on Kathryn's thigh through Roz's transparent cheeks. Roz slowly became a vision, then a smoky specter, until I wasn't sure if she was there at all. She slipped away, and Joseph took her place. Sharon kindly moved aside part of the way. Sharon kissed Joseph once, tenderly, and then continued to tease Kathryn's lips with her tongue as Joseph joined her. Kathryn's body seemed to move with the two of them.

Sharon knew what was required of her. She lowered herself onto Kathryn, her legs spread around Kathryn's face, tears dribbling down Sharon's face and onto her breasts. Sharon faded slowly, until she was nothing more than Roz had been at the end. Then she was gone.

Joseph's breathing quickened audibly as I came to see Kathryn's face through his back. Finally, when he cried out, he vanished. Kathryn lay unattended for several minutes as the remaining guests watched.

Several guests moved forward at once, each of them nervous and tentative.

It was Alice and Mario who next took their places atop Kathryn. Alice disappeared slowly as she rode Kathryn, mouth descending fiercely. Mario watched and assisted. When Alice was gone, he took her place, and his moans took him gradually onward.

And so it was, as each of the guests possessed Kathryn one by one after that, in supplication to the dark ghost for damned salvation. Until there were three of us left, the three of us who had been here for the past six years, resisting Kathryn's final embrace. Myself. Valery, my lover. And Ian.

He looked at us, sadly shaking his head.

"I can't stop it this year," he said. "I'm not strong enough. I'm sorry . . ."

I sighed. "I knew it would happen, eventually."

"It's gone on too long," he said. "It's time to end it."

I watched as Ian undressed. His body was thin but strong, muscled. His tuxedo mingled with the other rumpled clothing on the floor as he crawled onto the bed and made his way to Kathryn's body.

Valery turned away, choking back sobs. Neither of us had thought Ian would succumb this year.

Kathryn's body seemed to move underneath Ian. He grew translucent, then mostly transparent; then he was gone.

I looked to Valery. It was over. We were among the living.

Valery's eyes were filled with tears. They spilled over and ran down her cheeks. She shook her head.

"Oh God, Valery, don't."

She reached up and began to unfasten her dress.

"Don't!" I took her in my arms and kissed her, but she choked and sobbed and pushed me away. When I reached out for her again, she was like a vision, a dream, and my hand passed through her. I stood, powerless, as she let the dress slip over her body, then her slip, then her other garments, until she crawled nude onto the bed. Kathryn's blood-red lips seemed to twist in a death grin, and her arms seemed to lift to welcome Valery.

The tears ran down my cheeks as I watched my lover succumb to Kathryn's spell. The death dance gradually grew in its passion.

Gradually, she faded.

I could have sworn, then, that I heard Kathryn cry out as Valery disappeared. But I must have been mistaken.

Kathryn's corpse lay on the bed, stretched out, the blood from her wrists smeared across her nude form. I laughed, shook my head, and lit a cigarette.

So you've done it, you undead freak. You've taken everyone from me, and they've all gone willingly. Well, I can't say you didn't earn their souls. But you can't have mine.

With a grim determination, I held my lighter under the fringe of the blood-red velvet canopy. It took some time to catch, and the smoke curled around the room. Kathryn's corpse appeared to be smiling.

"Oh, fuck it," I said to no one, and kicked my way through the pile of formal clothes to the bedroom door. I did not glance back as I left the room, but I knew that the fire had gone out, that the velvet would never burn.

The limousine was waiting outside the front door.

I must have known, when we arrived that year, that Valery would open herself like a razorblade Valentine for Kathryn in the fashion that had been fated for a dozen ice-cold years. Her surrender had been inevitable, and Ian's. It was Kathryn's gift to me.

I sank into seat 12D and massaged my eyelids, faces ghosting my retinas as the page twelve headlines, read aloud in Kathryn's stage whisper, filled my ears. Roz drowned skinny-dipping at a lake near Minneapolis . . . Andrew a suicide in London . . . Alice an OD in a Catholic church . . . Michael and Lydia a drunken car wreck on the Pennsylvania Turnpike . . . Peter murdered by a horde of nuns. Yellowed clippings that arrived in manila envelopes now and then, postmarked nowhere in particular with no particular date.

I did not doubt that there would be clippings in my mailbox describing Valery's and Ian's sudden deaths a few days before Valentine's Day.

I did not doubt as I approached the airport that there would be a thirteenth Valentine's Day, travel arrangements made on unsigned credit slips from beyond the grave, a limousine to the party at Kathryn's mansion, page twelve razorblade Valentines taunting me from the mailbox. She had finally made her way to me.

For I was the one she had called, that night, to save

her. I was the one who knew what she was going to do. Valery had been away, and Kathryn had awakened me, begging forgiveness, telling me about her dreams and her visions of death and desperation, and a room full of blood-lipped ghosts possessing her dead body.

I was the one who had called Kathryn a freaky death-rock slut and slammed the phone down, thus consigning her (and, by association, myself) to oblivion.

This was her revenge. For I knew that I would return, every year, powerless to control myself, to watch Kathryn possessed by a room of pale ghosts, each of them a vision or delusion of a person who had once existed, with only myself being real. I alone in that dark room would be among the living. Until the day I succumbed to Kathryn, accepted her razorblade Valentine, gave in to her dark love. As Valery had done, and the others. Until then, I would dream of Kathryn's face, and taste her revenge so bitter at the back of my mouth.

Dawn had been breaking for some time now, but it was not yet light.

Quos deus vult perdere prius dementat: Those whom a god wishes to destroy, he first drives insane.

VAMPIRES OF LONDON

Rex Miller and Lynne Gauger

A fifty-six-year-old fat man lies sprawled across his enormous bed, one hand cupping the back of a young woman's head, the other fondling a slick, hard thing about five inches long. It is inscribed *Milano,* and the fifty-six-year-old fat man is only four—maybe five— years older than the small edged weapon he caresses. It is an Italian switchblade knife; the genuine article, circa 1942–43, made in Milan before the war short- ages turned such things into crap. He got it from the confiscated property room in some forgotten cop shop. It is very sharp, it will take a razor-edge hone, and the hard steel tapers to a dangerous stiletto point. It is good for absolutely nothing. Too short to be effective as a weapon, and the tapering point will rip trouser pockets to shreds. It looks very sexy, of course, as all the best weapons tend to do, and the spring is still quite strong, so it is fun to flick open. The fifty- six-year-old fat man uses it to cut twine on packages, things like that. He is claustrophobic and always carries the blade in his car, in case his driver's-side airbag would suddenly inflate and try to kill him. I know this guy like a book.

I wrote him, edited his fat ass, did the revisions, and finally—in recent years—produced the last draft. I'm reinventing him for the zillionth time as we speak. As I lie across my bed getting a first-class knob job, Eleanora Fagan cries from a remastered CD in my office down the hall. Ms. Fagan, Billie Holiday, assures us that love is like a faucet, it turns off and on. Ain't it the truth. After fifteen years or so, my wife and I turned our faucets off, but—for our sins—we stayed together in some kind of semiplatonic hell, a pretense of a marriage that dragged out for twenty-nine years. You can hear it in Lady's voice, she damn well knew what a bitch life could be.

The old fat man was proud to have lived by his own rules. Translation: loner. One day, he ... Jeezus, enough of that, *I,* I woke up to find I'd lost it. I'd lost everything that counted: my wife, my sense of purpose, my friends—our friends—the broken shards of family, all vanished. Success, modest or otherwise, suddenly meant zip. The money I'd counted, and counted on, was gone. She'd taken it, and the car and the CDs and the mutual funds. "I had to think of the future," she told me, on her way out the door. I'd sat there hunched over a keyboard like some idiot gargoyle pounding away at white pages until they resembled thirteen books—that was the sum of my life since 1986—and the net proceeds were now in a St. Louis bank, under a name I'd never heard before. When that faucet turns off, it's fucking brutal.

I didn't know where to turn. I grabbed the Bible and began reading the Lord's Prayer over and over, crying like a child, mumbling devotionals from youth in the hope of recapturing a day-to-day closeness with Him that I was positive I'd had as a kid. No friends, I told my guru, no sense of family, no lover, no abiding belief to hold on to. Can I return to whatever state of innocence once allowed me to seek redemption? That's essentially what I asked him. His reply hurt worse than the question.

"Not like this, you can't," he said truthfully. "You're only interested in your personal religiosity as a theoretical metaphysical key to the puzzle." That made even less sense than my asking about a lost innocence. I told him that I regarded my life as worthless and my work as junk.

"Wrong," he told me, probably working on his curve ball. "Life is a terrifying series of complexities. Because it is the deep, unsolvable mystery that it is, you serve a very therapeutic, soul-healing function. Your work, and the work of others like yourself, allows us momentary relief from our tensions, helps us to understand that we're not alone. As Doctorow says, you writers make the suffering a bit more bearable now and then. Wouldn't it be funny if your catharses in print proved to be your ticket into Heaven?" He actually speaks this way, which is how he got to be a guru, I suppose.

I never actually took all that mumbo jumbo to heart, unfortunately, but I did swipe it and began to insert it into various things I was writing. A girl in Chicago happened to read some of my stuff, and it touched a chord with her. We began a like affair by phone.

One day she showed up at my door, an absolute killer in black leather. I had the lady deleathered in about four seconds, and back where she belonged, in the big bed. Holy moley, sports fans, this was one sexy honey. For a guy who'd been celibate the last two years of his marriage, it was beyond all my fantasies. She left me slanted, reared, slithered, careened, caressed, spiraled, zigged, zagged, and stair-stepped.

What was so groovy about her? How about looks,

skill, attitude, and a sense of humor more warped than mine? She could have done stand-up: the first time she saw me naked, she remarked—not unkindly—"I've never seen such a belly on a land animal that wasn't pregnant." I was almost sure it was a line out of one of my books. If it wasn't, it was going to be. I told her she was so loose she thought monogamy was a board game. I tried to tell her other things, but her long, hot, pink, wet tongue kept getting in the way, and what was a man to do? I had to suck on it.

The hand that held her head cupped in it knotted a twist of hair and changed the tempo. Most women hate that kind of shit, but she was right into it as if she were the cartographer of my sexual map and had charted a course straight to Orgasm City. I realize this is awfully discursive, but *you* try telling *your* life story while a pretty woman gives you a world-class knob gobble.

For no real reason, I pull her head back far enough that I can see her big beautiful eyes staring up at me, and I flick Milano open in her face. Nothing changes in her gaze. The woman trusts me no end. This in itself can be a remarkable turn-on. If I tell her I want to slap her around a little, by way of freak foreplay, she begs me to do so, knowing I won't get carried away. I once asked her to hand me something, and she said in a very soft voice, "I can't, my hands are tied behind me," which of course they were. You can't imagine . . . well, maybe you can. You probably didn't get this out of the library at the seminary.

Her name is Gretchen, but she once stripped, table- and lap-danced under the name Burma Chavez, pronouncing it just the way you'd expect her to. We have had fun *out* of bed as well. We can talk about neural evolution, sun tea, mutations of the synaptic code, the sculpture in the Louvre, and quantum misterioso out the winkydoo.

I need to describe her to you: she's thirty-five, dark-haired, bangs, punk, tattooed, breasts the size of champagne glasses with nipples nearly as big as the corks, the greatest behind in Christendom, a model's coltish legs, actually just an ordinary-looking woman with a feral magnetism about her. She's right at home in the Year of the Spooky Chick, with translucent salamander-white skin and Fuck Me Red lipstick. If you were casting a thirty-five-year-old vampire with a heart of gold, you could do a lot worse.

She went to work on me for a serious couple of minutes, and the little Italian blade slipped out of my hand as I reached near-unconsciousness, which for me is a higher state, heart pounding like Chuck Berry's steam engine, gasping for oxygen like a beached whale, and moaning for my mama as I geysered into her mouth.

"Bless you, my son," she whispered, reaching for a damp washrag, making the sign of the cross with it over my flaccid gherkin. *"A coelo usque ad centrum."*

"Mortis causa," I said, *"timor mortis conturbat me,"* quoting Kenny Rexroth more than anything.

"You OK, big fella?" she whispered, hand against my chest.

"Nn." Just call me the Prince of Whales.

The second time we were together, she peeled out of a scalloped cut top in turquoise spandex and spent some time telling me about her tits.

"My dead ex-husband was a sadist as well as a coke fiend. The cocaine would take him into psycho rages, and he focused his violence on my breasts. To him, my titties were targets. He liked to stick pins in my breasts to wake me up. Another favorite pastime was when he could catch me sleeping and burn me with cigarettes."

"My God. Your breasts?"

"Look," she said, cupping them with her small,

black-polished fingernails. "See the burns?" Brown marks encircled the fleshy pink aureole around each prominent nipple. "He thought I was his fucking ashtray." She hugged me and buried her face against me. "Gone now, happy to say."

A less centered, more bent man might have been slightly turned on by such tales of tortured mammaries. Gretchen seemed to know instinctively everything to say and do to wind me up like a tin locomotive, which—by the way—is the best triple-edged pun since Lani Guinier said she was "disappointed." I asked her the second time we were together if she'd marry me. I could stand whole tons of this sort of activity. She smiled and gave me a sort of provisional yes.

"Yes, I will. Eventually. Unfortunately, a couple of things stand in the way of that at the moment, one of which is a husband in England. He's dying of leukemia, and we struck a kind of bargain where I've agreed to spend some time with him during his last months, and he's agreed to help me. Financially and in other ways."

"So it's a business deal?"

"No," she said, "not really." She flicked a gold Dunhill and touched the flame to a Players. The room filled with the blue smoke of a bog on fire. "I have cancer, so I was very sympathetic. I know what it feels like to have a doctor tell you your time is running out." She blew smoke away from me. I didn't say anything, but she read my reaction. "It's cancer of the lymph glands," she said, touching her throat. "They told me six years ago I had three years to live. I went the homeopathic route, and—what can I tell you? I haven't taken possession of my narrow underground apartment yet."

Gretchen took maybe two more drags on the nasty Players and stubbed it out, opening a voluminous purse. "I live in a more or less perpetual drug fog, but"—she shrugged her slender shoulders—"better than the pain." She lined up a row of bottles, jars, ampoules, a syringe, a thing with a small test tube sticking out of a rubber stopper. "Junkies would kill me fourteen times for this stuff." I believed her. Vanax, Valium, Dolophine, Darvon N 100, Rexamol MS solution—a regular Rexall-orama in her purse.

She told me her dead husband had been hooked on everything from coke to smack. He'd had the virus when he killed himself. She had cancer. Her dance card had been incredibly full—let's put it like that. Was I really ready for this? I mean, listen up, sports fans: if it walks like a duck, quacks like a duck, if it has a bill, nostrils, head, eyes, auricular region, neck, cape, shoulders, covers, wings, saddle, breast, second-aries, primaries, rump, tail, down, shanks, webbed feat, oily feathers, and if it likes water, well, Chuck, it's probably a fucking duck.

Any other time, with anyone else, my red bullshit detector would have gone off instantly, but what can I say? The lady had my fat ass nailed, from gemein-schaft to gesellschaft. Down cold and stone solid. Chumped off, pussy-whipped, and legs spread in the A-stance. I was meat, as in loaf. Humped and stumped, I swallowed hard and considered the op-tions, my heart slam dancing against the ticking inexorability of the cosmic jester's metronome.

The conclusion I reached was foredrawn, hell it was probably built right into the fucking DNA. The bulge in my pants had its own little brain, and a will that would prove to be stronger than a sauerkraut fart. Before Gretchen, no one could have begun to con-vince me that I'd continue such a dangerous relation-ship, but my heart and gonads had taken charge.

"Gothic rock is my scene," she'd said to me on more than one occasion, wrinkling her nose at the ancient be-bop that crackled from the speakers of my audio system. She played some of her faves for me: "Snake Dance" by March Violets, Type O Negative's "Christian Woman," "Temple of Love" by Sisters of Mercy. Witchy, sometimes sensuous dance music as epitomized by the play lists at London clubs like the Slimelight and the Electric Ballroom in Camden. The *Slime*light? Jeezus.

"These are dance clubs," she informed me, "and you can judge the popularity of a tune by how empty the bar becomes as people run to the dance floor when 'Mircalla,' or whatever, comes on. Everybody from the bartenders to the DJs has the gothic look: white faces, black or blond hair, black clothes, lace, lots of velvet, lots of silver—crosses, rosaries, ankhs, pentagrams—the London vampire look."

"A bunch of punk vampire wanna-bes."

"Fuck you. What's so bad about wanting to be beautiful and live forever?"

That night, she came to me in a black dress that appeared to be painted onto her—the Harlow look—a nipple- and cunt- and butt-accentuating thing that was soft, shimmery and seductive, long and mysterious, revealing everything and nothing, from her womanliness down to the tips of pointy patent stilettos.

She'd teased her hair into a loosely finger-dried nest, colored with streaks of indigo, purple, and lavender. About a pound and a half of silver jangled from her slender throat as she bent to the business at hand. I felt her take the old love snake in slim, opera-gloved fingers, and I winced out of surprise when she gently bit me.

"I'm sorry, baby," she whispered. "Did your wanna-be vampire hurt her baby?"

"You fucking freak," I said. "Be gentle."

"Sorry, darling. Please punish me—*please*," she

urged, obviously meaning it. "I need to be slapped and disciplined."

What could I do but comply?

"Please, sugar, slap me harder. Punish your bitch."

I was hard as rock. Old Moby Dick blew in about eight and a half seconds. Aye, Captain, sperm off the port bow.

She knew every button to push. I was nuts about the freaky bitch. I told her so.

"I want you to live forever, angel. Don't ever die—hear me?"

"I could live forever . . . if you'd help me." Her tone was serious.

"Hm?"

"If you'd share your blood with me."

"Say which?"

"It's how the vampire kids live so long. They drink each other's blood." Very matter-of-fact but not kidding. "You have to drink quite a bit of it, and it only works if it's somebody you're going with." Dead serious.

"Drink each other's blood?"

"Yeah, my husband and I used to do that—he'd probably still be alive if he hadn't killed himself." She was oblivious to the inadvertent hilarity of the statement.

"Let me see if I get this right: your husband, the one who died of *AIDS,* you and this junkie drank each other's blood, and now you've got cancer of the 'nymph loads,' and you want me to drink some of *your* fucking blood, and a lot of it. Is that pretty much your game plan?" I was fairly pissed and let it show.

"Well," she said, shrugging, "you said you wanted me to live forever, and this way you could do it, too."

I didn't bother to reply.

A couple of years ago, had someone suggested I

would even begin to contemplate anything so idiotic as drinking anyone's blood, or donating my own, for that matter—much less the notion of ingesting the befouled virus juice of some wanna-be neck biter— I'd have offered this countersuggestion: their lips to my hindquarters, pucker to pucker.

But that was then, and Gretchen is now.

You know those ads in the big-city personals? "Regina from West Vagina has a predilection for men or Labradors and will take them big, black, and buff. Regina is a funky bunk monkey who will make you so hard you can use your thing for a cat-scratch pole." Some promise of weird sex followed by the name of an escort service and a number? Gretchen has just told me a couple of experiences she had when she was with Sex-corts. When I get my strength back, she's promised to teach me some new tricks.

The fifty-six-year-old (that's 392 in dog years) fat man lies sprawled across his enormous bed, one hand cupping the back of a young woman's head, the other fondling a slick, hard thing about five inches long. He pulls the woman's face up next to his, and they kiss. Every orifice on the lady tastes pretty much the way Chanel No. 5 smells, which is to say delicious.

His hand turns her, directing and repositioning her with her back to him, and as always it's such a turn-on to note the complacence of her response to his touch. His huge arm is over her small one, and the arms cross her chest. With his other hand, he snaps the sharp blade open.

Fuck it, he thinks, nobody lives forever. Right?

TROPHIES

John B. Rosenman

*W*e'd all heard about Larry's wife, of course. From Larry. He told us endlessly about how beautiful she was, how intelligent, how talented. According to him, the sun rose and fell on his Mary, who possessed endless accomplishments to go with her old-fashioned name. For all we knew, she flew like an angel, too, and was followed by a personal escort of sweet-singing birds.

That she was, in addition to all this, simply unbeatable in bed, a sexual queen who reigned over his royal nights, was just too much. God, how we hated the guy.

Why did we believe him, you ask? Why did we believe a fat, balding slob when he rolled his eyes and poured forth a new litany of Mary's virtues? Maybe it was because we saw what this Mary had accomplished with him since he'd married her. Before that happy day, which he hadn't even told us about, he'd been a dead, distant last when it came to selling anything at Pinnacle Life ("Pinnacle Clients Enjoy Peace of Mind at the Peak"). In fact, Barker was even thinking of giving him the ax. But then Larry returned from a week's honeymoon a veritable ball of fire, reeking with confidence and nailing those leads like he'd had a personality transplant. Soon it became unusual for a client even to *think* of turning him down. Say no to Larry? Not on *your* life, excuse the pun.

Naturally, we all wanted to meet this amazing woman who had so turned Larry around, and we pressured him constantly to meet her. After Larry put us off with one excuse or another, though, Bert Lee, who used to be number one, snidely suggested that there was no wife and that Larry had found his salesmanship through his nose or at the end of a needle. But that convinced nobody, especially since we all knew that Bert held a grudge. Thanks to Larry, Bert's string of three straight Salesman of the Year trophies had been broken. Nope, if Larry was using, then Bert was a male impersonator who was actually a beer-hall blonde on the weekends. In the end, nobody knew quite what to think.

Then Larry invited me home for dinner.

It came unexpectedly. He simply asked me one day after work with that new, high-wattage smile of his, promising to drive me back to my car later. Within minutes, I found myself in his new Porsche, zooming down the highway toward the coast. He lived there in a small town called Green Meadows, which, near as I could tell, was located midway between Lost and Nowhere. In fact, it was so out of the way and hard to find that the few guys who had tried to drop in on Larry in order to meet Mary had just given up in disgust.

While driving, Larry beamed with pleasure as he told me how it had been Mary's idea to move out there for "privacy and seclusion." When I asked why none of us had ever been invited to meet Mary, he delivered his stock answer. "Mary's shy," he said, "afraid of meeting people."

Changing tactics, I asked if he had a picture of the little woman, only to have him adroitly shift gears.

"Ever been married, Bob?"

"Nope," I said, wishing I could manage just to keep a steady girlfriend. "Might as well serve a life sentence as walk down the aisle."

"Aw, it ain't so bad." He grinned. "Actually, it's heaven."

Heaven? Even if he were an oversexed sultan with a harem, that would be pushing it. Before I could say anything, he pointed up ahead. "Thar she blows. Green Meadows."

Green Meadows? If there was anything green or meadowy about the place, then I was sure missing it. As we entered, I saw parched fields and lawns that looked as terminal as my Uncle Fred. A few sad, faded homes and narrow, dustball streets tried feebly to break the monotony, but without much success. Larry drove up one stunted lane and down another—left, right, and left again in a maze of streets till I was hopelessly lost. At last, he stopped before a white house with a picket fence.

I blinked. It looked like a stereotype. The house even had a gate and *roses,* for gawd's sake, their heavy heads drooping over the fence, which looked freshly painted. White, of course.

I got out of the car, wondering at how green and neatly cut the front lawn was. To both sides of it, I saw only brown, bleak fields and what looked like abandoned houses.

"C'mon, Bob." Larry grinned. "Let's go meet the little woman."

He opened the gate and led me up a stone walk. The only thing missing was a cute mutt running out to meet us. Inside, all was neatness and order, pastels and chintz curtains. On the wall, an embroidered sign read: "A Good Marriage Is Made in Heaven."

"Sit down," Larry chirped, pointing to a pink sofa. "I'll get us some drinks."

Drinks? What about Mary? But he proceeded directly to what I assumed was the kitchen. I glanced around, seeing that Larry's trophy for being Pinnacle Life's Salesman of the Year sat on a nearby table, needing only a spotlight and a twelve-piece band to make it more prominent. The gold-plated prize featured a miniature mountain and a man who stood proudly grinning on top of its narrow pinnacle.

I sighed and sat down, thinking that I'd be a top salesman, too, if only people would *listen* to my presentations. But for some reason, they had great sales resistance when I was around. To tell the truth, my record was getting to be as bad as Larry's *used* to be.

Glumly, I stared at a fireplace. Where was everybody? No Larry. No Mary. Well, maybe Mary was out in the kitchen and she'd come back with him.

Within a minute, though, Larry returned alone, bearing a drink in each hand. "I know you're a beer hound, but I thought I'd try you on this. Mary's special concoction."

"Thanks," I said, accepting a tall, chilled glass. "And speaking of Mary . . . ?"

He winked and toasted me. "All in good time, Bob boy."

Something—maybe the cold glass—made me shiver. *All in good time, Bob boy.* Hadn't there been a "time" when Larry had been almost dour and definitely not the flippant type? I hoisted my own glass and took a tentative taste.

It was delicious.

Crisp, mildly sweet, and richly layered, the liquid seemed to dance on my tongue and caress my taste buds. Taking another sip, and immediately yet another, I vowed then and there never to drink beer again.

Larry winked. "Like it?"

"*Like* it? It's the best thing since malt liquor." I took a deep pull and leaned back on the sofa, which was so soft I seemed to melt into it. Larry himself sat down in an easy chair next to the table bearing his trophy and hummed an old song.

"You know," I said, trying my best not to finish the drink too soon, "you surprised the whole office when you got married like that. And then, when you started to sell policies like they were going out of style, you simply blew us away."

He smiled, humming. "That so?"

"Yes." I struggled up on the sofa and tried to lean forward. "How does it feel, Larry?"

"Feel?"

I nodded at the trophy beside him, trying to remember the last time *I'd* had a decent year—or a girl hadn't dropped me like a tin-plated Edsel. "Yeah, how does it feel to be a hot-shot rep? The hottest there is? A few months ago . . ." I stopped, not wanting to embarrass him.

He glanced at the trophy and laughed, his belly quaking like jelly. "A few months ago," he said, "I couldn't have given away free ice water in hell." He nodded. "I know. I was bad."

"What happened, Larry?" I sneaked a glance around, wondering where Mary was.

"What happened?" As he gazed at the trophy, his face seemed to darken. Then it was sunny again. "Why, I met *Mary,* that's what happened. And when I did, my whole life changed." He took a deep sip of his drink, patted his stomach. "Thanks to Mary's cookin', I've gained nineteen pounds, and thanks to *her,* I've gained peace of mind and a world of confidence. Ya know, used to be I'd go to bed every night worrying 'bout making a living and keeping my job. Now I sleep like a newborn babe."

"After a little loving, huh?"

"Actually, after a *lot* of loving." His lips twitched, and he fumbled with his glass as if he'd forgotten what he was going to say. Then the smile was back, brighter than ever. "I'll tell you somethin', Bob. I've never been one-tenth as happy as I am now."

"Larry," I said, "do you mind me asking why you invited me here? I mean, I'm not the only one in the office."

He didn't answer. I watched him look at his glass and take a sip.

"Larry?"

Footsteps sounded on the stairs. Footsteps descending.

Larry put his glass down and rose quickly. Clumsily, I worked my way to the edge of the sofa and gained my feet. I looked at Larry, who was watching the stairs, then turned to follow his gaze.

Footsteps coming closer. Soft, childlike steps. Then I saw a pair of tiny, delicate feet. On an impulse, I raised my glass and drained it.

A shadow appeared on the lower steps, reaching toward us. I raised my eyes just as Mary began to appear.

First, I saw her feet, then her legs. And then . . .

Then the whole world simply went away, and I saw only Mary as she reached the floor and came toward me with a smile. I watched her hand reach out and take my free one, holding it between hers.

"Hello, Bob," she said. "I'm delighted that you could come."

I tried to turn my head to Larry, but it wouldn't move. Opening my mouth proved equally ineffective. I could open it, all right, but nothing came out.

Mary's smile widened. I cleared my throat. Despite my bum sales record, I remembered that I sold insurance and made a living with my voice. But nothing had prepared me for this beautiful, voluptuous, blond-haired creature. From her tiny feet to the tip of her chin, she was more curvaceous and delectable than any woman I'd ever seen, a sensual embodiment of all that a man could desire. When I gazed at her face, though, my stomach twisted, for its appearance constantly seemed to change in subtle ways, perhaps because of the room's lighting. Now there was something strange about her nose, and now her mouth and chin flowed into a shape I could almost define. The illusion made me shiver, and I tried to pin down just what it was that disturbed me. But her features continued to shift and elude my eye, staying just out of reach. They were like slippery rocks on which I could find no footing.

Soon I forgot the matter, for her beautiful, riveting eyes, which I *could* see clearly, drew my own so strongly that I could attend to little else. During that first minute, therefore, it was her eyes that held me most. They and her hands on mine, kneading it like a mound of dough.

"I'm delighted we could have you for dinner," she said brightly.

Finally, I snapped out of my stupor. Her voice, I noted, was sweet and melodious—a little like the drink she had prepared.

"I . . . I'm happy to be here," I said.

"And hungry, too?"

"Oh, yes. Uh, starved."

"How delightful! So am *I!* Larry," she said, turning to her husband, "shall we escort our hungry guest to the dining room?"

Larry jumped. "Oh, sure! Uh, come on, Bob, it's over here."

Mary led me to the dining room. Dimly, I was beginning to sense that, besides her appearance, there were other things different about her. The way she talked, the way she smiled. There was something about the way she smelled, too, something I could not name that made me want to pull away despite her voluptuous body. And her *eyes* . . . there was something odd about them as well.

Clutching my arm closely, she winked up at me, licking her lips with a delicate tongue. Though I was mesmerized, something about her lips bothered me, and I sucked in my breath.

In the dining room, she released me and glided toward the kitchen, her hips swaying in her dress, which I noticed for the first time was green. "Seat yourselves and be comfortable, gentlemen. Dinner will be served soon."

I sat down in a chair at one end of the table, relieved that she was no longer holding my arm. Why did she speak so formally? Was she a foreigner of some kind? Blinking, I stared at the blue tablecloth before me. Plates, glasses, and utensils were meticulously arranged. Napkins lay neatly beside them, their necks inserted through gold rings.

Larry sat to my right halfway down the table, a knife and fork already in his hands.

As Mary returned from the kitchen with a tray, the smell of food grazed my nostrils. I took one breath and almost moaned. Such fragrance! Never in my life had I smelled anything so delicious, so divine. My taste buds swelled and burst into action, filling my mouth with saliva.

I glanced at Larry, whose wet lips trembled with anticipation. "I remember you saying she could really cook," I said.

He didn't answer, only stared at an ornate silver bowl as Mary laid it on the table. As she lifted the lid, thick steam issued forth, smelling like ambrosia and almost dazing me with pleasure.

"I hope you will deeply enjoy my Padulanka."

Padulanka? Inhaling, I watched her serve me first, her full, firm breast pressing briefly against my arm. Then she did the same for Larry, who ignored us and began eating at once. Serving herself, Mary sat down at the other end of the table. She licked her lips, smiling down the table's length at me.

"Please proceed, Bob. I believe the expression is 'Down the hatch!' "

I tore my eyes away. Lifting a fork, I studied what looked like a meat pie. The crust was golden brown, the smell intoxicating. Almost choking on saliva, I broke the crust and stabbed what looked like a piece of chicken. I raised it to my mouth—and swallowed.

It was heaven.

Wave upon wave of flavor filled my mouth, pleasure such as I had never known. If this was chicken, she had done something to it you couldn't find in a cookbook. Another bite, and I knew that her magic extended to peas and carrots. Potatoes were also transformed, anointing my tongue with delectable dimensions of taste.

Besides the Padulanka, we had only ice water. It didn't matter. I was so happy, I didn't come up for air until I was almost through with my third helping. Looking around, I saw Larry forking down the food like there was no tomorrow. Mary herself sat without eating, her eyes fixed on me.

I felt a chill. Her eyes ... for the first time, I noticed they had no irises. Enormous brown pupils gazed back at me, eyes immensely soft.

"You really ought to get married," Larry said.

I started. Larry stared at me, holding a fork laden with food.

"Larry is correct," Mary said in her sweet, cotton-candy voice. She eyed Larry like he was a plump dumpling on a fork. "His work has improved immensely, and he himself has never been so . . . content."

I gazed enviously at the Salesman of the Year, wishing I had his record. If marriage was what it took . . .

I started to say something, then stopped. It was like I was being petted, stroked like a dog, only from *inside.* Stroke. Stroke. Stroke. It felt soft and strange, yet at the same time stimulating and arousing. Within seconds, I started to respond to Mary. I thought of what it would be like to strip her luscious body naked, to caress her nipples and smooth round thighs. And then I'd kiss her . . .

I pushed my plate away, wondering why part of me was so repulsed by her. The strong attraction I could understand, but not my fear and queasiness. Surely, her differences were not only elusive but minor. Compared to her sensuous body and hypnotic gaze, which kept drawing my attention, such trivialities should hardly matter. I swallowed. What did these people want, anyway? Why had Larry asked me here? And why was I feeling so strange, having such weird thoughts?

Mary smiled, the details of her face subtly changing, slipping away from me. Then, for an instant, I glimpsed something that staggered my mind and made the manna I'd eaten heave in my stomach. It had almost looked like . . .

My mind approached the brink, then cringed, cowered away from knowing. My fingers twitched helplessly. Mary's sweet voice, though, quickly soothed me, calmed my pounding heart. "Bob," she said, "I hope you find my food tender and succulent enough. I know that is the way *I* prefer it." Slowly, she licked her lips. "Would you like some more?"

Her eyes. Her enormous brown eyes. I could melt in their depths.

. . . Somehow I was out in the chintz-filled living room again, sitting on the quicksand sofa. I blinked and shook myself, trying to remember how I'd gotten out there. Larry, I saw, sat nearby, next to his proudly displayed trophy. I rubbed my eyes. Somehow he looked as if he were on display himself.

Softly, Larry started to sing the same song he had hummed before. I struggled up on the sofa, my hands slipping on the smooth surface. As best I could, I tried to catch the words.

"The girl that I marry will have to be . . ."

I knew it, a song from *Annie Get Your Gun.*

". . . a girl to possess me, e-ter-nal-ly . . ."

No, wait, that's not how it goes, I thought. The new version troubled me. Glancing around, I saw no sign of Mary. Could she still be in the dining room?

"Larry," I said.

He stopped singing.

"Larry!"

"Uh, yes, Bob."

I thought of him sleeping with her and for some reason experienced conflicting feelings. Envy and pity competed with each other, as did lust and loathing.

"She's some woman," I said.

He blinked. "Don't I know it," he finally said.

"But she does seem . . . different."

"Different?"

"Strange," I said. I searched for a word. "Even . . . unnatural."

He should have been offended, but he only sighed. "When I first met her, I felt . . ."

"You felt *what,* Larry?"

He wet his lips. "Hard to remember. I think I . . . didn't even find her beautiful then."

"You didn't?"

"No, isn't that strange? I mean her body *is* so wonderful. I'd never seen anything like it." A dreamy smile crossed his face. "I even seem to remember that at one time I found her almost repulsive. The way I couldn't quite see her face, the way she talked and smelled, the way she stared at me with those weird eyes and constantly licked her lips. Though I couldn't put my finger on it, she made me . . ."

"Made you *what?*"

"She . . . made me c-c-c-cringe." His expression tensed, and he gripped the chair. "Isn't that odd? Why would I say such a thing?" He hesitated, his lips moving silently. *"Mary's the most beautiful, wonderful, kindest woman in the whole world,"* he said in a flat voice. "I must thank God each and every day that I was fortunate enough to find her. She's made such a wonderful difference in my life." He sat still for a moment, then looked at me. "Bob," he said.

I glanced toward the dining room. "What, Larry?"

"I have wonderful news for you. You have been found acceptable."

"Acceptable? Acceptable for *what?*"

Before he could answer, Mary's lovely form entered the room. I pulled back, expecting her to stop, but she continued past on those tiny feet of hers. I watched her go to the stairway and gaze up it.

I swallowed, looked at Larry. Something was wrong. But *what?*

Footsteps.

They sounded like Mary's had on the steps—light and delicate, as if a fairy were slowly descending to Earth.

Larry squirmed. "Mary told me a secret once."

"She did?" I waited for the next footstep.

Tap.

"Mary said she was a mutation."

"Mutation?"

Tap.

"Yes. She also said she was lonely, almost as lonely as her sister."

Sister? I found myself remembering the feeling I'd had at the table of being stroked from inside by Mary. Why should I think of it now?

"Anne is even lonelier," Larry continued. "She needs someone, Bob."

Tap.

I remembered him saying earlier I should be married, and Mary praising what marriage had done for Larry. But for some reason, Larry didn't look particularly happy at that moment.

Tap.

Feet appeared on the steps, tiny, delicate ones just like Mary's. Trembling, I tried to rise but found that my whole body was numb, as if I'd been given a massive dose of novocaine. Somewhere deep inside me, a small voice started screaming.

Tap.

No, I *mustn't* look. Raising my fists, I drove them hard against my legs, anything to feel pain, to feel *something*. Groaning, I managed to rise an inch from the sofa, only to fall back like a fat, overturned turtle. Another try produced the same result.

Larry stiffened, seemed to come awake. "Bob!"

"What?"

Abruptly, his mask crumbled, and I found myself staring at the Larry I remembered. He opened his mouth in horror.

"Run, Bob!" he screamed. *"Her sister's horrible, a THOUSAND TIMES WORSE!"*

Panic seared me. With a desperate lunge, I made it to my feet. Staggering, I stared at the creature who had finally reached the bottom of the stairs. If anything, she was even more ravishing than her sister, a seductive goddess beyond compare. But, as with Mary, her features seemed to flow and elude my mental grasp, never quite coalescing into form. Somehow, though, I glimpsed enough to know that Larry was right, for as bad as Mary's face was, Anne's was immeasurably worse. It kept changing like a bizarre kaleidoscope, bearing Medusan horrors I dared not see.

Mary, who was closer to me than Anne, swept toward me and reached out.

At last, I roused myself and pulled back, but too late. Her fingers caught my wrist and held tight.

Struggling was useless. It was as if she'd locked a pair of handcuffs on me. Seeing Anne move toward us, I whimpered. An instant later, I felt an unseen hand stroke me from inside again. STROKE. STROKE. STROKE. This time, the sensation was far stronger. Unlike with Mary, it was intensely sensual, profoundly stimulating, and this time I *knew* that it came from *Anne*. I could even sense her feelings. To her, I was some kind of beloved pet, a possession that she not only desired in order to fill her lonely existence but which she also disdained as an inferior creature. Despite my horror and disgust, I felt myself begin to respond. In seconds, I grew hard and erect, my body aching . . .

No! The part of my mind that was still sane screamed. *Oh God, no! Anything but THIS!*

I wrenched, twisted, shoved, but Mary held me fast. And behind her, just a few feet away, came an even richer prize . . . Anne.

Desperately, I looked around for something to use, a weapon. An andiron from the fireplace? No, it was too far away. A cup Larry had set on the floor? No, it was too light. No matter where I looked, there was nothing I could use!

Larry's trophy.

Stretching toward the table, I reached out for the trophy, only to find my fingers were inches away. Pulling against Mary's grip, aware of Anne's approach, I strained again toward the table. This time, I managed to seize Larry's golden prize by the man perched on its pinnacle, and I turned. Raising it, I struck Mary's hand as hard as I could. Once, twice, three times, and still she did not let go. My mind screamed. How could she hold on? What kind of creature *was* she?

Raising the trophy again, I made the mistake of meeting Anne's beautiful eyes.

"Don't fight, Bob," she said in a sweet, incomparably lovely voice. "You know you don't really want to."

I hesitated, feeling myself weaken. Anne's hand reached out and touched my cheek. Almost at once, I felt the rest of my resistance fade. The trophy sank in my hand as she moved close and bore me back to the couch. I seemed to fall in slow motion toward it, floating down for an endless time beneath her. Moaning, her lips covered mine, moist and soft.

Sometime later, I sat passively watching as she rose and stripped a gossamer-thin gown from her body and cast it aside. She stood there in full magnificence—long, smooth, sleek thighs glistening, her firm breasts pointing up. Her nipples, I saw, were erect, the aureoles broad and golden.

Kneeling, she opened my fly and teased me out, took me in her mouth. I felt myself throb and snap to attention as if obeying a command. Yet I was numb, couldn't even move!

"Bob," she moaned. "Oh, my dear Bob."

She rose and lowered herself upon me, the golden fleece of her pubic hair feeling like velvet as it slid down my shaft. She was moist and eager, and I smelled the scent I had detected earlier on her sister.

Only this was heavier, a musk rich with pheromones and laden with her desire. Part of me abhorred and detested it, but at the same time it stirred me profoundly, like the super aphrodisiac I sensed it was.

She started to move, murmuring endearments as she feverishly kissed my lips and face. Despite the strange feel of her lips, I responded. My penis throbbed, stiffened still more, and shot jets of sperm deep inside her. The orgasm was so intense as to be painful, seeming to come from the base of my spine. I screamed, and she sobbed, her vagina feeling alive, as if it were a separate part of her with a mind of its own. Grinding against me, she straightened and cried up at the ceiling as her own orgasm approached.

Then, incredibly, I was responding again. I gasped—it must have been less than a minute since I'd come the first time! As my excitement rose, I saw that Mary and Larry were standing there watching us as if sealing our union, witnessing its consummation. This, what we were doing, I realized, was all a perverse marriage ceremony—and *I* was the reluctant groom!

And all the time, Anne stroked and caressed me and moaned strange endearments. "Oh, my love, my heart's true cry. I have waited through long, empty nights for you to come and complete me. Please fear me not!"

But fear turned cartwheels even as my organ swelled and climaxed again, this time even more violently than before. Despite the intense pleasure, I knew that to her, I was no more than a plaything for which she felt a perverse passion, a drone to serve and perhaps impregnate her. Thinking of what our children would be like, I fought feebly to resist her, only to feel my penis stiffen yet again before it could even soften. Obviously, something in her body replenished my own before it became sated, and could do so again and again!

In the minutes that followed, my body repeatedly transcended its limitations, passing from one shattering climax to another. Clasped and caressed by her vagina, which seemed to possess tiny, silken fingers, I erupted till my voice grew hoarse and I felt faint. For the first time, I realized that she might drain me, wring me dry. My balls ached, and I saw myself shriveling up like a mummy, crumbling to brittle pieces.

Sensing my fear, she shifted her weight, forcing an erect nipple between my lips. Milk spurted into my mouth—thick, rich, aromatic fluid which quickly restored me, flooded me with life and lust.

Oh God, how was this possible? Desperate, stricken by a vision in which I grew plump as Larry, a lamb fattened for psychic slaughter, I wrenched my lips away as Anne continued to pound against me. Mary and Larry, I saw, were smiling, their skin flushed. And no wonder, for the union they watched meant they were no longer alone!

At last, Anne stopped moving, her beautiful pink skin wet with sweat. She sighed and pressed her face against my shirt.

"Now you are *mine,*" she sobbed.

The words sounded like a death knell, and I felt my will return, perhaps because she was exhausted. Forcing myself up on the sofa, I shoved Anne aside, then scrambled to rise as she fell to the floor. Six feet away, Mary started toward me, followed by Larry.

Staggering up, I snatched Larry's trophy just as Mary reached out and seized me again.

I shrieked and struck her face with all my strength. She groaned and sagged, relaxing her grip. A sharp twist, a savage pull, and I was free! But now it was

Larry reaching for me! I pulled back, feinted, and kicked him in the gut, then dodged around him when he fell. As I did, a hand seized my shirt from behind and held tight.

I whirled and swung, smashing the trophy directly into Anne's face. Bone broke, and blood erupted in a bright spray. As she collapsed, I turned back. The door looked a mile away. I dove toward it, feeling like a bug trying to run in amber, as if Anne were renewing her control. Eventually, though, still clutching Larry's trophy, I reached the door, tore it open, and plunged out into the front yard. Even as I raced across the grass and cleared the fence, I heard Anne's sweet, forgiving voice.

"Don't run, Bob," she called. "I LOVE YOU."

I run for hours, up and down narrow, dusty streets. Sometimes I cross blighted fields, wondering why everything looks so lifeless. Though I don't have a car, I tell myself it should be easy to get out of a small town like Green Meadows. But every road I take only seems to lead me back where I came from.

Once, during a brief rest, I belch. What rises to my mouth tastes both of Mary's Padulanka and the delicious drink she made, as well as of Anne's rich, thick milk. They all linger on my tongue as if I just swallowed them.

Not only that, I feel something caress me inside. Something that is also familiar.

Stroke. Stroke. Stroke.

I moan as an unseen hand pets me just as if I were a dog. Despite my fear, it feels so soothing.

With an effort, I shake it off and start running again. After that, I run some more. No matter where I go, though, it all looks the same.

Eventually, I sense that something more than the

town's layout is to blame for my inability to escape. But what can it be?

At last, with the sun drooping like a dead flower, I approach Larry's house. The grass seems so lush, the roses supremely ripe—just aching to be cut. I linger at the picket fence, tempted to pick one, then look up as the door opens and Anne steps out on the porch. Though I still can't quite make out her face, I can tell that it has already healed and bears no sign of my violence.

She stands there and waits, occasionally licking her lips.

Part of me wants to scream. But I know now I can't run, that all paths ultimately lead right back here. It is useless even to think of escaping.

Besides, I find that a part of me, a *growing* part, actually wants Anne, actually *loves* her. What did Larry say—that his Mary was the most beautiful, wonderful, and kindest woman in the world? Strangely, that description seems more appropriate for Anne as I stop struggling and let my gaze linger. And as I do, I begin for the first time to really *see* her, to behold parts of her face. Though her mouth alone might unhinge others' minds, perhaps I need to change my thinking. After all, Larry did, and look what it got him.

I look down at the trophy I still clutch with white fingers. Odd, the man standing on its mountain peak looks like he's about to jump. But maybe, just maybe, he can still fight back. I remind myself that the trophy itself can be a lethal weapon. All I have to do is be willing to use it.

I open the gate and start up the walk, seeing Anne smile. I smile back. How striking Anne is, how . . . desirable. Dimly, I wonder if she could help *me* to sell insurance like Mary did Larry. Somewhere, a fading voice screams at me to resist, and I struggle to remember why I should. After all, I've all but reached Anne now, and her beautiful arms reach out to receive me.

Laughing, I feel the trophy slip from my fingers as I run up the steps into Anne's arms.

INTERSTATE 666

Max Allan Collins

*H*ave you heard this one?

It's another of those stories about Interstate 666, which is only one of the nicknames bestowed on I-66 over the years. Maybe you know it as Bad Luck Highway, the Devil's Turnpike, or possibly the Highway to Hell . . .

Anyway, on a lonely turnoff just off the I-66, back in '66, three cheerleaders found themselves with a flat tire on the way to the big game. It was a cold fall night, but all three girls wore their little short-skirted red and white cheerleader costumes. Ronni, a cute brunette, had borrowed the shiny red Mustang from her boyfriend, Larry; but it was the equally cute LaVonne, the cheerleading squad's only Afro-American member, who took charge, opening the trunk.

Betty, blond and, yes, very cute, seemed on the verge of panic. "What are we gonna do, Ronni?"

"What else, bubblehead? Change the tire! Haven't you ever changed a g.d. tire before?"

Betty's blond locks bounced as she shook her head no. "I don't have driver's ed till *next* semester."

LaVonne was looking down into an empty trunk. "Have *you* ever changed a tire, Ronni?"

"*Of course* I've changed a tire . . ."

LaVonne shook her head no, and her Afro bobbled. "Not on this car, girl. There's no spare—damn! We're already runnin' late." She frowned at Ronni. "If only we hadn't had to drop your little sister off . . ."

Ronni put her fists on her hips, like Superman. "Oh, I suppose it's *my* g.d. fault that baby-sitter lives out in the boonies!"

"Are we gonna miss the big game?" Betty asked, her eyes wide, and, as if in answer, the whine of brakes caught the three girls' attention, headlights suddenly illuminating them as a semi bore down on them.

"Here's somebody who can help us!" Betty cried in relief, as the truck pulled over, bringing itself to a gear-grinding stop.

"We'll hitch a ride to I-66 Truckstop," Ronni said. "It's close. We can have the g.d. car towed."

"And maybe catch a ride to the game!" Betty added.

"Go if you wanna," LaVonne said. "I'll stay with the wheels—I'm not sure I *believe* that good ol' boy's smile . . ."

And the burly trucker, climbing down out of his cab, did wear a grin that was maybe a little too wide. He also wore a Peter Bilt cap and a lumberjack shirt, his gait a trifle bowlegged, his paunch hanging over his belt like a smuggled watermelon. As he planted himself before the awkwardly grouped girls, the cold night wind brought the odor of chewing tobacco to their nostrils.

"You young ladies in distress?" he asked, his voice gruff but his manner affable.

Betty touched her chest. "We have a flat."

He raised his eyebrows. "Uh, yeah . . . got a jack? Be glad to help . . ."

"We have a jack," Ronni said, "but no spare."

His grin got even wider. "I don't think one a *my* spare's gonna fit this cherry little buggy. . . . Why don't you kids pile on into my cab? Truckstop's just a hop, skip, and a jump . . . getcha some help."

"That's white of you, Mister," LaVonne said. "But I'll just wait here."

Somewhere an owl hooted.

He shrugged. "If you like. . . . So I guess they musta caught that Hook character, huh?"

Betty swallowed. "Hook character?"

"Didn't you hear about it?" He shook his head, made a *tch-tch* sound. "That insane feller with the hook, in the papers last year? He busted outta the nuthouse last night. Couple kids parking, over by Mad Crick, kinda goin' at it hot and heavy, when they hear a *scratchin'* at the door . . ."

Betty hugged Ronni's arm. Each girl could hear her own heartbeat.

"So they take off like a bat outta hell!" he said, and the girls jumped a little. "And when this fella drops his little gal off t'home, and goes 'round to open the door for her—a *bloody hook* was caught on the door handle!"

Betty gasped. "That's horrible!"

The trucker shrugged. *"Horrible* thing is, they got the hook, but not the guy that used to be attached to it."

"I heard about him," Ronni said thoughtfully. "He . . . he's a g.d. *molester,* isn't he?"

"Oh, yeah," the trucker said casually. "And a homicidal maniac." Then he smiled yellowly at LaVonne. "But I'm sure you gals'll be just fine here, 'long the roadside. Maybe you should all three stay, and I'll just stop at the stop, and send the wrecker—"

"No!" LaVonne said. "We'll all go with you."

But as the girls followed the trucker to his vehicle, LaVonne brought up the rear, so that nobody could see the tire iron tucked behind her back.

They rode about half a mile in silence, all crowded in the cab with the burly trucker, light from the dash casting an eerie glow, the vehicle lurching as he shifted gears, and soon they were on the interstate.

"You know," he said finally, "I'm doin' you little gals a big ol' favor, what with the Hook at large and all."

"We're really grateful," Betty said.

"Yeah, thanks a lot," Ronni said, pointing to an exit as they rolled past. "But isn't that the turnoff?"

"Oh, damn!" he said. "Pardon my French. Well, we can turn off up at the rest stop—we can use the phone from there . . ."

"I guess that would be all right," Ronni said.

He grinned over at them, and the affability had been replaced by something lascivious. "We can pull off to one side, nice and private . . ." He gestured behind him with a thumb. "And I can show you gals where I *sleep* and things."

"No thanks," LaVonne said.

He took one hand off the wheel and reached inside his jacket, as casually as if he were plucking a pack of cigarettes from a pocket; but what his hand came back with was a gun, a little revolver.

As the girls recoiled in fear, he said, "Kids today! You girls are gonna show me some goddam gratitude. I saved your pretty asses!"

LaVonne sat forward, turning toward their "savior."

"See, I always had me this fantasy about cheerleaders," he was saying, his lips glistening with saliva in the dashboard glow. "Me and three sweet young things, goin' rah rah rah on my sis boom bah . . ."

That was when LaVonne whapped him across the chest with the tire iron.

His yelp of pain accompanied a reflexive jerk of the wheel, and the huge semi rammed into a bridge abutment, the sound of the girls' screams and breaking glass and tearing metal soon engulfed by an explosion as gas ignited and an orange fireball blossomed in the night.

"But," Dr. Janet Vanguard said, "the Tale of the Stranded Cheerleaders does not end there . . ."

Vanguard paced slowly before the blackboard as the small classroom of college students listened with rapt attention. She was thirty-five, her long dark hair was pinned back, her glasses were wire-framed and functional, her gray tailored suit with blouse conservative; but none of these efforts to downplay her natural beauty was entirely successful. Behind the glasses were large dark eyes, and she had the high cheekbones, clear skin, and slender shape of a fashion model.

She acknowledged a male student seated toward the front. "Yes, Steven?"

"Dr. Vanguard, we all know the Hook story is one of the oldest urban legends around. Has it *always* been a part of the stranded cheerleaders story?"

"Good point, Steven," Vanguard said, and sat on the edge of her desk, unaware she was further undercutting her efforts to maintain a cool professorial image by showing off perfectly formed nyloned limbs. "No, the first logged occurrence of the Hook legend converging with the Stranded Cheerleaders' Revenge is '81—whereas the cheerleaders tale in its purest form dates to '66, a year that has clung to the legend because of its echoing of the 'true' story's locale, Interstate 66 . . . or I should say, 666."

There were smiles around the room as she continued.

"In virtually every variant of the legend, the story picks up exactly one year later, to the night. Two truckers are in a truckstop parking lot, and one of them is drunk and getting drunker, swigging from a brown-bagged bottle. His friend suggests he's hitting the booze a little hard, and the drunken trucker takes offense. The drunken trucker is then seen, by his friend, being lured into the back of a truck by three beautiful young girls in cocktail attire—in the earliest versions of the tale, the girls are wearing Playboy Bunny costumes."

"And I suppose," Steven offered, "one girl is a brunette, another a blonde, another black."

"Exactly," Vanguard said with a smile. "The drunken trucker disappears into the back of a semi, which his friend takes for a bordello on wheels. The next morning, the drunken trucker is found in a ditch—stone dead. And when an autopsy is performed, he's found to have no blood in his veins . . . but pure, one hundred percent alcohol."

The ironic ending of the tale elicited more smiles and a few nervous laughs.

"Dr. Vanguard," Steven said, "in your book, you list no fewer than twenty-five variations on the trucker's demise—including several where the victim isn't even a trucker, but some unlucky male traveler."

Vanguard raised a gentle finger. "Unlucky *horny* male traveler . . ."

And that prompted more smiles and gentle laughs.

"Actually, Steven," Vanguard said, "that can be viewed as a simple variant on a theme. Or we may be talking about multiple victims. You see, the Stranded Cheerleaders are said to reappear every year, on the anniversary of their tragedy, to lure men with a promise of erotic fantasy fulfilled by a horrible, ironic death. . . ."

The busty blond cheerleader was shaking her pom-pons (among other things) to a Z. Z. Top tune as appreciative males looked on. On another stage, a stacked black cowgirl was twirling a lasso (and the tassels on her breasts), while on the last of the three stages, a brunette was slipping out of her negligee down to pasties and G-string undies that you wouldn't find at Victoria's Secret.

Around the stages of the glittering mirrored strip club sat hooting, horny guys, white- and blue-collar alike, stopping in after work for the chance to stuff dollar bills in the G-strings of the dancers. Along the mirrored walls were tables of more passive observers, including an afternoon bachelor party in progress, four guys in their early twenties who still looked like the frat brothers they'd been not so long ago.

The one who seemed to be having the least fun was the man of the hour, Jason Peterson. The dark-haired, boyishly handsome young man seemed alternately bored and ill at ease.

His friends—Al, Bobby, and Bill—were doing their best to get him with the program.

Al—tall, skinny, leering at the cheerleader—said, "Jay, why don't you get your ass up there, ringside, and jump-start your dick?"

Bobby—chubby, curly-haired—said, "Come on, Jason, when did you shrivel up and die? You used to be such a *hound!*"

"I'm sorry, guys," Jason said, shrugging, sipping his Coke. "I'm just not into it."

"You used to be into *anything* female and friendly," Bill said. Bill was a little older than his pals, a broad-shouldered ex-jock with thinning blond hair.

"Hey, I always had my standards," Jason said, then pointed a finger at Bill. "You, on the other hand, would shtup mud."

Bobby leaned in conspiratorially. "See that little cheerleader?"

"I think I can just barely make her out from here," Jason said.

"Barely is right." Bobby grinned. "I slipped her fifty bucks for a table dance. For you. Sort of a going-away present for your balls."

Bill let go with a slow whistle. "You know what kinda table dance you get in this joint for fifty bucks? I hope you wore your rubber jockey shorts."

"This is truly a Hallmark moment, guys," Jason said. "Bobby, you better collect on that yourself."

Bobby, getting up, threw Jason a disgusted wave. "Some bachelor party!"

Bill rose and said to Bobby, "I'm with you, man! Jeez, you'd think the condemned man woulda wanted his last meal!"

And the two went over to find themselves seats at center stage ringside, hooting and whistling as they went.

Al said, "I remember when you used to live in places like this."

"That was before Jenny," Jason said.

Al's sigh was wistfully nostalgic. "You used to say your idea of heaven would be a titty bar where you were the only customer."

"You're right. I also used to be thirteen. Some of us get older."

"What, and wiser? She's really changed you."

"Maybe I changed myself."

"Hey," Al said, sitting back in his chair, "girls don't come any nicer than Jenny, or better lookin' . . . but, Jason, she's so . . . so . . ."

"Nice?"

Al held his palms up. "Hey, if you wanna marry some preacher's daughter, some Young Republican Stepford Wife, that's your problem. But I'll tell you one thing—*I* wouldn't buy a car without at least drivin' it around the block a few times."

"Is it too late to get another best man?"

"That hurts. So—you and Jenny are leavin' tonight? Driving to her folks?"

"Yeah. We'll probably stop for the night someplace on I-66."

"Separate rooms, of course."

Jason got up; he'd had enough needling, good-natured or not. "Listen, I'll see you this weekend. Tell the guys thanks."

"Yeah, sure," Al said, toasting him with a beer glass, then adding cheerfully, "See you in hell."

As he left, Jason noticed Bobby sitting in a chair over by a wall, with that cheerleader sitting in his lap, grinding herself into him. Jason shook his head and escaped from the smell of cheap perfume and smoke into the fresh late-afternoon air.

Dr. Vanguard used a corner of her classroom as an office, just one of the indignities of teaching at such a small college. She was correcting papers when a door slam startled her, and she looked up to see an incongruous figure step into the classroom, closing the door on Vanguard and himself.

While neither tall nor strapping, his was an imposing presence; his well-worn apparel—workboots, jeans, work gloves, lumberjack shirt, and stocking cap—suggested a trucker or perhaps a construction worker. But his eye patch and scruffy beard lent him a sinister sailor aura.

"Thought we might want some privacy," he said, his voice a throaty growl.

She half-stood at her desk, working to keep the

alarm out of her voice. "Who the hell are you? What do you want?"

He removed his cap; his head was Yul Brynner bald. "Few moments of your time, ma'am."

"Open that door," she said, pointing, "or I promise you a scream that'll wake the dead *and* bring campus security running."

"We need to speak of things that only you and I can understand, ma'am." And he began to move toward her, dragging his left leg as he came; his left arm remained motionless at his side. "You have nothing to fear from me, Doctor. Might I sit?"

"What do you and *I* have to 'speak of'?"

"A mutual interest. Even an obsession."

She was interested despite herself, and heard herself saying, "Sit."

He did. "Might I ask what a famous person like yourself is doing at an insignificant institution like this one?"

Rather stiffly, she said, "My specialty is not in much demand, except for the very top people."

"Folklore," he said. "With an emphasis on urban legends. But you *are* one of the 'top people.' Your book, *The Stranded Cheerleaders' Revenge,* got you on Leno and Letterman."

"That was five years ago," she said, annoyance rising. "Who the hell *are* you?"

"Jack Talion," he said. "Retired Teamster." With his thick-knuckled, callused right hand, he patted his useless left arm. "Been on disability some time now."

"How fascinating. Is there a point to this?"

"That big university out east—why did they fire you?"

"Petty campus politics and jealousy."

He nodded. *"Because* you got on Leno and Letterman, and the best-seller lists. But what was their *excuse?"*

She shrugged. "My views were at odds with the conventional wisdom of the field . . ."

"You believe urban legends are rooted in fact. That if proper, in-depth research were done, you could find 'the core of truth at the heart of the beast.'"

Her big eyes got bigger. "My words exactly. How—"

"They were reported in the *American Folklorist Journal.*"

She smirked, shifted in her chair. "No offense, Mr. Talion, but you don't look the type to follow scholarly journals. What is your interest in this subject?"

His eyes seemed almost to glow. "Personal. You see—I was the only one of their victims to survive."

She frowned. "Only victim to survive . . . *whose* victim?"

"Those bitches from hell," he said, coldly matter-of-fact. "Those succubus cheerleaders that got you your fifteen minutes of fame. Here . . . look at these."

And from under his navy coat, he withdrew a manila folder and handed it to her. Within were yellowed newspaper clippings, which she spread out before her, reading them slowly, carefully. Ten minutes had passed before either of them spoke again.

"This certainly *could* be the right case," she said. "The year is even 1966. Truck rams a bridge abutment, the driver and his three teenage passengers are killed . . ."

"Cheerleaders on their way to the big game," Talion said. "A perfect fit, and you *know* it . . . keep reading."

"Good Lord," Vanguard said. "A year later, within miles of the accident—"

"A trucker turns up dead in a ditch with what the coroner calls 'an ungodly amount of alcohol in his system,'" Talion said, drenched with self-satisfaction. *"Ungodly!"*

She smiled, gestured dismissively. "This is certainly worth further research, and I owe you a debt of thanks, Mr. Talion. This could be my ticket to a full professorship at a *real* university."

"The talk-show circuit," Talion said, his gruff voice strangely seductive. "Best-seller list. Connect those two incidents to the inception of the 'legend,' and you get another fifteen minutes of fame . . . maybe half an hour."

She was nodding, her eyes glazed. "No one in my field has ever isolated the beginnings of *any* urban legend."

"The core of truth," Talion said.

"At the heart of the beast," she said.

The grizzled trucker sat forward. His good eye narrowed and gleamed. "The 'beasts' are coming out tonight, Doctor. This is it—this is their time."

She looked at the date on the clipping in her hand. "My God, you're right. This *is* the anniversary of their deaths."

"Once a year," Talion said, sneering, "they come to claim victims whose only crime is their manhood. Like the Flying Dutchman of yore, they emerge, to seek their vengeance."

Suddenly, he sat forward, and his hand gripped hers tightly. His face was clenched like a fist.

"Come with me, Doctor. Help me find them. Help stop them."

Jason unlocked the motel room for his fiancée, Jenny Chase, and held the door open for her. Even in jeans and cutoff sweatshirt, Jenny was a stunning young woman, her gold-highlighted brown hair brushing her shoulders, her features sharply pretty, her big, dark brown eyes a lovely contrast to her creamy complexion.

Jenny, train case in hand, stepped in and stopped short, saying, "Oh dear."

She was reacting to the gaudy cupid-themed honeymoon suite before them, dominated by a heart-shaped bed and lots of red satin and mirrors.

"I'm sorry, honey," Jason said, closing the door, carrying a suitcase. "It's the only room they had left."

"I'm so disappointed in you," she said. But there was nothing bitchy in her tone.

"I know," he said. "I'm sorry, I shoulda called ahead. It's just that I wasn't sure how far we wanted to drive tonight."

She pointed accusingly at the heart-shaped bed; even in the suite's low lighting, its red satin winked reflectively. "When I agreed we'd sleep in the same room on this trip, to save money, you promised you'd book twin beds."

"Baby," he said, "let's turn right around and *un*-check in and keep driving."

"No." She sighed. "No, I'm in for the night."

"Honey, I didn't plan this—honest."

Her brow was furrowed over the lovely brown eyes. "I hope not. After we've waited all this time, been so good, and just a few days away from the big day . . ."

"I'll sleep on that sofa."

She held up a "stop" palm. "No! We're going to sleep in this bed together, and we're going to exercise self-control. We're going to prove our love for each other by doing . . . nothing. All night long."

She marched into the bathroom and closed the door. Jason, thinking maybe he should have taken Bobby up on that table dance, stripped to his shorts and was folding his clothes neatly onto a chair when the bathroom door opened and Jenny emerged in a neck-to-floor frumpy robe.

"Is *that* what you're wearing to bed?" Jenny asked, gesturing to his boxers.

"My suit of armor is at the cleaners," he said.

Jenny moved quickly past him, saying, "I don't think sarcasm is necessary." Still in the frumpy robe, she climbed under the satin sheets.

"Oh yes it is," he said, joining her. "If I wanna preserve my sanity."

"Ready to go to sleep?" she asked, covers up to her neck.

"Soon as I say my prayers."

Her frown was more hurt than angry. "I don't find your attitude amusing."

"I don't find your distrust in your future husband anything to smile about, myself."

"I *do* trust you," she said doubtfully.

"Right. That's why you're wearing that seat cover to bed."

Now she really seemed hurt. "It's all I have."

"That's what you *always* wear to bed?"

"No. It's just that my nightgown is something . . . special I'm saving. For, you know—*the* night."

He half smiled. "And I suppose I just couldn't control myself if I saw you in it."

"Okay," she said, sitting up. "Judge for yourself."

And she got out of bed and opened the frumpy robe, letting it slip in a puddle to the floor. She was wearing a sheer baby-blue teddy. Her full, round, rosy-tipped breasts were visible; every rounded curve of her was visible, in fact, as was the gentle triangle of wispy brown.

"You see," she said, "I do trust you."

And she flounced under the covers.

"Our Father," Jason whispered, "who art in Heaven . . . lead us not . . ."

Heavyset, hairy Harry Simmons and his friend Earl sat sipping coffee in a booth at the sprawling I-66 Truckstop, discussing the sexual attractiveness of several waitresses. One of the waitresses in question was a pleasantly plump black woman in her early thirties.

"Nice saddle on 'er," Harry commented.

"I thought you hated coloreds," Earl said. "Didn't you lose your dispatchin' job to a black guy?"

"Yeah." Harry sighed. He lighted up a cigarette. "Now I'm back out here in no-man's land, makin' the long hauls. Musta been one of them quota deals."

Earl smirked. "Didn't have nothin' to do with you screwin' up and him bein' better qualified?"

Harry leaned forward and shook the cigarette between two fingers at his friend. "Listen, pal, spades ain't better qualified for *nothin'* except maybe peelin' bananas or somethin', like the black-ass apes they are."

The black waitress swayed by, and Harry turned to watch her fine rear view.

"Love that dark meat." Harry sighed.

Earl chuckled over his coffee. "At least your pecker ain't prejudiced, Harry."

Harry was smiling, shaking his head. "You know what they call them big ol' glorious heinies of theirs? Booties. You know what 'booty' means, don't ya, dickweed? Treasure. Buried treasure . . ."

Earl was sliding out of the booth. "Catch ya down the line at some other waterin' hole, Harry."

But Harry was still lost in poontang reverie. "I bet they're wild in the sack, man. Savage. They come down outta the trees later than we did, you know. They got natural instincts."

Earl shook his head, grinned, waved. "Later, Tarzan."

Before long, Harry was heading out to his own rig, in the rear parking lot, when from between two parked trucks, a lovely black girl in her late teens stepped out. She wore a tightly belted trenchcoat.

"Hey, big boy," she said. "You up for a romp in the jungle?"

And she opened the coat, flashing him a glimpse of her skimpy jungle-cat-pattern bikini.

She was belting back up as Harry, licking his lips, said, "I can make time for you, Brown Sugar. How much?"

"Who said anything about chargin'?"

She slipped her arm in his and walked him toward a parked rig.

"I thought they chased you workin' girls outta the motel," he said.

"We're not in the motel, Harry. We got our own portable playland."

She was guiding him to the ramp of the parked rig.

He frowned at the pretty chocolate face. "How did you know my name was Harry?"

"You told me," she said, her smile beautiful and white. "Remember?"

The door slid up, and red light engulfed him. Soon he was in a place that didn't seem to fit logically within the trailer portion of a semi; but he was so caught up, he didn't care. Why doubt reality?

And this reality was a jungle world of trees, leaves, bamboo, mosquito netting, displayed animal hides. Slipping out of her trenchcoat, the girl led him under the canopy of the bed.

"Relax here, Bwana," she said. "Jungle Girl serve you."

Harry stretched himself out on the waterbed. "Hey, you ain't gettin' no argument from me."

The girl plucked a banana from a hanging bunch, waved the phallic fruit under Harry's thick nose. "Bwana like banana?"

"Ain't crazy about 'em . . . but don't let me stop you."

He could feel his heartbeat increase as he watched

her suggestively peel the banana and slowly insert its tip into her mouth. Then she clamped down hard, taking a big bite, which made him jump a little.

She tossed the banana peel aside and began unbuttoning his shirt, playing with the thick hair on his chest, nuzzling his neck, sending him into ecstasy.

"Will you be my new bwana?"

"Sure will, Brown Sugar . . ."

"Old bwana gave Jungle Girl fur coat."

Harry frowned. "Hey . . . what kinda money are we talkin' about here?"

"Coat was gift. Bwana no give Jungle Girl gift 'less Bwana wish."

"I mean, I don't mind payin' a fair price . . . maybe we oughtta establish the goin' rate before—"

Her eyebrows rose over big brown eyes. "Bwana like see Jungle Girl in fur coat? In *nothing* but fur coat?"

"Uh, yeah. Bwana could go for that, just fine." He licked his lips. "Bwana want see Jungle Gal's fur . . ."

She waggled a finger and gave him a little-girl singsong. "Bwana not leave?"

"Bwana ain't goin' noplace, Jungle Gal."

She scampered out of the hutlike canopy, and Harry said to himself, "Cute little monkey . . ."

He was leaning back, elbows winged behind his head, when he heard a terrible bellowing cry, an animal cry, the thundering howl of something huge . . .

Then it was in the hut's opening, filling it, a huge beast, a *gorilla* . . .

. . . only it was an absurdity, a gorilla out of the Three Stooges, obviously a guy in a gorilla suit.

Except this was a *girl* in a gorilla suit, wasn't it? What kind of stupid sex play *was* this, he wondered.

"Fur coat, my ass," he said irritably. "Well, *my*

fantasy ain't no goddamn girl in a goddamn gorilla suit, so go take that ridiculous thing off—*right now!"*

But then it was on him, and its powerful arms were swatting at him, knocking him around as if he were a ragdoll, and those paws had claws that tore his flesh, and Harry scrambled out of the canopy, screaming for dear life. He didn't see the banana peel.

Harry hit the peel perfectly and sent himself flying, and falling, and landing, with a resounding *whump!*

When Harry looked up, that absurd gorilla face leaned in to fill his field of vision, and Harry began to scream again, a scream that escalated when the phony gorilla yanked Harry's arm from its socket and proceeded to beat him with the bloody thing. In fact, Harry's scream continued, in varying stages of pain and hysteria, until the beast gripped Harry's head in its paws and yanked it off, sending a geyser of blood that painted the ceiling of Harry's fantasy.

Outside the parked rig, a blonde and a brunette, both in cheerleader attire, waited patiently. Ronni filed her nails. Betty sat on the edge of the ramp, swinging her legs like a bored kid. Neither of them seemed to notice the trailer rocking, or the muffled cries of agony, mixed with gorilla snarls, within.

And after a while, the trailer door swung up and open, and LaVonne—her jungle bikini traded in for her cheerleader outfit—handed out a large garbage bag, tied at the top and filled with things that poked here and there. Harry's body parts.

Betty took the bag. "Ooooh! It's heavy!"

"Put that in the Dumpster over there, sweetie," LaVonne said. "White trash."

Dr. Janet Vanguard, at her passenger's request, pulled her little white Geo over to the shoulder of I-66. Talion had pointed out a road sign he wanted her to inspect, a sign that clearly read "I-666." Which she, of course, assumed was a prank of some kind, adding an extra 6.

She turned to Talion and said, "I can't believe I let you talk me into coming along on this white-whale hunt of yours."

"You think I'm crazy?" he asked smugly. "Let's find out."

And Talion got out, even as a semi whizzed by. Vanguard followed, and soon she was examining the sign, only to find the third 6 *wasn't* graffiti!

"Painted on, isn't it?" he asked. "Pretty elaborate 'prank,' if you ask me. And every damn sign you see tonight is going to be that way."

"Really?" she said archly. "And this happens every year? Every sign along Interstate 66 transforms itself magically into '666,' and nobody notices? Or if they do, nobody believes them?"

"Use that instant camera of yours," he suggested. "See what happens."

She fished her Polaroid out of her big purse and flashed a photo. As she waited for it to develop, she faced Talion and said, "Just what do you hope to accomplish tonight?"

His eyes were crazed as he replied, "These little girls have been taking revenge for nigh onto thirty years. Now it's Talion's turn."

She looked down at the developed photo in her hand. The sign clearly read "I-66." "Oh my God," she said, looking over at the sign that still bore its extra 6.

"Never occurred to you that the supernatural elements of these urban legends might hold that core of truth you're looking for, did it, Doctor?"

Soon they were at a booth at a truckstop, and Talion was spreading out a roadmap on the tabletop.

"You aren't expecting us to cover the entire length of I-66 in one night, are you?" she asked.

"Every dot is an incidence," he said, pointing to the occasional red dots on the black line drawn to highlight I-66's path parallel to the Mississippi River. "The first incident was within miles of where they died in that fiery crash. Then they began working their way up to Canada, leaving a trail of bodies. Didn't cross the border—All-American girls, you know."

Vanguard, frowning, shook her head. "Why hasn't the FBI's behavioral unit picked up on this? Technically, at least, these are serial killings."

Talion shrugged. "The occasional disappearing trucker, or traveler, or hitcher, what's to pick up on? When bodies are found, there's never a similarity of modus operandi. This victim is killed by an arrow, that one's head is cut off, here a dismembered body, there a pureed one . . ."

Vanguard was aware that eyes of other diners, disturbed by this grisly dinner-table conversation, were on them.

"Keep it down, would you?" she asked him in a whisper.

"Over the next fifteen years," he said, ignoring her request, "they worked their way down to the Mexican border—then they turned back again . . ."

"Where are they now?"

"On their way home," he said.

In the rear parking lot of the I-66 Truckstop, between a couple of parked rigs, long, tall, cool, laid-back Danny Watkins was confabbing with short, fried, nervous Fred, his friend and occasional customer.

"I don't know, Fred," Danny was saying, feigning reluctance. "I stopped dealin' a long time ago—all I got's my own private stash."

"Don't hand me that b.s., Danny—everybody knows you're still the biggest connection on I-66!"

Slipping his arm chummily around Fred's shoulder, Danny patted the trucker around the chest and waist, gently, with his other hand.

"You wouldn't be *wired,* now, would ya, Fred?"

"Hell no!" Fred said, pulling away. "I wanna *get* wired—so I can make it to Cleveland by five A.M. and not get my ass fired!"

Danny reached in a pocket of his brown soft-leather jacket and withdrew a prescription-type bottle of pills. "OK . . . but it'll cost ya a C note."

"That's highway robbery!"

"Think of it as interstate commerce. Yay or nay?"

"Shit," Fred said, and dug into his pocket for the cash, handing it over, holding out his palm into which Danny placed the pill bottle.

"Be careful now, son," Danny said. "More'n one of those hummers can send ya flyin' into outer space."

Fred popped a pill. "I don't wanna get to the moon—just Cleveland."

Danny slipped his arm around Fred's shoulder again. "Well, if you *do* want a little space odyssey, when your run's over, you and your personal Barbarella pop enough of *these* puppies, you'll be humpin' in orbit."

Fred was already walking away. "That's not my idea of a good time."

Danny shrugged. "Don't know what you're missin'."

Once Fred was out of sight, Danny withdrew another pill bottle from his pocket and scarfed down a handful of his own product. "One small step for man," he said, smacking his lips, "one giant leap for pharmacology."

Danny was heading toward his own parked rig when a lovely little blonde, no older than her late teens, stepped out from between two other rigs. She wore a tightly cinched trenchcoat and a coy smile.

"Are you the bad man who gives little girls candy?" she asked.

He ambled toward her. "Stranger things have happened." He withdrew one of the pill bottles from a pocket. "If I bring the snacks, will you provide the party?"

The blonde opened her trenchcoat and flashed him a look at her cherry-red vinyl bustier and G-string; the only other thing she was wearing, he noticed, were moon boots. Then she smilingly cinched her trenchcoat back up.

"I'm gonna take that as a yes," he said.

She led him up the ramp of a parked rig; the door began to slide up of its own accord, and a red glow beckoned him.

Inside, however, he found an area larger than you would think might fit inside the trailer, a chamber whose walls were painted with starry skies, moon boulders decorated the floor, a moon car served as a bar, and a space capsule with flashing lights sheltered a round bed.

"Whoa," Danny said, holding on to his forehead, trying to get his bearings. "Those babies are kickin' in quicker than usual."

The blonde peeked out from behind a boulder. "Ever do it on the moon before?"

"How'd you get in here? I thought you were *behind* me . . ."

The blonde, stripped to her vinyl outfit, stepped out and approached him. "Anything's possible in science fiction."

"Anything's possible on acid, too."

She looked up at him with big eyes in her babydoll face. "Is *that* what we're going to do?"

"Naw," he said. "Uppers."

She put her arms around his waist, brushed her breasts against him. "Do you need an upper to get . . . up?"

"Not with you around, baby."

He was loving this. He'd always been into science fiction, "Star Trek" and all; wanted to be an astronaut, as a kid. But as a teenager, he'd found other ways to get high.

"I want this to be perfect for you," the blonde said. "Everything you ever dreamed of."

"You know how I'd *really* like it, baby?" he asked, and he whispered to her. She put her hands on her bottom and looked at him like a little girl afraid she'd get in trouble.

"Ooooh," she said. "I've never *done* that."

"Great," Danny said. "I can go where no man's gone before."

"Okay, if that's what makes you happy," she said with a perky smile, and went to the moon cart where a jar of Tang and two glasses of water awaited. She began stirring up two servings.

"That's my wish upon a star," he said. "Short of makin' it in free fall, anyway. You know—doin' it antigravity-style."

"Oh, we can do that," the blonde said matter-of-factly. "That's easy. Tang?"

"No thanks—never touch the stuff."

"I'll just hit the antigrav switch, then. Be right back."

"Yeah. Yeah, you do that."

He watched the little babe wiggle to the capsule and climb onto the bed; as she reached for the control panel, her pretty, heart-shaped, dimpled ass was in the air, displayed just for him.

"The moon is really out tonight," he said to himself. "What a little space cadet."

She hit the switch, and Danny flew suddenly upward. She didn't see him hit, but the *splat* turned her head, and when her two cheerleader friends, Ronni and LaVonne, peeked in, all three of them were looking up as blood and goo dripped down.

"Ick," Betty said.

"What happened?" Ronni asked as the gory glop dropped down.

Betty shrugged. "I guess he ran out of space."

Jason stared sleeplessly at the motel-room ceiling, suffering in silence as Jenny slumbered peacefully next to him, her brown hair beautifully tousled against the pillow, her creamy bosom spilling generously out of the top of her teddy.

He kept stealing looks at her until finally he couldn't stand it. He leaned in and, ever so delicately, tentatively, kissed her neck.

She smiled in her sleep and moaned pleasurably.

So he kissed her neck again. Harder.

And she turned to him and slipped herself into his arms, and they kissed. He pulled her close to kiss her again, when her eyes popped open.

"Oh, my," she said. "This *is* hard for you, isn't it?"

He filled his hand with a full, perfectly rounded breast. "What difference does a few days make . . ."

He buried his face in her neck, nuzzling her, and she was moaning in delight, really getting into it, when suddenly she had second thoughts and pushed him away.

She gathered the covers around her. "No. Not now. Not tonight. Jason, this is my fault, I shouldn't have tempted you!"

She flew out of bed and slammed herself into the bathroom.

He sighed. Hauled his ass out of bed. Trudged over to the bathroom.

"Look," he said to the door, "I can't sleep, and I'm

trouble for both of us. That truckstop next door's open all night. I'll be over there havin' coffee for the next, oh . . . why don't you join me for breakfast in, say, eight hours?"

And he got his clothes on and left.

The full moon gave the concrete ribbons of I-66 a lovely, lonely glow as Vanguard drove her obsessed passenger from truckstop to truckstop. They'd hit four so far—nothing. No sign of anything unusual.

"Next up is the I-66 Truckstop itself," he said. "It's the one closest to where the girls met their fiery fate back in '66. Where that rapist trucker promised to take them."

His intensity was amazing.

She said, "You really think we'll find them."

"Oh, they're out there tonight. I can smell them."

Her mouth made a wry twist. "Perfume?"

"Brimstone," Talion said.

They drove awhile, and Vanguard said, "How do you intend to stop them, anyway? Stake through the heart? Silver bullets?"

"Do I look like the Lone Ranger? Anyway, they don't have hearts."

"What, then? Exorcism? You don't look much like a priest, either."

He was shaking his head no. "Incantations won't kill them. They're demons. I have to destroy them to send them back to hell."

"Why not heaven?" she asked. "They were sinned *against,* you know. You remember what the urban legend says."

Talion's grunt was sarcastic, dismissive. "Their search will end when they find a man 'pure of heart.' The man who resists them frees them."

"That's the way the story goes, in most forms."

He snorted. "Well, I'm here to give the lie to that. *I*

147

resisted them . . . and they're *still* on their Satanic rampage."

The sound of the wheels on pavement was a steady *thrum.*

"Are you ready to tell me?" she asked.

"Tell you what?"

"Your story. Did they grant you *your* secret fantasy?"

"I'm a common man, Doctor." Talion sighed. "I had a common fantasy. Nothing lurid. Nothing exotic."

"Tell me."

His face was red in the glow of the dashboard lights. "I was hauling produce from Des Moines to points north. She accosted me in a truckstop parking lot, and I'll be damned if she didn't look exactly like Becky Sue Matthews, the girl I loved and lost in high school, and when I followed that little prostitute into the back of that truck trailer, it turned into the backseat of my old Chevy!"

Vanguard tried to keep her eyes on the road, but the hypnotized expression on Talion's face kept drawing her attention to him.

"Buddy Holly was playing on the radio," he said, "and she kissed me, and it was sweet at first, but then it was shriveling, and she was kissing the life out of me, sucking me dry, and I screamed and climbed out of there, and I opened the door and dove into the parking lot . . . and the bitches almost ran me over!"

As if punctuating Talion's story, a semi streaked by in the passing lane.

"Almost ran me down, in that big truck—the blonde and a brunette and a colored girl, in the cab . . . and I've dragged my sorry ass up and down I-66 ever since, praying that God would grant me one more night with those Satanic sluts!"

His good hand was raised in a trembling fist. Then he let out some air, relaxed, and Vanguard did the same.

"Thanks for sharing," she said.

In a booth at the I-66 Truckstop, Jason sat nursing his fourth cup of coffee—he was really pushing the "free refill" concept—when Jenny, back in her traveling clothes, slid in across from him.

"Am I too early for breakfast?" she asked, almost timidly.

He wanted to dive into those big brown eyes.

"No!" he said. "Are you hungry?"

"Not really. I . . . I couldn't sleep."

"I'm sorry."

She was shaking her head. "Don't say that. You don't have anything to be sorry about. This is my fault."

"No," he said. "It's mine."

She was busying her hands with a napkin, fooling with it as she said, "I know you didn't . . . plan any of that, next door. And I don't know how I could expect you to sleep next to me with me in that . . . nightie." She swallowed, embarrassed.

"You ever consider," he said gently, "that maybe we're just not compatible?"

Her expression was horrified. "No!"

"Jenny, I'm not very religious. You know that. I think I'm a pretty good person, but I just don't buy any of it, heaven and hell, life after death . . ."

Her brow tightened. "I haven't tried to force my beliefs on you."

"I know you haven't. But we gotta live with each other, and how do two people grow old together if they see the world so differently?"

"I don't understand."

"We supposedly love each other. We made a commitment. We're on our way to get married! And you treat me like a kid on prom night, tryin' to get laid."

"I want you to respect me."

He could see the tears welling up in her eyes, but he pressed on anyway. He couldn't help himself—it *had* to be said.

"But *you* don't respect *me*," he said. "That's the *real* problem, isn't it? To you, I'm just some horny asshole—"

A trickle of a tear rolled down her cheek as Jenny slid out of the booth. Her chin was trembling, and she was struggling for dignity as she said, "I think you're cruel."

And then she was gone.

The waitress came over with coffee and said, "More, Cowboy?"

"No," Jason said. "No thanks. I've had enough."

Soon he was walking across the rear parking lot, shoulders slumped, when a lovely brunette stepped out from between parked rigs. She wore a trenchcoat and a sexy smile.

"Lookin' for some live entertainment?" she asked.

"No thanks," he said.

He walked on, and then there she was, in front of him again.

"First table dance is free."

He swallowed. "Tempting—but no."

He kept walking, and there she was again. How did she move so quickly?

"Business is slow at the club tonight," she said. "You'd have it all to yourself."

Then she opened her trenchcoat and showed off her nearly nude, slenderly curvy, devastating body draped in stripper bra and G-string.

"Of course," she said in sultry tones, "if you've got something better to do . . ."

He thought about it. Looked toward the motel. Shook his head and said, "Goddammit, I don't have. Lead the way, beautiful."

And he found himself taken by the hand and led up the ramp into the back of a trailer that opened impossibly into a replica of the strip club where he'd had his bachelor party, an identical foggy, light-flashing, chrome-and-mirror palace, except he was the only patron present.

He touched his forehead, as if checking for a fever. "I've . . . I've been here before . . ."

"It's a franchise," the brunette said.

"In the back of a *truck?*"

The brunette leaned in and nibbled his ear. "Don't question it. Float with it."

And she guided him to a ringside seat by center stage.

"Welcome to the 666 Club!" a DJ's voice bellowed over a throbbing ZZ Top number.

Jason turned and looked back at the DJ's booth, but it was empty.

"We have an out-*standing* lineup of centerfold lovelies for you tonight. And tonight only, everything's free! You want a table dance, just ask for it! Now, let's get started with bouncing Betty!"

And down the runway onto center stage came a blonde so cute it made his teeth ache, decked out in a skimpy cheerleader-style outfit. She began a very sexy version of a cheerleader routine—just for him.

"You want a lap dance, just whisper in your filly's ear! You want *more?* Well, let your conscience be your guide . . . these little gals left *their* conscience with their clothes! They were put on this earth solely to satisfy your every whim . . . every desire . . . every fantasy . . ."

"That's all right with me," Jason said to nobody.

* * *

In the rear parking lot of the I-666 Truckstop, near the parked Geo, Talion was withdrawing two bulky flare guns from a canvas bag.

"What are *those* for?" Vanguard asked him, gesturing with an open palm.

He thrust one of the flare guns into that palm. "They're not silver bullets," he said, "or wooden stakes—but they'll do."

Her head bobbed back as if she were evading a blow. "You expect me to *shoot* somebody? Please."

He got right in her face; his breath mingled coffee and bourbon. "Not somebody, some *thing,*" he said. "They're hell spawn. They're born of fire, they'll die of fire . . ."

"You *are* a lunatic," she muttered. "But what's *my* excuse?"

Then Talion began to prowl the rear parking lot. "If they're anywhere, they're here . . . and I *know* they're here. They died within a few miles of this truckstop."

Vanguard had to work to keep up with him, despite Talion's draggy leg. "Listen," she said, "I don't believe in violence."

He whirled and faced her. "You believe in the core of truth at the heart of the legend, don't you? You *know* these creatures exist—otherwise, you wouldn't have made this journey."

And he stalked off, exploring the lot, eyeing each parked rig suspiciously.

She was glancing behind her when she bumped into him; she hadn't seen him stop, frozen to the spot.

"There it is," he said. "That's their home."

And her gaze followed his pointing finger to what, at first, seemed just the rear of another parked semi. But from under the slide-down door came an eerie red glow.

"That's just a truck," she said.

"You don't think I can recognize the quarter-ton of

steel that almost ran me down?" He nodded toward the rig. "But for the sake of argument, check out the personalized plate."

She did: on it was the number 666. *Nothing* but the number 666.

Suddenly, she realized she was trembling. "So . . . so where *are* they?"

His smile was more a sneer. "You know the 'legend,' Doctor. Didn't you write a little book or something? They're *inside*."

"What do you expect me to *do?*"

His eyes were wild. "There are three of them. I'll shoot one, you'll shoot one, and we'll both pray to sweet Jesus I have time to reload for the third."

Then he strode toward the ramp up to the back of the truck, the gimpy leg not slowing him down a bit.

And she followed.

Stripped to pasties and G-string, the blond cheerleader was down off the stage giving Jason some up-close and personal attention. Then the blonde plucked the pasties off her breasts, baring pert pink nipples, and unsnapped the G-string, revealing a downy tuft as blond as her bouncing shoulder-length locks. Woozy from her perfume and pulchritude, Jason allowed the blonde to touch him but remained passive.

He closed his eyes, moaning with pleasure as she ground her bottom into his lap. Then the pressure eased up, he opened his eyes—and she was gone.

"Bouncing Betty will be back later," the invisible DJ was saying, "but right now, feast your horny eyes on Luscious LaVonne."

And now an Afroed black girl, with a generously rounded figure, was strutting down the stage in a purple satin fringed bikini.

"Remember, there's no cover at the 666 Club, and

no minimum, but there *is* minimum cover on our foxy ladies! Keep in mind, if you want special attention, just ask and you shall receive."

Soon the black stripper was down off the stage, and the bikini was gone, and she, too, removed her pasties and G-string, and dark, erect, pencil eraser nipples were stroking his face, mounds of soft firm bosom engulfing him, making him drunk with sweet-smelling female flesh.

Then, in an eyeblink, the black girl was gone and the ZZ Top tune gave way to a romantic Whitney Houston ballad, as the DJ said, "And now it's time for your dark dream to step aside, but don't worry— Luscious LaVonne will be back . . . but right now we want to honor our special guest tonight, here at the Club 666—this one's especially for you, Jason! Ravishing Ronni!"

An incredible brunette who looked a little like Jenny was striding down the runway onto the stage, in a lovely sheer teddy. Hell! It was the *same* teddy as Jenny's!

The brunette had a similar rounded body, and there were no pasties or G-string beneath that sheer teddy, just rosy-tipped breasts and that dark secret between her legs as the dancer gyrated sensuously, gracefully, her eyes gazing down at him with the promise not just of sex but of love.

At times, the dancer seemed literally to be Jenny, but then he would blink and it would be the lovely brunette again. What a strange, delirious, wonderful, awful dream he was caught up in!

Then, still wearing the teddy, she came down off the stage and straddled his lap and stroked his face sensually, devouring him with those bedroom eyes.

* * *

When Talion yanked up the sliding door at the rear of the rig, the red glow intensified; but when he closed the door behind them, Vanguard was startled by the glow disappearing, and they were stepping through a doorway into the foggy, music-throbbing chamber of a chrome-and-glass strip club.

"Nice threads," Talion said with a nasty smile.

And she realized her conservative professorial suit had vanished, replaced by a skimpy gold lamé bra that barely concealed her small, well-formed breasts, and sheer red harem pants over a gold lamé G-string that left the cheeks of her behind exposed. Her hair was no longer tied back but full, a dark cascade of curls. Her glasses were gone, her feet bare.

"What . . . what's *happened* to me?"

Talion smiled, shrugged. "A marked improvement, I'd say."

"This is insane!"

"No," Talion said, somber again. "It's just that you're inside *his* fantasy."

And they could see a handsome young man, seated ringside at center stage, a lovely brunette in a sheer teddy straddling his lap. Two naked dancers, a lovely blonde and a black girl with a '60s Afro, came floating up and began smothering the young man with loving attention, from all sides.

"This world is constructed from each victim's secret desires," Talion whispered. "This guy gets a damn nightclub, and all *I* rated was the backseat of a Chevy!"

They began moving toward the young man, who, strangely, seemed to be having second thoughts; he was gently pushing the brunette in his lap away.

"No," he said. "You're very beautiful, but no . . ."

"We have unexpected guests here at Club 666!" the DJ announced.

The three strippers turned with surprise toward the approaching Talion and Vanguard.

Talion planted himself, the flare gun thrust forward. "Remember me, ladies? I'm the little man that got away."

The romantic song stopped, and a Buddy Holly tune—"That'll Be the Day"—replaced it.

The blonde was suddenly wearing a sweater, pleated skirt, bobby sox, and saddle shoes. She was beaming. "Jack! Jack Talion! I've *missed* you so. You *remember* me, don't you? Becky Sue Matthews?"

Talion's eyes half-closed; he seemed almost feverish as he said, "Becky Sue . . . I've loved you so . . ."

"The car's right outside," the blonde said. "The backseat's waiting, darling. Tonight's the night . . . I'm ready to go all the way!"

The flare gun in Talion's hand was wavering, but then he had his resolve back. He almost spat. "It won't wash, ladies."

The Buddy Holly tune stopped, with a needle scratch.

"But," Talion continued, his smile an awful thing as he aimed the flare gun, "I *will* let you in on my deepest, darkest fantasy."

The blonde, the brunette, and the black girl were in cheerleader attire now. Their latest victim, the young man in the ringside chair, was frozen in time, eyes glazed, hearing and seeing none of this. The three cheerleaders frowned at Talion, as if he were a mean teacher who had scolded them unfairly.

"I've been dreaming of sending you harlots back to hell!"

"Not just yet, Talion," Vanguard said, lifting the flare gun to her companion's temple. With the young man in the chair frozen, she was back in her professorial attire again.

He glared at her around the gun at his head.

"What's wrong with you? Are you *insane,* woman? This is what we came to do!"

"It's what *you* came to do," Vanguard said. Keeping the gun to Talion's temple, Vanguard turned toward the cheerleaders, focused her attention on the brunette. "Ronni—it's Janet, Ronni. I'm Janet."

"Janet?" Ronni said, stunned. "Baby Jan?"

Vanguard nodded.

"You sure grew up," Ronni said.

"It's time to let go, Ronni," Vanguard said. "You and the other girls. No more revenge."

Ronni frowned, shook her head. "We can't go, Jan . . . not till we find what we're after."

Vanguard nodded toward the frozen young man in the ringside chair. "I think you found him."

The cheerleaders took a look at the frozen, slack-jawed Jason Peterson. Was he the man who could resist their hellish charms?

"Naw," LaVonne said. "I can crack this sucker."

"He seems kinda nice to me," Betty said, almost sadly.

"It's our *job,* girl!" LaVonne retorted. "If we can get a rise out of him, he's *soul* food!"

Vanguard asked, "What do you think, Ronni?"

Ronni was thinking about it. The Whitney Houston song began playing, and suddenly Ronni was again in the blue teddy, and the other two cheerleaders were completely, startlingly nude. They converged on their prey, Ronni straddling him, the other girls kissing and caressing him.

Vanguard kept the flare gun pressed to the sweating cheek of the furious Talion; but he, too, was watching the attempted seduction.

Ronni's teddy was gone; she, too, was nude, and whispering in Jason's ear.

And then Jason, gently but firmly, lifted Ronni up and off his lap. "No! No thanks . . ." He stood, tried to regain his composure. "You girls are really beautiful, but I'm just not into this anymore."

Vanguard smiled at Talion, who was frowning in disbelief.

"I'm *married,*" Jason said. "Or, anyway, I'm gonna be." And he began to walk away from the beautiful naked girls, saying, "I mean, I don't mean to hurt anybody's feelings or anything, but I got stuff this good waitin' at home . . . at least, I *hope* I still do."

Ronni's expression, at first disappointment, melted into bliss. Utter bliss.

"'Bye, Jan," Ronni said.

"'Bye, Sis," Vanguard said.

Then the three girls, in the cheerleader outfits, pompons in hand, were waving, waving good-bye, Betty giggling like a little girl, as they faded away.

And with a *whump,* Vanguard, Talion, and Jason landed on their butts on a bare patch of concrete in the parking lot. The truck had vanished. The two flares were scattered here and there, as were the cheerleaders' pompons—the only remaining evidence any of this had actually happened.

Vanguard, first to her feet, helped Jason to his.

"What the hell happened?" the young man asked.

"Whatever it was," Vanguard said, "want a piece of friendly advice? Don't tell anybody . . . 'less you want it to get around."

Which was, after all, how urban legends got started.

Confused, the young man at first stumbled away, then ran.

Vanguard helped Talion to his feet.

"Guess you had a vested interest in this yourself," he said.

"The core of truth at the heart of the legend," she said. "Why do you think I was so interested in the tale?"

"You blew your second fifteen minutes of fame, kid."

"I don't know," Vanguard said with a shrug. "There's *two* of us to claim all this happened. Who knows? A book, a movie, the talk-show circuit. Partners?"

Talion chuckled, shook his head, taking her extended hand. "You know, you didn't look half bad in that wacky outfit," he said.

"Really?" she asked, pleased to hear it. "Aren't there catalogs where you can order stuff like that?"

Then Vanguard looped her arm in Talion's, and they walked toward the truckstop for some coffee.

Jason was careful not to waken Jenny when he returned to the motel room. In his shorts, he climbed under the covers, just hoping to make himself disappear.

But it woke Jenny nonetheless; she smiled at him sleepily. "You . . . you came back."

"I love ya, baby. It's not going to kill us to wait a little while. What's a few days?"

She began to kiss him, then turned away. "Ugh! I have sleep breath. I'll be right back."

Still in her frumpy robe, she trundled off to the bathroom and shut herself in.

Leaning back in bed, listening to the sound of running water, Jason felt the glow of relief that his bride-to-be had forgiven him. He wasn't aware, really, how much had been at stake in that "strip club."

Then the running water stopped, the bathroom door opened, and Jenny was in the doorway, wearing only the teddy. The light behind her was making a radiant silhouette of her womanly curves.

"It's not going to kill us to get a little head start, either," she said.

Jason smiled and looked skyward. "Thank you, God."

Then Jenny was in his arms, and they were laughing and kissing and rolling on the bed together, and soon they were making glorious love.

And what the hell is wrong with that?

THE HEALING TOUCH

Terry Campbell

Megan Willard rolled off her spent partner and sat up at the edge of the bed. She lingered for a moment in the darkness—a black void diffused by the stark whiteness of the walls—and savored the primal smell of sexual fulfillment. Finally, the young nurse slipped her uniform on and stood, looking down at her unknowing, yet complying, partner. He had been admitted only that morning, but Megan Willard knew how to welcome a new patient to the Millman Center for the Disabled. The man had been born with no arms or legs. In fact, he was little more than a head, a torso, and a penis. The nurses on the previous shift had fed him, bathed him, fluffed his pillows, and made him comfortable—at least, it had to be assumed he was comfortable; because he could not communicate, one could never be sure. Working the night shift, Megan could only check in on her patients and make them feel good by performing services the other nurses couldn't, or wouldn't, do. Megan pulled his gown back over his hips and draped the sheets comfortably across him for warmth. She ran her hand along the patient's shriveling penis and removed the wrinkled, sticky condom.

Tonight, she was lucky; she didn't always climax with her partners. But that was all right. They were too inexperienced, or the intercourse was purely a responsive action. Most of the acts lasted only seconds, but over the years, Megan's own sexual sensitivities had heightened to the point where sometimes seconds were all she needed. She had also developed an affinity for the physically challenged during her years of working with them. She supposed it was some warped type of Florence Nightingale syndrome; she just wanted to do something special for the pitiful souls who crossed her path.

Megan couldn't pinpoint the exact time or event in her life that had led to the development of her fetish for physical anomalies. Overpaid pompous psychiatrists would have tried to blame an abusive father or some form of early sexual abuse, but that wasn't the case. Megan was just attracted to the unusual, the different.

She could recall being drawn to a boy in grade school who was confined to a wheelchair. She remembered sitting in the swings at recess, gently rocking in the breeze, oblivious to the other children, watching the boy as he sat by himself near the front steps of the school, apparently lost in thought. She always wanted to know what he was thinking. In her freshman year in college, she had taken a volunteer position with a psychiatric clinic for the disabled. She remembered a young man named Frederick, whose only physical deformity was his right hand. He had only one finger, what amounted to a pinkie with no nail where his thumb should have been. He had been her first actual sexual experience with a "freak." She had witnessed a group of ruffians kicking at him and making fun of him. He ran away, and Megan followed him. She found him crying in a concrete drainage tunnel next to a park. Megan had tried to comfort him, but nothing she could say or do could ever change what the other children did to the poor man. She could think of only one thing that, in some small way, might make it better. Megan had taken his deformed hand and pushed it up under her skirt, guiding the soft pinkie-thumb into her pussy, letting it explore her moist darkness, pumping the finger in and out like a narrow penis, soft yet firm. The skin of that finger had been so soft, like velvety gelatin. She could remember looking into Frederick's surprised bright blue eyes, at the wonder held within them, watching the drying tears streak his face. The sensation of the soft finger in her vagina and the heartwarming feeling that she had just made life better, if only for the moment, for Frederick combined to bring her a shudder of pleasure she had not yet known in her young life. That had been her first real orgasm. She had let other guys get to "third base," but the excitement just hadn't been there.

There were many more "freaks" after that. She had volunteered and interned at various clinics and rehabilitation centers throughout her college years. There had been countless encounters then, and they became more frequent when she began her career as a physical therapist.

Megan had found herself becoming less and less involved with so-called normal men. It wasn't as if she didn't have opportunities with all sorts of men. She looked as if she could still be in college, and her blond hair, blue eyes, and statuesque five-foot-ten frame with *Playboy*-centerfold measurements combined to form one definite dick magnet. But these men didn't interest her. They had too many problems, too many distractions. Hung up on their jobs, on themselves, on relationships in general. And worst of all, in every normal man, Megan could see the boys who had teased Frederick that fateful day long ago.

But the freaks were a different story. There was no commitment, no talk, no promises. Just a powerful bond shared by two people, an opportunity to relieve their pain the best she could. Most of them had limited mental abilities, and many were not even aware of what they were doing while performing with Megan. It wasn't difficult to make a penis harden, even if the mental flames had been extinguished long ago. The sex was just so simple, so natural. Especially in the feeble-minded, their bodies just took over where their minds were incapable of treading, and it became a primitive, continue-the-bloodline fucking. It never lasted long, but it often resulted in extremely intense orgasms for Megan, orgasms no normal man could provide.

Megan sat at a desk in the administrative office, wiping tears from her eyes. Stanley, a young intern who had asked her out several times in the past few weeks, had just let her know, in no uncertain terms, how he felt about her constant rejections. "Frigid cocktease" had been his term of choice. Megan didn't really know why she was letting the bastard's attitude upset her. Perhaps, deep down, she longed for a "normal" relationship, wished that she could feel for other men the way she felt about her special friends. Perhaps she really longed for something permanent with a man of not-so-normal physical status. Reaching out for comfort, Megan opened a manila folder and began reviewing the files of the center's newest patients, Glen and Galen Moore, an eighteen-year-old set of conjoined twins. The twins had come to the clinic for psychological counseling. After years of scraping for money, Glen and Galen's parents at last had the financial means to have the boys separated.

The young men were joined at the hip, sharing only two legs. The surgery would be simple enough, but the boys simply wanted no part of it. They had lived their eighteen years in this manner and were frightened beyond belief at the notion of going their separate ways.

Good for you, Megan thought. *Don't let them drive you into the world of the normal. Don't succumb to their pressures. You are unique; you are special.*

Megan retrieved the birth photo of the twins. To anyone else, the wrinkled pink monstrosity that stared out from the Polaroid would be highly disturbing. But not to Megan. To her, the boys were beautiful.

She leaned back in her chair and stared at the photo, looking forward to the next morning when she would meet these two special young men. And then, as it so often did, her mind began to wander into other, forbidden territories. Megan's fingers deftly loosened two buttons on her smock, allowing her hand access to her breasts. She rolled a hardening nipple between two fingers, pinched it with the tips of her nails, while her other hand slipped under her skirt and teased the soft hair between her legs.

Megan rubbed the tips of her fingers together, lubricated by the oily slickness of her arousal, and she continued to stare at the baby boys, imagining how they would look now, as adults in the same natural state. Though the boys shared only two legs, it was obvious from the reports of their medical history that each had a fully functioning penis.

"I'll make it better," Megan whispered. "You'll see. I'll make it all right."

"I just wanted to tell you that I support your decision not to have the operation," Megan told the twins.

The boys looked surprised and maybe a bit groggy; they were not used to being awakened in the middle of the night. Defensively, they pulled the bed sheets a little closer to their bodies.

"I'm here to tell you that you are both wonderful, unique human beings, and that no one should tell you otherwise. You're old enough to make your own decisions. If you had been separated as infants, that would be another story. But fate didn't play it that way."

The boys looked around their room. Diffused light from the lampposts outside filtered through the closed miniblinds covering the windows. The boys appeared nervous, as well they should be. They were in an alien place, surrounded by strangers—professional people in white jackets who took it upon themselves to decide what was right for Glen and Galen.

"Why are you here, then?" Galen asked.

"Just to talk, to get to know you," Megan said.

"In the middle of the night?"

Megan shrugged. "No one else is around. We can be ourselves. Tell me about yourselves; tell me what you're feeling."

"About being here?" Glen asked.

"About anything."

"They want us to be normal," Glen answered. "They think that by separating us, everything will be all right. But it won't be. We'll be two separate people with only one leg each. How can that be any more normal than what we are now?"

"It can't," Megan said. The boys were starting to loosen up in her presence. "But they're frightened of you. It disgusts them to look at you, so they want to change you, not for your sakes but for their own convenience."

"You're not like all the others," Galen said. "You understand."

Megan smiled. "I've had lots of experience dealing with matters such as this. I know how to make things better. I know how to make you forget your situation. When was the last time you were able to be free? When were you able to go away on your own, to be free of all others, to experience the joys of life and all it encompasses?"

"Never," Galen said, slowly shaking his head. "There's always someone else around."

"Someone besides yourselves?" Megan asked.

"Yes," Glen agreed. "That doesn't mean Galen. I don't consider my brother to be someone else. We are one."

"Have you ever experienced total happiness? Have you ever been so happy, so free, that you forget where you are, what you're doing? Have you ever experienced ecstasy?" Megan asked. She removed her smock, and her shaking fingers fumbled with the buttons on her blouse, unfastening them and letting the silky garment fall to the floor with a whisper, exposing her small breasts and erect nipples. The twins sat up in bed suddenly, their eyes growing larger in the dark.

"What . . . what are you doing, Nurse Willard?"

"Call me Megan," she whispered in a sultry voice dripping with the anticipation of sex. The twins' unfortunate situation made her want to nurture them all the more; she had to comfort them. She quickly unfastened her slacks and stepped out of them. She could already smell the musky odor of her aroused sex.

"You've never been with a woman, have you? Never even seen one nude, have you?"

Glen and Galen shook their heads. Megan was momentarily amused by the way their heads moved in unison. She approached the bed and slowly pulled the sheets off, letting them fall to the floor. Immediately,

Megan was aware of twin peaks jutting from the crotch of the specially designed pajama bottoms. Instinctively, her hands reached for them, taking each penis in her grip, stroking them through the thin cloth. The boys looked at each other and gasped, but neither set of arms made a move to stop her. Megan grabbed the hem of the pajama bottoms and pulled, feeling the boys lift their hips slightly. The twin erect penises bobbed slightly as the fabric slid across them, freeing them.

Desire took over the twins' minds, and they removed their pajama tops. Megan bent to kiss the head of first one penis, then the other. She had never made love to two men at once, but this was the same thing. The twins groaned, their heads lolling slightly, as Megan continued to kiss and suck one while stroking the other, then swapping. It only took a moment for both penises to erupt simultaneously in a flood of hot semen. Megan looked up, staring into the bright eyes of the two boys experiencing something they no doubt had thought they would never experience. She ran her hands across the sweat-soaked chests and bellies while cleaning the boys off with her tongue. When she was done, Megan stood and moved closer to Galen and Glen.

"That . . . that was incredible," Glen said.

"I had a dream once where that happened," Galen said, his eyes distant. "But it was only a dream. Until now."

Megan smiled at the twins and stroked the hair on their heads. "Nurse Willard . . . I mean, Megan. Can we touch you?"

Megan's smile dissolved slowly into a sultry stare. She took Glen's right hand and Galen's left hand and placed one on each breast. The boys gasped again as she moved their hands gently in a tight circular motion, pressing down in the center as her nipples strained to the touch. She guided them for a moment before realizing she was no longer controlling their motions, then let go. She let her head drop back, closing her eyes and concentrating on the feel of the warm, soft hands gliding across her shoulders, breasts, stomach, and buttocks, and reveled in the knowledge that the twins had momentarily forgotten everything that was wrong in their world. Megan could feel beads of sweat breaking forth from her forehead, her shoulders, between her breasts, as the hands continued to explore. She waited and waited, beginning to believe she would have to direct their touch to her vagina, but then one of the twins—was it Glen or Galen? it didn't matter—grew bolder and let his fingers run through the golden thatch of hair between her legs. Then she felt another set of fingers slide along her slick opening, circling teasingly before demanding entry. Megan released a long wail as many fingers—too many to count—explored her wet depths. Never before having experienced the touch of multiple freaks, Megan, too, didn't last long, crying out in a release of orgasmic bliss.

Her legs weak, she collapsed into the arms of the twins, pulling herself up onto their bed. Thoughts raced through Megan's head—thoughts of Frederick, of Michael, of all the freaks she had ever made comfortable. And then she thought of Stanley, a man who wanted her only for the pleasure and convenience of her orifice. As Megan lay back on the bed, she glanced at her smock lying crumpled on the floor. Inside were two unwrapped condoms, brought along with the twins in mind. Megan saw the selfishness and lust of men side by side with her own willingness to help and comfort and the twins' refusal to be normal, and Megan decided what it was she needed, what relationship was missing from her life. The condoms would stay in the pocket of her smock. Finding them erect again, Megan rolled onto her back and directed the twins to position themselves above her. Their two legs supported them well as they moved between her own legs. The boys held themselves up with one hand, still leaving two hands free to trace circles around her navel, to crawl upward to pinch her brown nipples. Wanting them like she had wanted no other freaks in her life, Megan began stroking one penis while directing the other between her moist labia. She shuddered as the full length slid into her while her hand worked the other penis frantically. After a moment, she allowed the penises to trade places, and the frenzied pace resumed.

Once again, the sexual inexperience of the twins and the heightened, almost spiritual arousal of Megan combined, and she screamed her pleasure just as she felt one penis explode, spewing forth its contents deep into her body even as the other splattered white hot semen across her belly. She hated to waste the precious fluid on the exterior of her body, but the sticky warmth felt so good on her skin, and six hands—the twins' and her own—traveled erotically up and down her body, smearing the semen across her breasts, along her ribs, over her navel, and the twins collapsed atop Megan in a spent, congenitally defective heap.

The three lay there for what seemed an eternity, a deformed and twisted pile of arms and legs, until Megan rose from the bed. The janitor usually made a final run through the halls of this wing toward the end of his shift, and Megan wished to be long gone when he did. She slid from the bed and quickly dressed. She helped the twins back into their pajamas and watched as they laid their heads down on twin pillows and fell asleep with smiles on their faces. Megan leaned over and kissed each one on the forehead.

"Don't ever let them tell you what to be," she

whispered. Megan smiled down at them. Her work was done.

Megan crept back to the door and opened it. The shadow creeping into the room didn't register in her brain at first. Then she noticed something was wrong. Megan looked up. Stanley's large frame blocked the doorway.

"Stanley!" Megan whispered loudly, her heart pounding.

"You sick bitch!" Stanley snarled through gritted teeth. "You fucked the twins? You slept with those fuckin' freaks?"

"Stanley . . . I—" Megan stuttered, her panicked mind racing. She was frightened beyond belief. Surely he would tell. She would be discovered, and everything that she had ever done to comfort her patients would become public knowledge.

She overestimated her would-be suitor. He quickly grabbed her delicate wrists in his large, rough hands and shoved her into the janitor's closet across the hall.

"You're a goddamned pervert, you know that?" he said, slamming the door. The sound made Megan wince. "How many of the freaks do you get it on with?"

"It's none of your business," Megan said, fighting to escape. Her willpower slowly overcame her fear, and she wanted desperately to be far away from Stanley.

"You wouldn't even go out with me, but you'd do it with these freaks?"

Megan backed up against the wall, knocking over several brooms and mops. Stanley's eyes were wild with anger and passion.

"Well, I got news for you, bitch," he said, his voice heavy. His hands went to the drawstrings on his scrub pants, loosening them. "You will now, or I tell everyone about your little escapade tonight."

Stanley's scrubs dropped to the floor. His erect penis pointed to the ceiling, looking disturbingly abnormal.

Megan Willard sat in the nurses' lounge studying the doctor's notes. Glen and Galen Moore had left the center a few weeks earlier, still joined at the hip, seemingly walking a little taller and prouder than when they had first arrived. The Millman staff had been unable to sway their beliefs, and Megan hoped that she'd had some influence on their decision.

She never told anyone about the night Stanley had raped her in the janitor's closet. Likewise, he had told no one about her nightly visits to various patients at the center. It would seem that everything had worked itself out, that everything had returned to normal.

Normal.

Megan chuckled, but there was no humor in it.

The damage had been done. Stanley had seen to that. He had ruined everything, had destroyed her plans for a normal life.

God knows she had tried to do everything right. The ashtray on the table was piled high with cigarette butts. She was up to five packs a day. She had small liquor bottles stashed throughout the hospital. A sip here, a chug there. The smack she picked up on the street corner she did only at home. Too risky to take at the center. God knows she had tried, but Stanley had messed it all up.

The ultrasound of her developing fetus had confirmed what earlier amniocentesis had indicated. Megan ran her hands across her slightly distended stomach and hit the Play button on the VCR's remote control. The writhing mass of colors and the tiny beating heart displayed on the screen only served to sadden her more.

The doctor's words still rang in Megan's ears:

Congratulations, Miss Willard. The sonogram checks out fine. The fetus appears to be perfectly normal.

Damn Stanley, Megan thought. *Damn Stanley and his normal sperm.* She couldn't be sure if one of the twins was the father, or if Stanley was. But that hardly mattered now.

Even with possibly congenitally defective sperm, even with Megan abusing her body, bombarding the fetus growing deep within her womb with poisons and chemicals, everything was turning out normal.

Normal.

God, how she hated that word. Now more than ever.

There was only one thing she could do, only one course of action she could take to make it right. What miracles God chose to refuse Megan would have to perform herself.

She stared at the videotaped image of her child's tiny, developing appendages.

Her patients needed her; her child *would* need her.

Megan reached into her locker and retrieved the large hunting knife, a knife whose blade could easily slice through the bones of the largest deer. She removed the sharpening stone and slid the blade across its coarse surface, honing it with nurturing care as she had done every day since the initial examination had indicated the fetus would be normal.

By the time the baby arrived, the blade would be perfect.

DEATH FETISH

T. Diane Slatton

*T*he dead woman lay facedown with doe eyes staring blindly at the pavement. Her forehead was furrowed, brows arched high in an expression of terminal shock. Legs spread immodestly wide revealed a dark, wet stain at the crotch of yellow silk panties, the only garment she wore.

"I-I'm coming down, OK?" said a voice from the heavens.

As one, the crowd of police, paramedics, and gawkers raised their heads to the twelfth-floor corner apartment. A cry went up to greet the young man who sat perched on a windowsill with bare legs dangling out.

"I helped Cathy come down, so now I-I . . ." The voice was carried off by a high wind, then dropped on the crowd like a slab of concrete, "O-fucking-*kay?*"

"Christ," Officer Harrison Jenko breathed. He broke from the now-screaming mob, which fellow officers had begun shoving back toward the curb.

Racing into the building's art deco lobby, he pounded the elevator button with the side of his fist.

"Wait, Jumper—wait, Jumper—wait," he chanted like a mantra during the seemingly endless ride up.

He stepped off the elevator and stopped. His internal compass spun wildly at the sight of five hallways stretched out like fingers awaiting a manicure.

The jumper screamed something incoherent that turned Jenko toward the second hallway and blasted him off his mark. Even with eyes fixed on the left-side-last apartment, he was acutely aware of sedate paintings, textured wallpaper, hanging ferns, tasteful wall-sconce lighting that passed him in a blur.

He hit the door shoulder-first. Twice more, and it gave way with a shotgun bang.

The man, clad only in blue boxer shorts, twitched, then turned his body until he sat sideways on the living room's windowsill. "I was coming down!" he protested in an adolescent squawk.

Jenko unsnapped his holster, unsheathed his revolver. "You still *are.*" He smiled and crept a few steps closer. "Dive," he ordered.

The young man's mouth fell open for a moment, then trembled closed again as red rage flooded his face. "Fuck you, OK?" he snarled in a voice that cracked like a fourteen-year-old's.

Jenko stretched his arm straight, cocked the gun's hammer, shrugged. "OK."

The young man spun, flung out his legs, and dropped from sight as silently as a dove taking wing. Even the crowd's renewed cries below could not stifle the poetic crunch of bones breaking on concrete.

Jenko replaced his weapon and stepped to the window. Placing his palms on the still-warm sill, he leaned recklessly out to take a mental photograph of the exquisite artwork below.

Tears hovered in his eyes at the beauty of young death times two. Blood rushed in his ears like ocean waves, and his legs trembled until he was kneeling. A voice came from his hip, calling his name until Jenko unhooked the walkie-talkie from his belt and reported with emotion-choked sincerity, "Sorry. I was too late."

It was four in the morning when Jenko arrived at the private hospital that was his daughter's permanent home. Kara slept her usual undead sleep with one machine *shush*ing breath in and out of her lungs, another removing toxins from her kidneys, another measuring the inactivity of her brain, another . . . and another.

Jenko bent down and plunged his fingers through the web of tubes and wires. He brought her tiny, limp hand to his chest, willing his own strong heart to strengthen hers.

With a sigh of reluctance, he forced himself to take stock of her thin arms, short waist, the shape of miniature legs beneath the sheet. Though Kara was nearly fifteen, her body remained the size of a six-year-old's. Only the head, with its increasingly beautiful face, had grown at a normal rate.

Dead-dead-dead . . .

Jenko whispered, "No," and rubbed the little hand between both of his to encourage circulation. The heroic intensity of his rubbing was such that if flesh were kindling, they would both burst into flames.

He had to keep believing. He was her only advocate.

It had taken no more than the words "brain-dead" uttered by a few faithless neurosurgeons to make Kara's mother hop a plane back to Czechoslovakia, that eastern European hell the woman had so desperately blow-jobbed her way out of before communism fell. But proof of Jenko's passion for the woman remained—dwarfish, ethereal, hovering between death and something less than life—Kara was *his*.

On the drive home, Jenko had to pull over and toss back two codeine-laced amphetamines to kill a crying jag. He lowered his forehead to the steering wheel, held his breath against an attack of hiccups, dreamed of his own snoring.

An urgent *rat-a-tat* at the passenger window jolted him awake. The delayed high swooped down on him like a buzzard onto carrion. His grin felt idiotic, plastered on, as he rolled down the window and said, "Oh, hey."

The hooker's worried expression disappeared beneath a half-pound of makeup. She shoved a fallen black bra strap up her freckled shoulder, stuffed it back under her sleeveless halter top.

"Hey, yourself!" She laughed. "Thought old Officer Friendly bit the big one for a second there."

"Unh-unh. The only thing Officer Friendly's gonna bite is sweet Bobbi." Jenko reached across and opened the door.

Bobbi hopped in, demurely tugging down her miniskirt while singing "I'm Just Wild about Harry" in her slightly annoying nasal honk.

Harrison Jenko despised being called "Harry." The only person who'd ever gotten away with it regularly was the mother of his child, and even then only when she handcuffed him to their bed and tortured him with her smell filling his nostrils, her taste on his insatiable tongue until he ached for—begged for—*screamed* for her to use the whip handle.

"Shut up," he snapped at the singing hooker beside him.

The light died in her eyes. "Sure, Jenko," she said through a tight-lipped smile. "Pay first."

Entering his cramped, dingy apartment, he saw her large-ish nose wrinkle up. Her reactions were usually ignored, since Bobbi knew good and damned well that, aside from the cash he threw away on tramps like her, Jenko spent every spare dime on his daughter's care. Today, though, with the dose shooting twin arrows to brain and groin, he felt a drop of resentment swirling around with the testosterone.

He told her to strip in the middle of the living room while he sat on his secondhand sofa and checked the local TV news. Though it was a sweeps month with naked breasts and naked death served up like a visual feast, he had to flick through three stations to find one that actually put the bodies from last night's murder-suicide on-screen. Even then, it was only a glimpse, just enough to call up the snapshot in his head.

He moaned at the pleasurable memory.

Bobbi did a spin on her high heels and said, "Thanks. Didn't think you'd notice."

His head jerked her way. Notice what? Her bleached hair was still lopped off in a bad pageboy. He narrowed his eyes. Maybe she'd lost five pounds. Or had her legs waxed.

"Nice?" she persisted.

The shoes looked kind of new, or . . . shit, what!?

Rage pounded at his temples. Why hadn't the whore-mother of his child cured him of caring about prostitutes?

"Get on the floor." He blew past her into his paint-peeling bedroom and dragged a cedar chest out of the closet.

With a deep breath to steel himself, he threw open the lid and exhaled blessed thanks to the gods of illegal medications. The drugs coursing through his bloodstream were all that stood between him and the urge to curl up in that hell-tangle of lace/silk/satin where he could close the lid and sleep forever, like a vampire too burned by the light.

Why on earth had he even found the strength to lug *her* abandoned lingerie from the house he'd sold to pay for their daughter's life support, but never discovered the nerve to burn it all two years later when the whore-mother did not return to him . . . or five years later . . . or seven . . .

He quickly dug out a pair of yellow silk bikinis and shoved the chest back into darkness where it could not mock his life of delusion. When he returned to the living room, Bobbi's lips curled as if loading up to fire off some insult. But when a fifty-dollar bill fluttered to the floor beside her, she only cooed prettily and slid the panties on.

Jenko bent, posed her facedown with legs spread immodestly wide. Something missing. He sat on the sofa and closed his eyes to search the photo in his head.

"Yes." He fell to his knees and crawled toward her like a panther, lowering his head to the apex of her thighs. His tongue snaked out, rolled saliva onto the silk-covered crotch until the dark wetness he'd seen on the dead woman earlier was perfectly recreated.

"Stay still," he commanded.

Breath shuddered from his mouth, a tear slid down his cheek, his heart beat joy and misery at the memory of youthful death. He sat on the sofa and began slowly to masturbate.

Approaching orgasm, he squeezed his own windpipe shut until lights exploded behind his eyes—

"My back hurts," Bobbi whined.

—just like when Kara's mother used to wrap his throat in a studded leather collar with the studs turned inward . . . pulling harder, squeezing tighter until he passed out or—

"Ow, if I waste any time at the chiropractor's, *you're* paying for it!"

Jenko's erection fell. He cursed himself for the stupidity of trying out Death Art on his "regular."

Anonymous hookers would never dare complain like this woman who considered herself his girlfriend.

"Go ahead and move," he said. A wicked smile slid across his lips, and he added, "O-fucking-*kay?*"

He quickly located the next item he needed in the bedroom. Bobbi laughed. "You gotta be kiddin'!" she said when he reappeared offering her a pair of blue boxer shorts. But when his hand moved to reclaim the fifty, she wriggled out of the yellow panties.

The shade of blue was all wrong. Her breasts were unsightly distractions.

Jenko compensated for these potential disasters by brutally shaking Bobbi's shoulders so that when he posed her in a faceup sprawl, she wore the same angry/frightened expression as the young man he'd forced to jump only hours before.

Much better . . .

His lower lip touched the outside of the cup; his upper lip loosely embraced the hot liquid inside. Instead of sucking, he blew to make gurgling bubbles swell and pop on the coffee's surface.

Performing the long-discarded ritual brought a bitter smile to his face. He stared around the diner, letting his gaze briefly alight on the cops who used to be his buddies. It seemed a lifetime ago when a dozen or twenty of them would push tables together and tell war stories, filthy jokes, whopping lies, before the start of third shift.

The macho banter would stop cold when Jenko invariably blew into his coffee in that strange, childish way. The other cops had laughed, ribbing him with baby noises and crude shouts of, "Blow *this,* Hairyson!"

Those times were dead now, sealed in a tomb with the rest of Harrison Jenko's happy past. Kara's accident had seen to that. He'd felt the impact hardest, emerged by far the most damaged . . . and he hadn't even been in the car.

His cup rattled, spilling as he set it back in the saucer. He mopped up the table with his napkin and whispered, "Stop it," to the waves of guilt crashing through him.

If only he hadn't gotten so uncharacteristically drunk after work that fateful morning, he and Kara's mother would never have argued. He would have been awake to drive his daughter to school like usual instead of passing out on the sofa. There was a dim memory of hearing his Mustang burn rubber out of the driveway, a dull realization that the worst driver in the world had lifted his car keys, then sleep like paralysis.

Why isn't your idiot-bitch skull busted instead of Kara's?

The words were like ice water dashed on his face every time they rose to taunt him. Blurting from his mouth in a moment of grief and anger, they were the killing blow that sent his first and final real love back to her Slovac gutter town.

"Fuck her," he said to his haggard reflection in the diner's Formica table. His voice cracked. Just like that young jumper's last night.

Jenko snorted laughter until he noticed other cops in the diner looking at him. "Fuck you, too," he said to none or all of them.

How many of his old buddies had been telling tales about him to the "suits" over at Internal Affairs? He learned of IA's long-standing interest in his state of mental health only that afternoon when they roused him out of bed to chat about his actions the night before. It appeared his written report didn't jibe with even *one* other eyewitness account.

"Why, Officer Jenko?" they asked in their deceptively friendly way. *"Why* do you keep insisting that your jumper panicked and took the dive upon seeing you enter his apartment? Everyone on the ground saw him turn around on that windowsill for half a minute, as if he were speaking with someone inside."

Jenko had kept his cool, stuck to his version of the story. After all, what earthly reason would he have to want a complete stranger dead?

"I get off at four," said a Minnie Mouse voice. "Wanna, like, *get off* with me?"

He looked up to accept both his bill and a wink from the scrawny, slightly bucktoothed new waitress. *Not in a million years, honey.*

For politeness's sake, he smiled a lying promise that made the woman's skin flush and her nonexistent chest heave. Jenko felt a pang of surprise as his smile became genuine in the face of her spunky sexuality. *Maybe in a million years.*

"Four A.M." He nodded.

The scent of loneliness and need that rose from her when she sashayed away, swinging bony hips for him, stung his senses like a hit of dimestore perfume. Jenko shook his head and dug out two quarters for the cup of coffee. Let her *earn* a tip from him.

The moon hung sensuously full and round at two thirty-seven A.M. Its beacon shone like heaven's last blessing into the car that had gotten caught in the middle of a gangland mini-feud.

A little girl dressed in crinolines and satin lay dead, shot through the abdomen, on the Lincoln's backseat.

Jenko stared at the callous shooter, who'd been easily apprehended. The punk said "Excuse me" for his "egregious error," because he had actually been aiming at a "rude gentleman called 'Diz-Lowboy'" who'd had the "unmitigated temerity" to wander through a rival gang's territory without paying "proper respect and the current pedestrian tax."

Made sense. No way could a snot-nosed sixteen-year-old nail a marksman's-class shot like that on *purpose*.

Jenko slapped on the cuffs, making certain to say "Excuse me" before he dropped the charming little asshole with a fist to the solar plexus. He smiled at fellow officers on the scene and whispered, "Write it down."

After loading the gasping punk into a squad car, he turned to concentrate on the moonlit carnage that fed his passions.

The Lincoln's driver was in pretty bad shape. Jenko could envision the sequence of events: a gunshot rings out, little Wifey sitting beside the driver screams, the kid in the backseat falls over, Big Daddy freaks out and wraps his car around a telephone pole.

While firemen cut his mangled legs free of twisted metal, the driver rambled that he was pastor of Christ in the Gospel Faith Holiness Church, on his way home from guest-preaching at Tongues of Fire Pentecostal Church in Detroit. He seemed very bewildered, as if his exalted station in life should have rendered him and his family bulletproof.

Thank God and the right reverend that the child's body wasn't mangled, Jenko thought. She was Art. He snapped a mental picture of her snug within the protective seat belt, sleeping like a well-dressed little doll, beautiful even with the abdominal opening that leaked bloody intestines onto the plush leather seat, the deep-carpeted floor . . .

The tot's barely bruised mother, who up to now had stood quietly sobbing into her white-gloved hands, suddenly screamed and lunged at the car like a woman possessed. Jenko grabbed her around the waist just before she threw herself atop her dead child.

Her husband did not seem to notice the commotion

and continued babbling his holy bio while the paramedics strapped an oxygen mask on him and wheeled
his dying carcass into the ambulance. A nosy cop
from the neighboring precinct shouted after them to
come give the grieving lady a sedative or something.
But the doors slammed and the siren blared as if the
paramedics were flipping policemen an audio middle
finger.

Get going, Jenko thought, watching the ambulance
just sit there while the cop angrily banged on its rear
doors. The "grieving lady" had all she needed now,
didn't she? Women were *always* just fine once they
killed the kid and shed the man. They just fucking
flew off to fucking Czechoslovakia and started over,
didn't they.

While everyone's attention was on the ambulance
driver, who actually rolled down his window to shout
back at the cop, Jenko clamped a hand over the
woman's mouth and began dragging her backward.
He kept his eyes on the Death Art Angel while
pushing himself tight against her mother's tweed-
covered backside.

Blood and sorrow and red, red hate ignited his
senses, poured like lava from his mouth. "Kill everybody that loves you, you selfish bitch! *You* should've
died!"

A fist out of nowhere exploded white balloons
behind his eyes, released the pain that had filled them.
When Jenko's hands came up to clutch his bleeding
nose, the woman now wailing "Lord! Lord!
Loooooord!" was taken away into gentler arms.

"You *are* crazy!" screamed a red-haired rookie cop
who stepped back and rubbed his knuckles, then
crouched into street-fighter stance in case Jenko
wanted more. "Go on—get out of here before I
hafta . . ."

The kid looked like Howdy Doody with his big ears

and freckles. "I *swear* it, Jenko. Go away! NOW!" The rookie's voice cracked; his eyes were dilated pools of fear.

Jenko laughed nastily and walked away, wiping his nose on his sleeve.

Driving along in the comforting shroud of night, Jenko let his mind tumble down the rabbit hole to a time when his life was almost a Wonderland. His father and bachelor uncle, locked in their twinship and lifelong sibling rivalry, vied for little Harrison's favor with the best Christmas gifts, the best summer outings, the best of everything they could afford. He'd once had to break up a fistfight between the brothers after each learned that the other had bought Harrison a red Toyota for his sixteenth birthday.

The ultimate battle for his soul was waged over what profession he would go into. His uncle was an undertaker. His father was a cop. There was no such thing as a third choice.

Though he had inherited his father's fiery intensity, Harrison also shared his uncle's keen aesthetic sense. He saw beauty in art, and artistry in the business of death. His uncle's career was filled with meaningful quiet, like everlasting peace. He saw himself eventually taking over, running things.

When he announced his sixteenth summer would be spent vacuuming the velvet interiors of coffins, polishing candlesticks, and seating mourners at wakes, Harrison's father started making boozy, jealous accusations against his twin. It all seemed like so much bullshit, like when his old man had pointed at the two identical birthday cars in the driveway and demanded, "Well? Which one do you like better—his or mine?"

What brought hell to the level of earth, though, was his uncle's unfathomable decision to change the sign outside "Jenko Mortuary" to "Jenko and Son." Harrison's father responded with three full days of deadly silence.

That Saturday night, after supper, the man finally spoke. "Leave the dishes, kid. I've got a surprise for you."

In the car, Harrison was blindfolded and warned not to peek. Right then, he had a gut feeling he wasn't going to like his surprise in the least. His father drove for the better part of an hour before he stopped, got out, led his son up a walkway.

Harrison was anxious, aware of a burglar's pick being jiggled in a lock. In a minute, the door creaked open, and he was led inside. "Can I look now?" he asked.

His father said no, and pulled him by the elbow so fast they were almost running. The smells—Woolite rug cleaner, Lemon Pledge, sickly sweet death—could they have spent so much time in the car only to end up at his uncle's mortuary three blocks from home?

"Stop!" Harrison gasped. He reached into space, caught a door jamb, but his father pried his fingers loose and pulled him down, down toward the place where bodies were prepped for final display.

In the narrow hallway below, his father started a low, gas-punctuated grumbling that couldn't be deciphered over the somber sounds of organ music. Whiffs of booze breath wafted backward every time the man in front of him belched.

"Daddy?" he said.

A sharp, surprising slap was his answer.

They abruptly stopped. From the smells—formaldehyde and fresher death—Harrison knew exactly where he was. His father put a hand around the back of his neck and pushed him forward until his chest was against the door.

Then the blindfold was snatched away.

His knees shook. His mouth opened soundlessly and wide. Through the small, thick square of glass in the reinforced door, Harrison Jenko saw his beloved uncle, looking so exactly like his father, atop the metal prep table slowly screwing a middle-aged, very dead male.

"Saturday night is *date* night," his father said scornfully at his ear.

Harrison tried to turn, tried to run, but the hand like an iron clamp squeezed the back of his neck and forced him to remain facing the hideous scene. Two candles lent the cold room a romantic glow. Festive hors d'oeuvres sat half-eaten on a sterling silver tray. Two fluted crystal glasses were filled with sparkling wine.

Two glasses. Harrison's face twisted; he began crying uncontrollably.

"Wassamatter?" his father asked with mock sympathy. "Huh, kid? Don't wanna be like *him* anymore? Huh? Don't wanna be a corpse fucker like your big, smart *hero?!*"

Harrison howled, and the live naked man inside the room turned, looked straight at his nephew's agonized face. Only then did his father release him.

He bolted into the night, tears burning down his face. Why hadn't he seen it before? Why hadn't he noticed anything? There had to have been a sign, some hideous little *something*. But Harrison couldn't come up with a clue any stranger than the way his uncle blew bubbles in a cup of coffee . . .

Reaching home, he fled to his room, where he stood staring into the mirror, watching his eyes become his father's eyes, his uncle's eyes—black as the pit of a boy's ravaged soul. One week later, he spent a single, last day at the mortuary arranging the funeral of a suicide all by himself.

His uncle's funeral.

No one cried over the coffin louder or longer than the dead man's twin brother. Harrison felt nothing.

Nor did he cry four years later when his father was ruthlessly gunned down in an alley—some say *over*killed—by a yet unknown assailant attempting a midnight jewelry store break-in. The slain officer's fat partner did not even pretend he'd tried to chase the suspect, described only as a six-foot male wearing black clothes and a ski mask.

Harrison arrived at the scene feeling invincible in his rookie cop's uniform. He wouldn't accept consolation. He just needed to be alone with his thoughts for a while. The other officers understood.

Standing apart from them, in shadows, he used his father's burglar's pick to dig stubborn bits of corn dog batter from between his teeth. He weighed the merits of dental floss while watching the Swiss cheese corpse zipped into a body bag and hauled off in the coroner's wagon.

Try as he did to hold on to that night's nonchalance, the passing years brought dreams of fear and desire that threw death into bed with sex until the only relationships that could stand up under his growing obsessions were *paid* relationships. Then he met the future mother of his child.

She was a prostitute, but one possessed of such love for the fouled-up thing Jenko was that she succeeded in channeling his worst inclinations into games of near-death sex. Now she was gone—his safety valve. And Harrison Jenko had been dangerously off his leash for a long, long time.

At the private hospital, he lowered the rail on Kara's bed, then bent and brought her tiny hand to his face. "Who'll take care of my little girl now?" he said softly.

After a few moments, he dropped her hand and posed her stunted limbs so that she looked more like the dead little girl in the Lincoln. Too bad he'd never thought to buy her frilly church clothes, but there was something else . . .

He raised the blinds to let fading moonlight illuminate her face. A sob rose, lingered in his throat, released itself in a rush when the raw beauty that was truly death overwhelmed him. Something missing . . .

Jenko drew his service revolver and blasted a ragged hole in his child's abdomen.

There.

All Kara's life-support systems flashed their horror, shrieked their alarm. When the pretty night nurse burst in, Jenko ordered her to undress and position herself on the cold, tile floor. The woman's icy refusal was surprising, even frightening. Maybe he should offer money . . .

What to do was answered when she turned to flee for help. He shot her in the back.

Instantly realizing his terminal fuck-up, he replaced the gun in its holster and considered his next move until the distinct sound of police sirens approaching made up his mind for him. He checked his watch—five minutes to four.

Jenko had little doubt that the spunky, scrawny waitress would still be waiting at the diner if he showed up late. He bet she lived alone and had a car he could "borrow," too.

"Daddy's got a date," he said, blowing a last kiss to his long-dead daughter. His mind snapped a picture of the nurse's breathtaking death sprawl, then he stepped over her body and out into sensuous night.

HAIR OF THE DOG

Ray Garton

*H*e opens his mouth before opening his eyes, and it makes a sound like sweaty flesh peeling off Naugahyde. The sound is only slightly louder than the one he expects his eyes to make when he opens them, so he does not. Instead, he becomes preoccupied with the thick, rusty ax someone drove into the top of his skull while he was sleeping. Pain radiates from it, pressing his eardrums and the backs of his eyes, threatening damage. In fact, that pain spreads through his entire body, gnawing at his muscles as if he'd spent the night engaged in exhausting physical labor. Even patches of his skin hurt, stinging as if rubbed raw.

Jeremy Culp opens his eyes slowly. Although the motel room is a dim gray, he flinches and groans with pain at the light, squinting as he lifts his head from the pillow. He sits up and clumsily slides his legs out from under the tangled sheet and over the side of the bed. He isn't sure what annoys him most, the hangover itself or the fact that he let himself get so drunk the night before. As he massages the back of his stiff neck with one hand, he winces when his hand rubs over one of the sore spots. There are others here and there, as if he was attacked by fire ants in the night.

He can't remember getting drunk. He can't remember *anything,* not at first. It takes a moment.

The digital clock on the nightstand reads 3:14 P.M., its big red numbers glowing accusingly. He croaks the time aloud, rubs his eyes, and mutters, "Middle of the afternoon, for crying out loud."

The air in the motel room is slightly cloying and redolent of perfume, liquor, dead cigarettes, and sex. It is that smell combined with the sight of two mostly empty liquor bottles on the dresser that make Culp remember the two women.

He eases himself to his feet, dipping a bit when the room seems to lurch to one side, and turns around to look at the bed. It's empty, and when he looks around the room, turning his head with stiff-necked caution, he sees no clothes, no purses, nothing. They are gone, though he does not remember them leaving.

They probably had the good sense not to get themselves hammered, he thinks as his stomach cramps and roils. But then, as he thinks about it, he doesn't remember drinking much himself, certainly not enough to justify a hangover of such proportion. Culp isn't much of a drinker, never has been, and he can't remember having a hangover since college, and never one quite like this.

Three despondent balloons hover halfway between floor and ceiling over by the dresser, and confetti and noisemakers litter the ugly copper-colored carpet.

"Happy New Year," Culp mutters as he lifts his robe from the floor and slips it on. His feet barely clear the carpet as he makes his unsteady way to the bathroom. The flesh between his legs is sore and burns as he walks.

The face in the mirror is an unfamiliar one: pale and long, with shady crescents beneath the puffy eyes, his brown hair, thinning on top, splayed around his head, lips cracked and pallid.

After splashing some cold water on his face, he leans both hands flat on the sink and lets his head hang low as the tap runs. He thinks about the two women. The events of the night before come to him in jittery, disjointed images, just vivid enough to make him smirk and shake his head in disbelief. He cannot believe what he did. Where did a doughy, married, forty-nine-year-old high school English teacher find the energy to do such a thing, not to mention the nerve?

Culp thinks that perhaps he is not suffering from a hangover alone; perhaps he is feeling the aches and pains that come from indulging oneself in something as silly and ultimately embarrassing as a midlife crisis.

Culp walked out on his wife on the first day of his Christmas vacation, and ever since then, every time he thought of himself as a married man, he amended that, considering himself instead to be a soon-to-be-divorced man. He knew that after twenty-two years, it was going to take a while to make the mental adjustment, but he intended to make it as soon as possible.

Culp had spent the first afternoon of his Christmas vacation preparing an elaborate dinner while Norma was at a UFO seminar. The meal was to be an effort to breathe some life back into their marriage before the death rattle sounded, to create a little romance . . . to remind her that he was there.

In their second year together, Norma had taken up the harmless hobby of macramé, which led to crocheting, which led to knitting. She went from one hobby to the next, like a hummingbird in a flower garden. Culp did not object, although he found hobbies to be impractical and had none himself. But over the years, Norma became more and more consumed by her hobbies; by the time their kids were in school, she was juggling three at once. She went from rock collecting to Middle Eastern cooking, from learning Esperanto to growing roses, from collecting Tarot cards to bird-watching, and more, so many more. After the kids left for college, conversation no longer seemed necessary at the dinner table. He stopped trying to keep up with Norma's hobbies, and she stopped trying to include him in them. Over the intervening time, a chasm opened up slowly between them.

Nearly a year ago, Culp had realized that he was lonely in spite of the fact that the kids visited frequently and he was happily married. That was when he realized that he was no longer happily married. Not exactly unhappy, and certainly not miserable . . . just married. The revelation panicked him, and he began to make an effort to scale the wall that had been constructed, one slow brick at a time, between himself and Norma.

He tried talking to her more, asking about her hobbies and fellow hobbyists, none of whom he knew. Norma talked, but with an air of distraction about her, as if there were someplace else she'd rather be. Sometimes when he spoke to her, she'd look at him with surprise, as if startled to find a total stranger in her house. Culp tried to take her to dinner, to movies. She usually didn't have the time, but the couple of times they did go out were very awkward; she was always running into people she knew from her UFO-watching club or from the Crystal Society, and Culp would stand around while she talked with them about sightings or about the metaphysical properties of crystals. It was awkward because Norma never introduced him, and it made him realize he had no friends of his own.

The candlelight dinner he'd prepared for her on the first day of his Christmas vacation was to be his final effort, although he didn't know it at the time. Norma arrived home just as Culp was lighting the candles and turning down the lights. But she arrived with eleven other members of the Crystal Society. She sniffed the air and said pleasantly, "Oh, you cooked dinner. Is there enough to go around?" Culp said, "Sure," then went into his bedroom, packed a couple of suitcases, and left the house while Norma and the girls chatted in the kitchen. After a dinner at Lulu's Café, he went next door and checked into the Thunderbird Motor Lodge, then started thinking about what to do with the next thirty years or so. Just like that, as casually as if he were rearranging the furniture in his office rather than his entire life. His only regret was that he'd let the relationship with Norma, which once had been so intimate and joyous, just slip through his fingers.

He'd gone home early Christmas morning, because he knew the kids would be showing up and he didn't want to ruin their holiday. Peter came with his wife and baby, and Beth brought her boyfriend. It was a noisy, festive gathering, and none of them seemed to notice anything unusual. Seconds after the kids left, Culp was on his way out when Norma stopped him at the door. With genuine curiosity but no emotion whatsoever, she asked, "So, have you found a place?"

After splashing more water on his face, Culp turns away from the mirror, sick of the sight of himself. The thought of a shower is just too much. He prefers to come slowly back to life; coffee first, then a shower. Culp decides to go over to Lulu's.

As he goes to the closet, he notices his clothes from the night before scattered all over the room. He remembers tossing them. They took turns removing articles of clothing, Culp and the two women, almost as if they did not want to separate even long enough to undress, touching and kissing and licking. The memory amazes him, but he is shamed by the fact that he must think a moment to remember their names: Pam and Valerie. They were so oral, both of them, their mouths all over him. And they were less than half his age, probably younger than his kids. But they were so beautiful, so carnal, as if they'd been fantasized rather than born. They looked like they could make him forget he was ever married, happily or otherwise. They almost did, too. Almost, but not quite.

He puts pants and a shirt on the bed, takes a clean pair of socks from the dresser, then mounts a search for his shoes. On hands and knees, he finds one beneath the chair beside the dresser, then gropes beneath the bed for the other.

His hand slaps onto smooth, cold flesh, and a gasp catches in his throat as he jerks his hand back, crawling backward quickly. He doesn't move, doesn't even breathe as he stares slack-jawed at the dark space beneath the bed. For a moment, his confused mind ceases to function properly as it claws for some shred of logic to hold on to. But it finds none. That was flesh he touched under there, and it does not, it simply *does not,* belong under the bed, not cold naked flesh, no way.

His breath comes in tremulous bursts as he lowers himself very slowly until he is lying flat on the floor, head turned to look into the darkness beneath the bed. There is a shape of some kind in the murky space, but it takes a moment for his eyes to adjust themselves, to bring the thing into focus . . . to see the hair. Valerie's lovely red hair.

Culp and Norma had never paid much attention to New Year's Eve. Another holiday a week after Christmas seemed like overkill. But a celebration of some sort was in order. After all, it wasn't just another year that was beginning; his whole life was starting over. Besides, he'd spent the last week looking diligently and unsuccessfully for an apartment. He deserved a few drinks, maybe a few games of darts if there was a board. Whatever he did, he decided he wasn't going to sit in that motel room and watch Dick Clark rock in the new year; he'd done that with Norma too many times.

Outside, the Shack was just a flat, nondescript building attached to the side of a coffee shop; inside, it was mostly the same, only darker and smokier. Country music was playing on the jukebox. Normally, Culp hated country, offended by its feigned, self-righteous wholesomeness, but he figured if he was going to start a new life, he might as well try new things, and he gave the song a chance. By the time he reached a barstool, he decided his new life wasn't *that* new and simply ignored the twangy music.

A small, exhausted Christmas tree twinkled half-heartedly, and balloons floated among festive streamers, all of it draped in a veil of cigarette smoke.

Culp perched at the bar, ordered a vodka gimlet, and looked around. It was busy, as Culp had expected it to be on New Year's Eve. There were only two empty stools, all the booths were full, and just one of the cocktail tables stood unoccupied. There was no dartboard, but two video games and a pinball machine stood against the back wall. Beneath the country music there were voices, laughter, the vague sound of ice clinking against glass.

As the bartender put the gimlet on the bar, the song ended and the voices became louder. Culp took his drink and walked to the jukebox over near the games. Taking a sip, he read over the patchwork of country, blues, and pop as he jingled change in his pocket. Another country song started as Culp put in a couple of quarters and punched up some blues, preferring B. B. King's guitar to Merle Haggard's. He took another swallow of his drink as he headed back to the bar, and that was the first time he noticed them.

They were sitting in a booth leaning over their drinks and smoking. And they were watching him. He nearly tripped over their gaze, immediately wondering what was wrong. Was his fly open? Had he put on a stained shirt? Suddenly nervous, he returned to the security of his stool and took another swallow.

The bartender set a bowl of peanuts on the bar, and Culp popped a couple into his mouth. Slowly, he sneaked a look over his shoulder to the booth where the two women were sitting. They were still watching him but looked away the moment he caught them.

One was facing away from him. She had hair the color of raw honey that fell in luxurious waves to her pale bare shoulders; he followed the line of her arm down to her hand, where the tips of her unpainted nails rested on the scarred tabletop. The other woman was facing toward him and had long, thick, straight red hair. They wore tight clothes, party clothes, the kind of clothes you'd wear to a nightclub, not to the Shack. The redhead wore a simple, short black dress, and Culp looked at her bare legs beneath the table, shapely ankles crossed. But he did not stare. He was already embarrassed enough by their stares; he didn't want to get caught gawking at them.

The long-faced bald man on the next stool watched Culp watching the women and finally chuckled. "You oughtta buy one a them a drink," he said. "I saw 'em checkin' you out over at the juke. Shit, buy 'em *both* a drink, maybe you'll get lucky. Write a letter to *Penthouse* about it."

Culp had been caught. He was reaching his embarrassment threshold. He laughed it off and ate some more peanuts. A minute or so later, the man sitting next to him was chatting with the bartender. Culp snatched another cautious look.

The redhead was leaning forward, smirking as she said something to the blonde. She was staring directly at Culp, but she didn't look away this time. Instead, she leaned back, tilted her head to one side, and stretched a leg beneath the table as she shifted position, giving him a good look. Then she returned her attention to her companion.

Culp's face became very warm, and he almost laughed out loud at himself, sitting at a bar on New Year's Eve staring at a couple of beautiful young women and blushing like a shy teenager. It was laughable, no doubt about that.

A noisemaker squealed somewhere in the bar, and another quacked in response. The man beside Culp pulled a disgusted face and shook his head as he slowly got off the stool, leaving Culp between two empties.

"That's my cue to go home," he said. "The later it gets, the louder it gets, and I'm all holidayed out." He put some money on the bar, nodded at Culp, and walked away.

Culp turned on the stool and watched as the man went to a coat tree by the door and slipped on a rumpled overcoat. He let his eyes wander from the man to the women in the booth, but he felt an immediate shock of embarrassment and turned back to the bar quickly.

They were *both* looking at him, hunched forward

and chattering intently over the small round candle holder in the center of their table.

Culp frowned at his drink for a moment, then took a sip, wondering why they kept looking at him like that. Did they know him? Maybe they were former students. The possibility made him consider going back to the motel to watch Dick Clark after all.

The country song ended, and a moment later, Culp's first song began to play. He tapped the bar to the beat and scooped up some more peanuts, leaning his head back and dropping them all into his mouth. He nearly choked on them when he looked over his shoulder to see the women coming toward him with their drinks and purses, smiling and walking like they were in a music video or something. He gulped the peanuts down and wet his mouth with a sip of the gimlet.

"You look awful sad for New Year's Eve," the blonde said. She didn't speak very loudly, but he could hear her plainly above the music and voices, and he watched her lips form the words, moist and smooth as rose petals.

"Yeah," the redhead added. "You look like you need a little help."

Culp felt his mouth working independently and fought to control it. "Uh, help? Doing what?"

"Having fun," she said, and they both eased onto the stools flanking him.

Hookers, Culp thought, feeling a little better. That explained a lot. But why were they targeting him? He certainly wasn't the only man in the crowded bar. Did he look *that* needy?

The bartender stood before them, smiling. "Pam? Valerie? Anything for you?"

"No thanks, Phil," the redhead said. "But another for our friend here." She put her hand on Culp's shoulder and squeezed ever so gently.

The bartender grinned at Culp, winked, then went to make the drink.

"That's very nice, thank you," Culp said, nodding, "but you didn't have to do that. I haven't even finished this—"

"People who only do things they *have* to do are not happy people," the blonde said.

With her hand still on his shoulder, the redhead added, "In fact, they're usually pretty miserable." She touched his earlobe with a fingertip. "You're not from around here, are you?"

Culp almost said he was, that he'd lived there for nearly twenty years, but thought better of it. Instead, he just said, "No, not . . . really."

The bartender brought his drink and winked again.

"And you're all alone on New Year's Eve," the blonde said.

"That's how it's turned out," Culp replied, finishing his first drink.

"Well, you aren't alone anymore," the redhead said, touching the fingertip to his hair. "I'm Valerie."

"And I'm Pam. Who are you?"

"Steve." He spoke the name without a second's hesitation, surprising himself.

"Well, Steve, you've certainly got better taste in music than most around here."

"Thank you."

Pam put her hand on his knee. It was cool through the material of his pants as it inched upward along his thigh.

"What's a tasteful man like you doing alone on New Year's Eve?" Valerie asked.

Culp started to give some inane response but stopped, thinking that it was a very good question. Why *was* he alone on New Year's Eve? He wasn't married, not *really*. He had no intention of purchasing the services of the two lovely women, but he might as well enjoy their company until they realized he wasn't interested and moved on to better prospects.

"I was just wondering that myself," he said, sipping his second drink.

"Well, you don't have to wonder anymore," Pam said, running her nails over his crotch.

The touch sent shock waves through Culp's body, and his back stiffened. So did his penis.

Valerie leaned over and pressed her breasts to his arm, lightly touching his ear with her lips. "Now you've got us, Steve. Wanna dance?"

"Uh, no, no, I'm afraid I don't dance. I've never had any rhythm. My wuh—" He almost said "wife." He almost told them how his wife had laughed at his dancing when they'd first met. He corrected himself quickly. "My wuh-worst, um, memories are of, um, high school dances."

"You don't have to be embarrassed," Pam said, cupping him in her hand and massaging his erection through his pants. "We can go someplace else. Someplace where it's just the three of us. We won't laugh at you. Promise."

"Yeah, we'll find your rhythm," Valerie said. "It's in there somewhere, you just gotta—" she flicked her tongue over his ear—"pull it out."

His face hot, Culp knew he had to bring an end to this or he was going to break out in a sweat and stain his shirt. "Look, uh, ladies, I'm . . . flattered. Really. But I'm afraid you're not, uh . . . within my budget."

The women laughed. It was a beautiful sound, their laughter, and it held no cruelty or condescension.

"You're too hard on yourself, Steve," Pam said.

"Yeah, we aren't ladies of the evening." Smiling, Valerie bit his ear and hissed, "We're ladies of the *moment!*"

"And at the moment, we wanna teach you to dance," Pam said, stroking and squeezing his erection. "So why don't we go someplace where nobody's watching us?"

"Uh, like I said, I'm not—"

"We don't charge, honey," Pam said, leaning close as she scraped her fingernails over his balls. "We *want* to teach you how to dance. Just dance your little heart out."

"Don't worry," Valerie said. "Your wife will never know."

He looked at her, startled, about to ask how she knew.

"Unless she's got your ring bugged," she added with a throaty laugh. Her fingers teased the back of his neck and nuzzled his hair with her nose.

Culp looked down at the wedding band still on his finger. He hadn't thought to take it off; he'd forgotten it was there. He'd gained some weight, and it was squeezed into the flesh. He figured he'd probably have to have it cut off and thought he wouldn't be surprised to find the skin beneath it black with moist rot.

The women smelled of alcohol, of course; who in a bar on New Year's Eve did not? But they'd probably had too much to drink. If they weren't prostitutes, that was the only explanation Culp could think of. Pam's restless hand between his legs and Valerie's lips against his ear were going a long way to convince him he should take advantage of their drunkenness.

"You staying near here?" Pam asked, brushing her smiling lips to his cheek.

"Next door," Culp replied. He regretted it immediately and squirmed away from them. "Thank you for the drink, but I think—"

"*I* think you're a sad case," Valerie said, smirking as she pushed herself against him again, ignoring his squirms. "You've got two women coming on to you, and you're wiggling like a boy in church. I thought that was every man's fantasy."

Pam went back to what she was doing as well. "Most men can't handle having their fantasies come true. Did you know that, Steve? They can't. Too much for them. They talk a good game, but when the cards are on the table, all bets're off. You're not gonna be like most men, are you, Steve?"

He looked first at Pam, then at Valerie, back and forth. They were beautiful . . . and they were driving him out of his mind. His hands trembled as he took a few healthy swallows of his gimlet, then asked, "You're not prostitutes?"

"We're missionaries, Steve," Valerie said, and her words were slightly garbled because she was sucking on his earlobe and sending an electrical current straight to his groin. "We spread the word. And tonight, the word is *legs* . . . or maybe *lips*."

"We wanna do this because we *want* to," Pam assured him. "For free. No strings attached. In fact, we'll even buy you another drink." She turned away from him. "Hey, Phil. Another one for Steve, here." Then, to Culp, she said, "We're gonna hit the ladies' room, Steve. You enjoy your drink. When we come back, we can go to your place, and I can make you dance. With my tongue. My tongue'll make you dance, Steve, I promise."

Suddenly, they were gone, and once again, Culp was sitting there alone with his drink. The music and voices had faded out before, but they came rushing back from all around him.

He could still feel them on him, Pam's hand, Valerie's lips, and he could still smell their perfume. But they were gone. He shifted position on the barstool, reaching down to surreptitiously adjust his erection in his pants. It was a powerful erection, hard as brick and almost painful, and he was struck with the certainty that it would never go away. Not unless Pam and Valerie came back. Not unless he left the bar with them that night. His erection would not go away unless they made it go away, he felt sure.

It was absurd, of course, but he was feeling his vodka, and Pam and Valerie had been feeling *him,* so he was worked up; he allowed himself the silly thought, then dismissed it. But it would not go away. And neither would their ghostly touches, still on him, teasing him, making him feel things he hadn't felt in years. He tipped the drink back, finishing it off as Phil brought another.

"Looks like you've made a couple friends," Phil said with a harmless leer.

"Do you know them?"

"Not really. They come in here maybe three times a month."

"They're not prostitutes?"

"Wouldn't let 'em stick around if they were. They're just real friendly. You're new here. From outta town, are you?"

Culp nodded vaguely.

"Yeah, they seem to like outta-towners. But they're not hookers." He chuckled, shook his head, and started down the bar saying, "Just real friendly."

His hands were trembling so hard he used both of them to lift his drink. It was his third, and it didn't live as long as the first two. The alcohol warmed him, made him feel a bit giddy, but it could not numb the hunger he felt for the two women in the restroom.

They were on him again, their hands and lips, and Culp was elated that they had come back, that it hadn't been a nasty joke with blue balls as the punchline.

At that moment, Culp decided he couldn't think of a better way to start a new year and a new life than doing something about which he could write to *Penthouse.*

Culp does not know how much time has passed since he crawled crablike away from the bed, as far as he could get, until his back was against the wall. Maybe an hour, maybe thirty seconds, he doesn't know. His mind is too busy to keep up with time, too busy going over the night before, trying desperately to remember everything. Sometimes, as he stares at the space beneath the bed, his thoughts slip out of his mouth.

"A witness," he says, his voice high and soft and breathy. "They've got a witness. He'll identify me."

He is thinking of the bald man who sat beside him at the bar. And the bartender, of course. Who else? Who else in the bar will remember him, the last man to see those two beautiful young women alive?

"I didn't do it!" he gasps, pulling his knees up, hugging them. "I didn't, I couldn't, I—"

—*can't remember,* he thinks. *I can't remember, so I don't know* what *I did!*

He stands suddenly, winded, feeling panic in his throat. He can't see them while he's standing, but he knows they're there, flat on their backs, arms and legs straight, almost as if positioned that way.

It occurs to him that they might not be dead after all; maybe they were just still passed out. But he remembers that white skin, cold as marble.

"No," he says, moving decisively toward the bed, "they can't be dead. Can't be." Moving with erratic, jerky motions, he slides the bed to one side, until the two women are unhidden.

Their clothes are balled up between their feet with

their purses on top. Their eyes are closed, and their hair is pooled about their heads. There is no blood, none that he can see. But they do not move as he watches them closely, not even to breathe.

With nerves humming just beneath his skin, Culp gets on hands and knees and crawls to Pam's side. He presses a hand over his mouth as he reaches down and touches two fingertips to her neck, feeling for a pulse. The roiling in his stomach worsens when he feels no sign of life. He touches her face reluctantly, rolls her head back and forth, holds his palm over her mouth and nose. No breath.

"Oh my God," he whimpers. "Oh my God, oh my God, oh my God." He says it over and over again, realizing after a moment that he is crawling on hands and knees in a small circle. There is movement inside him, and he scrambles to his feet as he heads for the bathroom. His insides explode just before he reaches the toilet, and some of it splashes onto the tile floor. He hunches over the toilet for a few minutes, groaning into the bowl. He wants to keep vomiting, to heave up the fear in his gut, the terror filling his chest and smothering his lungs.

Culp staggers out of the bathroom and goes to the dresser, grabs one of the bottles, and tips it back, taking a couple of gulps. It scalds his raw insides, but he takes a couple more. He is beginning to sweat as he turns and looks at them again.

The clock on the nightstand reads 4:03; more than forty-five minutes have passed, but it feels like seconds. Culp is shocked that so much time has gone by. If he could let nearly an hour pass without realizing it, what *else* might he do without realizing it?

"No," he says, shaking his head. "I didn't. I couldn't." His cheeks are moist, and he realizes he's been crying. "I *couldn't!*"

Then who did? he wonders. *Did somebody get into the room, kill Pam and Valerie without waking me, then hide them under the bed? How would*—why *would somebody do that?*

He looks at Valerie's purse, then Pam's, and kneels down at their feet. He opens Pam's first. It appears nearly empty at first, its black lining clean as if it were new. There is a billfold, a checkbook, some keys, and a black notebook. He opens the billfold and looks at her driver's license. Pamela L. Gleason. She is twenty-one years old.

Was twenty-one, Culp thinks.

There are fold-out pockets with credit cards and photographs in them. There is a black-and-white snapshot of Pam with her hair in a beehive; it looks old, its white border yellowed with time. He finds sixty-eight dollars and change in the billfold. The black notebook contains phone numbers, addresses, shopping lists, meaningless reminders. She hasn't been robbed. That would make it too easy, a robbery-killing; he would call the police, and after the initial suspicion blew over, everything would be fine. Although he is certain she has not been robbed, either, he opens Valerie's purse anyway.

The inside of Valerie's purse is almost identical to Pam's: perfectly clean and mostly empty. Culp frowns. He has never seen a woman's purse so neat and tidy. Norma's purse is always a pocket of chaos, with chunks of lint and old breath mints and bits of tobacco from stray cigarettes clinging to the lining. His mother's purse was always a mess. His sister's, too. But these purses look freshly shoplifted.

There is a folded-up manila envelope in Valerie's purse, bulging with its contents. He pulls it out, unwinds the red string from the tab, and opens it. The envelope is filled with what look, at first, like business cards. But they are not. Some are driver's licenses, some are credit cards; there are a number of Social Security cards, and in the bottom he finds half a dozen passports.

Each driver's license has a picture of either Pam or Valerie on it, each under a different name and with a different address. So many identities . . . and just two people.

The envelope slips from Culp's hands, and the licenses and cards and passports spill onto the carpet. He is paralyzed by fear, unable to move, even to blink. Although he thought it impossible, the situation has just become worse somehow. Two women with an envelope full of identities? Good ones, too. Those driver's licenses must be fake, but they are *great* fakes, professional. So who are they *really,* these two gorgeous women who, one New Year's Eve, just suddenly get the urge to team up and seduce a middle-aged man with a puffy paunch and an occasional problem with gout? That sort of thing doesn't happen in real life, not even in the real lives of people who write letters to *Penthouse.* Culp begins to think there is something else going on here, something much stranger and more ominous lurking beneath the already horrible surface.

Culp feels sick again but does not vomit. The poison stays inside and tries to eat its way out. He stands and paces, his body prickly with sweat beneath the robe. The sweat is stinging him in places.

Stinging the wounds, he thinks, only vaguely wondering what wounds he might have. Were they *that* rough last night?

The light outside the drawn curtains is dimmer. The first day of a new year is winding down. Culp can hear traffic outside. And rain, it is raining.

I'm going to have to go out there, he thinks, staring

at the door. *I'm going to have to call someone . . . the police, an ambulance, someone. And they're gonna come and take me out there in handcuffs.*

He hurries to the bathroom, wets a washcloth, and dabs his face and neck with it, then continues pacing, thinking now, trying to remember everything. There are blank spots . . . gaps in his memory . . . images that skip a beat, jump ahead in time, like those old damaged black-and-white movies on television in the middle of the night. Those skips get bigger, more jarring, until the memories stop. But he goes over them again, and again . . . and again.

Once inside the hotel room, Pam and Valerie were at him like two cats on a scrambling rodent. They'd bought two bottles of whiskey at a liquor store on the corner, and Culp dropped them in their brown bag onto a chair. He felt a panicky moment of claustrophobia as they closed in on him, kissing him, groping him, removing his clothes, their own, and each other's. He was still wearing his underwear, socks, and unbuttoned shirt when they pushed him onto the bed, faceup. Valerie pinned his arms to the mattress, and Pam straddled his legs.

Culp's shirt was the first sartorial casualty of the night. Valerie's fingernails ripped into it and began peeling it off him as she sucked hard on one nipple, then the other. When she kissed him, he feared she was going to suck his tongue out of his throat by its roots. She chewed on his lips, nipped his flabby chest, teasingly at first, then harder, almost too hard.

Pam pressed her mouth to his cotton briefs and wrapped it around his erection, which was straining the material. She gnawed on his cock, her tongue wet through the cotton, and pulled at the shorts as her fingernails clawed teasingly at his balls.

Culp's heart was hitting his ribs like a police battering ram, but very fast, and he suddenly regretted not sticking to that diet he'd started about five years ago because he feared he might have a heart attack and die beneath these women. A blissful way to go, yes, but not so soon. His heart continued to hammer without consequence, and he soon became too lost in the things Pam and Valerie were doing to him to worry about dying.

He heard the sound of material ripping again, his underwear this time. He tried to lift his head, but Valerie wouldn't let him. Pam tore the briefs away from him and took him in her mouth.

Someone in the room made a sound like a deer in pain, and Culp was shocked to realize it was *his* voice, that *he* was making the sound, but he had no control over it, over anything. *They* controlled him, completely, as surely as if they possessed his soul like demons. And that sound coming from Culp's throat was one of delirious joy. He reached out his hands and felt delicious flesh, soft round breasts, and rigid nipples. Their skin was cool, and he found the sensation of it exciting.

As Valerie kissed and licked and sucked her way around his neck and over his abdomen, Pam's tongue licked around the base of his cock, then down, over the wrinkled flesh of his scrotum, then down even further as Valerie reached over and stroked him while she kissed and chewed his belly.

There was another sound in the room: lusty, throaty laughter. Pam and Valerie were laughing as they devoured him, laughing in a buoyant way, with relish.

Culp felt heat rising inside him, between his legs, growing thick and unbearable, and he was going to come, he knew it. But he did not. Valerie stopped stroking him and squeezed his erection in a fist, then let go of him and—

—that is where the first skip occurs.

Culp folds his arms on top of the dresser, drops his head onto them, and groans as he goes over it again and again, that one moment that just seems to blink out in his memory, one second on his back and the next—

—he slid in and out of Pam, his movements slow, controlled by Valerie, who clutched his ass with both hands, guiding him as she pressed her face between his legs and licked and sucked his balls.

And they never stopped laughing. Sometimes they even talked to him, and each time they pressed him for a response.

"You enjoying this, Steve?" Valerie asked, and when he didn't respond, just kept grunting, she said, "C'mon, Steve, you enjoying this? We're not boring you, are we?"

"No, no, yuh-you're not," he gasped.

Pam smiled up at him and said, "You look so serious, Steve. How come you're not smiling? Fucking is *fun!*"

After a while, when he was beginning to feel the heat rising again, Valerie pulled him off Pam, her voice trembling slightly as she said, "My turn, Steve. On your back, baby, it's my turn."

Once he was flat, she mounted him, fell forward on him, engulfing his face in her long red hair as she kissed his face and throat, licked and sucked on his ears, and humped viciously. She sat up straight as her fingernails dug into his doughy flesh, and her bucking grew faster and faster. Culp turned his head to the right and saw Pam lying on her side, her grinning face inches from his. She ran her left hand through his hair as her right nested busily between her thighs.

Valerie became frantic and cried out as she came. She said something. It startled Culp because it was in a foreign language. French, or maybe German, he wasn't sure. He had other things on his mind. She kept moving on him, grinding, her head back, lips open on clenched teeth, and—

—he cries out in frustration, pounding a fist on the dresser. He empties the bottle and lets it thunk to the carpet as he begins pacing again.

His memory decays rapidly from that moment on, and there's no way he can fill in the blanks. The sex is just a series of disjointed images that simply end.

He remembers, at one point, being on the floor. He was on the bed, then—*skip!*—he was on the floor with them, rolling around, limbs entwined, rutting like animals, their cool, smooth skin rubbing frantically against his. One of the women—he couldn't remember if it was Pam or Valerie—opened one of the bottles and poured some whiskey over his head. Valerie drank some, then kissed Culp and spit it into his mouth. He drank some from the bottle, too, but he doesn't remember drinking much. Maybe two or three swallows. Not enough to have blackouts, not nearly. Unless he'd become very sensitive to alcohol without realizing it over the years; after all, he isn't as young as he used to be.

Just flesh, that is mostly what he remembers, tongues and breasts and moist lips hidden in thatches of kinky hair. And the laughter, of course. They never stopped laughing, and Culp joined in after a while, enjoying himself as if for the first time in his life.

He stops pacing to look down at Pam and Valerie, wondering how long before they will start to smell. He steps over to Pam's side and looks down at her throat.

Like Valerie's, it is unmarked. If he *did* kill them, how did he *do* it? Strangling would leave bruises, and there is no blood, so he didn't stab or bludgeon them to death.

Feeling sick again, he hurries to the bathroom, just in case, but nothing comes up. He stands over the toilet a moment, staring at the puddle of vomit on the floor. The sobs surprise him in their suddenness and intensity. He puts the lid down, sits, and cries until his lungs ache. With his tears comes resignation.

Culp stands, getting himself under control, wiping his eyes. He walks to the phone bolted to the night-stand, picks up the receiver, and punches 9-1-1.

On the second ring, a female voice says, "Nine-one-one operator, what is your emergency, please?"

His voice fails him at first, and he coughs a few times. "I've, uh, found . . . there are two, um . . ."

"What is the emergency, sir?"

"I'm at this motel, and . . . when I woke up . . . there were two dead bodies . . . under my bed."

"You found . . . excuse me, sir, did you say you *found* them under your bed? When you woke up?"

"That's right."

"Who are these two people."

"Two women. Young women."

"Do you know them?"

"I did . . . sort of."

"How did these women die?"

"I don't know, I . . . didn't do it. Really. I don't re—" He coughed again. "I didn't do it. I don't know. They're just dead."

"What is your name, sir?"

"I'm at the Thunderbird Motor Lodge. Room Twelve. I'll wait here until they come." He hangs up the phone.

The room is very dark now, and Culp turns on a lamp. It lends a garishness to the two corpses.

Sweat clings to him like honey, burning in his wounds. He frowns as he wonders again how he got cut in so many places. He feels sweat dribble down the middle of his back and down his sides from his armpits, and he drops the robe and goes straight into the shower, swinging the bathroom door shut behind him out of habit, although the door only closes halfway. He turns on the cold water and begins to rub a bar of soap over his skin halfheartedly as he stands beneath the stream.

He winces as he passes the soap under his left armpit; something stings sharply. Reaching under his arm, Culp feels a few small puncture wounds. He inspects every spot on his body that stings as if raw: behind his neck, in back of his ear, between his legs just behind his scrotum, and between the folds of flesh where his legs join his groin.

Culp's insides turn cold. He feels a dread that he cannot quite identify.

Who were they, really? What had they done to him?

He turns off the shower and steps out, grabs a towel, and begins to dry himself, his mind numb, perhaps beyond repair. He is unable to concentrate enough to think of what he will tell the police. He freezes with the towel over his head.

There are voices in the room. Quiet, sneaky voices.

Culp jerks the towel from his head and looks at the half-open door, his eyes gaping as he wonders if the police have already arrived.

But they are female voices. Two female voices, chattering in hurried whispers, giggling mischievously. There is movement as well. Culp sees shadows flitting over the dresser and hears whispers of fabric. His throat begins to close, and, to prevent it, he makes a startled, coughlike sound.

The movement stops, and the voices are silent. A hand pushes the bathroom door all the way open, and

Pam and Valerie stand in the doorway, smiling. They are all dressed and carry their purses. And they are still beautiful. But something is different. They look much paler than he remembers.

"Well," Valerie said hesitantly, "this is an awkward moment, isn't it?"

"Sorry, Steve," Pam says. "We don't usually do this sort of thing. Stay over, I mean. We just stayed too late and had to crash here till sunset."

Culp backs away from them, saying, "You . . . you're both . . . you were . . ."

Valerie steps forward and reaches out to touch his face, but Culp throws himself backward, slamming painfully into the aluminum towel rod on the wall. She places a hand to his cheek, and it is very cold. It's as cold as they were just moments ago while lying dead on the floor.

"You don't look so good, baby," she says. "You look like you could use a little hair of the dog that bit you."

"Unfortunately, we've gotta go," Pam says.

Culp tries to speak, but his mouth moves silently.

"Don't worry, Steve," Valerie purrs, leaning forward to kiss him. Her lips feel repulsive on his. "You'll only remember the good parts, I promise. And you *were* good." She turns and steps past Pam and out of the room.

Pam licks her lips and winks. "You were *real* good, Steve." Then she, too, leaves the bathroom.

Culp realizes he is shivering. The punctured flesh on his neck and behind his ear and under his armpit and between his legs stings cruelly as he hears the door of the room open, then close.

With his mouth hanging open, he staggers out of the bathroom to the window and pulls the curtain aside. Just cars in the parking lot and traffic in the street outside. Pam and Valerie are nowhere in sight.

Culp turns around and stares a few minutes at the

empty space on the floor, the place where, just minutes ago, two corpses lay still and naked. The unidentified dread he felt earlier is replaced with a sickening fear as the dimly lit room becomes bathed in the pulsing red-and-blue glow of a police car. He turns to the window again and looks at the light bleeding through the frayed curtain as three hard knocks sound on the door.

ONE LAST TIME

Michael Garrett

We touch.

We lie on our sides in bed, face to face, the overhead ceiling fan feathering our hair and cooling our skin. My hand caresses her breast, and hers traces a path through my pubic hair to grasp my erect penis.

We kiss.

I hold her tightly; her arms slide around me to gently scratch my shoulders with her fingertips. I squeeze her buttocks and pull her closer. My penis throbs against her pubic mound as we exchange passionate kisses, one after another. I reach below to feel her wetness.

She is ready.

A brilliant crash of midnight lightning cast sharp-edged shadows across the room like an out-of-control X-ray beam. Thunder rattled portraits on the wall; a thin aluminum ashtray on the credenza clattered from the resulting vibration.

Frank Anderson clicked the mouse to save the on-screen document, then leaned over to switch off the computer before a power interruption destroyed his manuscript. A tear glided down his cheek and splattered against the keyboard. Trying not to think of her, Frank ran his fingers through his thinning hair and hoped to temporarily erase her image from his mind, to escape an unexpected rush of grief as the lights flickered once, twice, then out, and he sat in darkness, his efforts to forget her overcome by a memory of the night they'd made love by candlelight inside a rural cabin as a sudden downpour battered its rusty tin roof. Now, torrents of rain lashed against a nearby window; a brisk wind whipped the trees along the perimeter of the house, scraping scraggly branches against the exterior walls.

God, how he missed her. It was foolish to think he could concentrate on anything else, even for a mere moment, particularly after tonight's discovery.

Kathy had been laid to rest just three weeks earlier, and only moments ago the reality of the loss struck Frank like a seizure as he recalled the tragedy. He had been numbed but strong throughout the ordeal, from the moment the police first reported the accident until he'd watched her coffin gently lowered into the ground in a private graveside service. The funeral home proprietor had urged him not to stay for the actual filling of the grave, had suggested that he leave the cemetery until her burial was complete, her plot of loose soil camouflaged by flowers. Kathy's parents had complied and had taken the kids with them back to their car, but Frank insisted on staying with Kathy until the last possible moment, assuring his own parents that he would be all right.

"Don't forget—it's cuddle time tonight," she'd teased as he kissed her good-bye the last morning of her life. Though her sex drive had never been as persistent as his, Kathy had always made it known when she was "in the mood." Her last words that day, her secret way of telling him she was ready, had tipped him off to an evening of passion that would never be. He would never forget the last time he'd laid eyes on her beautiful face—a face that had aged gracefully enough that she appeared ten years younger than her actual age.

Her body had been so mangled in the wreckage that the mortician hadn't even attempted to reconstruct her soft, delicate features. Her coffin remained closed throughout the proceedings. Frank knew he couldn't have viewed her remains on display anyway, even if she had been made up to appear normal. He preferred his final memory of his wife to be that of the moment she'd kissed and hugged the kids good-bye as she left for work. He would always remember the smell of her perfume, the fresh scent of her hair that morning, and how he had patted her on the bottom as she'd rushed out the door toward the car that within minutes would be crushed like an accordion between an eighteen-wheeler and a bridge abutment.

The lights blinked momentarily, restoring the power and interrupting the painful memories, but Frank was so overcome with grief that he collapsed onto the nearby sofa, a river of pent-up sadness flowing from his eyes as he tried not to disturb the kids upstairs. They were too young to understand the loss they had suffered, too innocent to realize that their mommy would never again tuck them into bed or dress them for school. Frank knew that he was unable to fill her shoes; nor could any other woman, and he feared that he couldn't be supportive enough to the kids, as he himself, after three weeks of unyielding emotional stability and determination, was now so distraught that he could barely function.

Frank returned to the computer and dried his eyes to study again Kathy's two-page manuscript on the desk beside the printer. Earlier in the evening, the missive had been delivered to him as if by a messenger from heaven while he'd sat alone in the den, the kids finally asleep, a cool autumn breeze whispering through an open window. A gust of wind from the approaching storm billowed the sheer draperies and fluttered the papers atop the desk, whisking two sheets from the paper tray and sweeping them across the room to rest at his feet. He'd turned the volume down on the TV and switched on a lamp to examine the ink-jet pages, a shock wave racing through his veins at the discovery.

Frank recalled how he'd laughed at Kathy when she first entertained the idea. She'd wanted to document how it felt when they made love, so that when they were elderly and the kids were gone, they could recall the passion they'd once enjoyed. Despite his friendly teasing, he now knew she had been serious and had secretly proceeded with her plan, having actually committed her thoughts and feelings to paper. He'd been wrong to make light of her idea, for calling it corny, and tonight her recorded observations sent chills through his body as a reminder of the splendor he would never again experience.

He feels so warm inside me. His arms hold me tightly but tenderly, and I feel safe, as if nothing in the world can harm me. His hands caress me all over. He makes love to every part of me, not just to my vagina. I love him, and he communicates his love to me through gentility. I want to please him. I want to do what he asks me to do, but I can't, because the act repulses me. But I wish I could. For him. I know other women do it, and some actually enjoy it, but for me, it's different.

But I'll try.

Someday I'll surprise him. I'll take him into my mouth and give him the pleasure he deserves. But for now I feel the warmth of his breath against my neck as his hands tighten around my bottom, and I know that he's approaching orgasm. I feel his release. He gasps for breath beside my ear. I feel him withdraw, and know that he will satisfy me a second time, as he most often does.

But I tug at his neck as his head slips beneath the covers. I tell him it isn't necessary. Once is enough for tonight. I explain that all I need is to have him with me. I find strength in his embrace. He holds me, and I feel a special closeness that few couples on earth can ever claim.

The manuscript pages shook in his grasp as Frank absorbed every word before switching the computer back on. He and Kathy had teamed up to write nonfiction articles before, and now, even from beyond the grave, they were collaborating again on their most special project of all. Frank knew that he must match her description with one of his own, imagining how their last act of lovemaking might have been had he known in advance he was about to lose her.

Outside the wind screamed, the storm intensified, but the power was back on, and visions of lost opportunities clouded Frank's mind.

I kiss her neck, her earlobes, and our lips meet again. I lick her breasts and massage her inner thighs with my fingertips. I want to make her happy. I want to fulfill her every need. She whispers in my ear and asks me to hold her. I thank her for being my wife, for being the mother of my children, for giving my life meaning and purpose.

She closes her eyes and goes to sleep. I watch her breast rise and fall in the moonlight. I am hers, in life and in death.

Forever.

* * *

The computer monitor blinked off as another crash of thunder and lightning rocked the house, the power interrupted again. Though these last passages were lost to the storm, Frank knew his words would be easily duplicated later, for he could never forget how it felt to make love to Kathy.

"Mommy!" Carly's frightened voice screamed from her upstairs bedroom. Frank jarred himself from the computer, chilled by the thought that Carly, still in a state of denial, had called for her mother instead. He stumbled upstairs in the darkness, feeling his way into his daughter's room to find Carly sitting up in bed, clutching her worn and ruffled teddy bear, with tears on her cheeks that sparkled from intermittent flashes of lightning.

"It's OK, honey," Frank whispered in her ear, holding his daughter tightly. "There's nothing to be afraid of. The storm will be over soon, I promise."

Carly clung to her father, trembling as if she were dangling over the edge of a cliff. "When will she be back? When will Mommy come to see me again?"

Frank took a deep breath. Lightning spilled into the room, illuminating a scattered assortment of toys. "She won't be coming home, honey. She's in heaven now, with Grandpa."

Carly shook in his arms, and Frank so desperately wished he could soothe her and take the hurt away. "How about if we get you a brand-new teddy bear tomorrow?" he said as he reached for the worn bear that leaked stuffing from its seams.

"No!" Carly objected sharply, tugging the bear away to herself. "Barry is special. I don't want another bear."

Soft footsteps padded into the room. "Daddy? Daddy, I can't sleep."

Little Frankie wandered through the darkness to crawl in bed beside his father and sister, dragging his pillow behind him. Jammed between his kids in the narrow twin bed, Frank held his children until the storm passed, until they were fast asleep, knowing he must be both father and mother to them now, and for a moment he found peace, as if Kathy, too, were in bed with them.

Frank awakened in his own bed at the earliest light of dawn, rain still draining from the roof and splattering into puddles outside the window. He had almost dozed off again before a swirling, vaporlike green mist began to form like a cloud at the foot of his bed, like nothing he had ever seen. Realizing that he must be dreaming, Frank turned his head away and rubbed sleep from his eyes. But when he reopened them, the glowing mist was growing thicker, expanding and circulating at the foot of the bed until it began to transform like state-of-the-art special effects in the movies, taking shape into a vague image of Kathy as she looked in her prime. A deadly silence chilled the room.

Frank's heart pounded. Had he slipped over the edge? Had the loss of his dear wife driven him to insanity? But as the vision sharpened, Frank experienced a strange calming effect and admired her nude form, his pulse slowing to a more normal pace. Still, it was difficult to believe that his imagination wasn't merely working overtime from the severe stress he'd endured. Suddenly, the sound of Kathy's voice reverberated through Frank's mind—not audibly but telepathically. His breath stopped for the slightest of moments. His heart pounded against his chest.

Frank! Kathy whispered. *It's so wonderful to see you again.* Ghostly tears ran from her eyes. Frank lay speechless, his own eyes barely blinking. *I was granted permission to return again,* she continued. *I'm so thankful. It's so seldom allowed.*

Frank shook his head so quickly to awaken himself that he pulled a muscle in his neck but was oblivious to the pain. He was awake after all, and there, at the foot of the bed, floating mere inches above the floor, was his beloved wife—not in earthly form but translucent, with color shifting softly between shades of green and blue.

But it was definitely her.

Kathy.

Kathy.

Frank's mouth opened and closed, but words refused to come. As she drifted closer, the lower half of her body seemed to dissolve without substance, disappearing into the bed through the blankets at his legs.

Frank swallowed hard in disbelief. "I d-d-don't know what to s-say," he mumbled. She looked both happy and sad, and he reached out for her, but she motioned him away. Obediently, he settled back in bed and finally thought to ask, "You said you've come back again. Does that mean you've been here before?"

Kathy smiled as her tears began to fade. Her mistlike form still slowly sank into the foot of the bed, and now only her head and breasts were strangely visible in a holographic image. Frank could see nothing of her lower half, yet he could see *through* her and feel a tantalizing warmth somewhere around his knees that crawled slowly toward his groin. Despite the bizarre nature of the experience, the sensation brought an immediate erection.

I was here once before, just last week, for only a matter of minutes, she said, *and I had to spend every precious moment with the children. I hope you'll understand.*

The feeling between his legs grew more and more intense. Frank kicked the covers away to see what was happening. Kathy's lower form was breaking apart, narrowing and spiraling like the base of a tornado, snaking its way up his leg and seeping into the crotch of his underwear and tickling his scrotum. He grasped the elastic band of his briefs and pushed them past his knees for a better view.

Kathy's warmth was unlike anything he'd ever experienced, a few degrees hotter than normal body temperature. The steaming sensation was overpowering; his penis stiffened to a rigidity that seemed almost frightening.

Frank nodded numbly.

I have no substance, so you can't feel me, but I can feel you, and I can generate warmth. I vaporized inside Carly's teddy bear and felt her arms all around me. She cuddled me so closely, and it was wonderful. And then I went inside little Frankie's pillow. I wanted to hold them both, to speak to them, but I didn't want to frighten them. It was the most difficult thing . . . I couldn't touch them, but I could feel them touching me, she admitted as fluorescent green tears floated from her eyes. *But I could at least keep them warm. In the cool night air. I kept them warm . . . warm . . .*

The heat at Frank's penis was so tantalizing he could barely comprehend what she was saying.

Carly awoke as I left to go to Frankie's room, Kathy continued. *I convinced her it was just a dream. Has she ever mentioned it?*

"N-n-no," Frank gasped from a feeling of ecstasy he had never before imagined.

Her head drifts between my legs, and she takes me into her mouth. I tense but can feel nothing other than the mysterious warmth enveloping my shaft. In the dim light of morning, I watch my penis slipping in and out of her translucent cheeks, as if I am viewing her ministrations through an X-ray, but all I feel is her mystical warmth.

She stops and makes eye contact, then her green-blue

hair begins to dissolve and swirl, her facial features fading along with her breasts and shifting into a smokelike whirlpool circling above the tip of my penis which now lies flat against my stomach, pointing directly at my face. The steaming whirlwind that was once my wife narrows to a pencil point and enters the opening at the tip of my penis. I tense. The humid warmth flowing into me feels like a reverse ejaculation. I gasp, clench my teeth, and grasp the wrinkled bedsheet with both hands. My entire body stiffens to the most irresistible sensation imaginable.

The warmth inside my penis is sultry and damp. I watch the pulsating, greenish glow of my foreskin throb as if I am being masturbated by waves of light.

The overpowering warmth, the most incredible stimulation overcomes me. My legs stiffen. My penis is about to explode—not in the usual sense, but with so much force it is almost frightening.

I gasp for air. The sensation is indescribable. I feel the heat of my wife inside me, and I wonder if the feeling compares in any way to the warmth of my penis inside her. My feelings sharpen to such incredible sensitivity that I actually feel my testicles move to a rhythm of their own, then draw up inside my scrotum, preparing for ejaculation. Waves of pleasure flow through my penis from the base to the tip, and I grab myself in preparation for ejaculation and point it straight up to avoid being blasted in the face.

The waves of pleasure fail to stabilize but instead grow steadily; I'm not even certain that I can withstand such an overload of stimulation without suffering some kind of harm as I groan uncontrollably. A massive green glob of semen erupts from the tip of my penis, not with the velocity I might have expected but slowly, and amazingly it floats in ball-like globules to the white ceiling, where it splatters and rolls in circles like mercury searching to merge into one larger mass.

Orgasm after orgasm occurs, each emitting a lower volume of ejaculate than the last. Exhausted from passion and pleasure beyond belief, I pass out, regretting later that I was not conscious to say good-bye to my most precious wife, and ask if she will ever return.

Frank lay awake, lonely and distraught. It was weeks later, and except for the unusually loud humming of the refrigerator downstairs, the house was silent. The kids were sleeping over with his sister, and he'd been to a movie and a late-night cup of coffee with a male friend, but Frank felt strangely uncomfortable socializing so soon after Kathy's death.

He tossed and turned, having given up days earlier on a return visit from Kathy. Sleep evaded him. The numbers on the bedside digital clock changed as if in slow motion. Frank switched on a bedside lamp and examined the bedroom carefully for the first time since he'd lost his wife. Her collection of porcelain dolls adorned the dresser across the room, and a smile actually creased his face when he noticed the wallpaper border around the room, remembering when Kathy and her mom spilled wallpaper paste all over each other and thought they'd never get it out of their hair. He slipped out of bed and walked slowly to Carly's room, noticing details of the house along the way as if for the very first time. The presence of Kathy was everywhere. In Carly's room, he reached across her bed and found Barry resting against the adjacent wall. Frank held the worn teddy bear tightly against his chest and returned to his own bed to slip beneath the covers. A peaceful calmness settled over him as he stroked the imitation fur of the stuffed animal.

Tears again streamed from Frank's eyes.

The bear felt unusually warm.

CLOSE ENCOUNTERS OF MADISON COUNTY

Gary Brandner

Fat black clouds erased the stars from the Maine sky. The boards of the old farmhouse creaked and snapped. Inside, Matthew Creighton lay between sweaty sheets and swore at the mosquito singing in the darkness above his nose.

On the nightstand, a single typewritten sheet fluttered in the humid breath that wheezed through the window screen. The words jumped off the page and danced a mocking jig between Creighton and the mosquito.

Dear Matt: (At least they were still on first-name terms. It was the only positive note in the whole damn letter.)

Thanks for the look at "Vampire Moon." I have to tell you it misses the mark. I wouldn't want to say horror is dead, but it is evolving. (What the hell does that mean?) *Your vampire is yet another Dracula clone, a gimmick that was used up in the 1970s. What I need from you is something '90s.* (What you need is a good fuck.) *Cutting edge, if you know what I'm saying.* (As a matter of fact, I don't.) *And the women in your story are badly dated, too. We are not victims today. Women are strong, spunky, and smart.* (And a huge pain in the ass.) *We never swoon, we do not scream. We take charge. Good luck if you want to try "Moon" with another agent. If you come up with something fresh and state-of-the-art, I'll be glad to look at it.* (Look at *this,* mama.)

Best regards,
Leona

Good old Leona Seltzer, his agent for twelve years, was blowing him off like some no-talent wanna-be at a summer seminar. Worse. Like he was a burned-out hack always a step behind the trends, who couldn't write a decent horror quickie.

Thunder grumbled in the distance. Creighton flipped a finger toward the window. *"Blow, winds, and crack your cheeks! Rage! Blow!* What do I give a shit? Let the weather match my mood."

He erased the rejection from his mental screen and scrolled down the titles of his published books. *Canyon Trail, Assault on Red Beach, Death in the Morning, Megablaster, Burning Planet,* and a score of others. Westerns, militaries, mysteries, technothrillers, sci-fi. Even a romance, something about *Lust* that he could not remember. Two shelves of paperback novels under a dozen pseudonyms for as many publishers. But nothing in the past four years. Now he couldn't get a fucking vampire story past his agent.

Creighton rolled over onto his stomach and buried his face in the damp pillow. How difficult would it be, he wondered, to asphyxiate himself?

A blast of light from outside registered on his eyeballs, even with his face deep in the pillow. Lightning? No, the storm was still somewhere over Boarstone Mountain. The light waned and waxed. An unpleasant buzzing, crackling sound filled the bedroom.

Creighton sat up and blinked. A blue-white glow pulsed outside. The buzzing became a deep, ominous hum.

Auto accident? Uh-uh, the highway was a mile away, and the narrow road in was on the opposite side of the house. Neighbors up to something? Nope. The McNaughton farm was three miles away.

Matthew Creighton had a logical mind not given to fanciful images, but one idea now overrode logic: UFO. Weren't they always setting down in some remote area like this? If the tabloids could be believed, witnesses were usually semiliterate types named Billy Bob. Maybe this time the space visitors had chosen a spot occupied by somebody who could speak in complete sentences.

He levered himself out of bed, pulled on a bulky sweater over his pajamas, shoved his feet into a pair of Kmart sneakers. He dug a flashlight from the nightstand and went out into the humid dark.

The source of the undulating glow and the baritone hum was somewhere on the far side of a stand of bigtooth aspen that bordered the property. Creighton picked his way across the farmed-out field toward the trees. A gust of wind off the mountain bit through the thin pajama bottoms, raising gooseflesh on his legs.

He edged around the clump of aspen, nerves ajangle with anticipation. After years of barely hanging on, Matthew Creighton saw himself about to board the express to Successville. He crept into the clearing beyond the trees and scanned the scene. The express jumped the tracks, the towers of Successville crumbled, leaving him smack back in Loserstown.

"Shit."

One of the high-tension lines strung between steel towers had popped loose in the wind. It sparked a brilliant blue-white whenever it made contact with metal. The tower itself hummed like a thousand angry bees. The ozone smell of electrical sparks made his eyes water, and for a moment he felt dizzy.

Creighton shook the cobwebs from his brain and swept the ground with his flashlight. The beam revealed an irregular patch of freshly scorched sawgrass. In the center of the browned area bobbed the probable cause of the short circuit—a silvery metallic balloon. The softened sphere trailed pink ribbons and bore the printed message, "Happy Birthday, Varna!!!"

"Shit," Creighton said again. "Fuck you, Varna."

As he spoke, the steel tower groaned, the flapping line snapped back into place, the sparking ceased, and the humming died. Creighton picked up the limp balloon and tried to pop it between his hands. People should know better than to let these things loose. The metalicized skin proved too tough, which pissed him off. Carrying the offending balloon by the ribbon, he clumped through the trees and across the field to the house.

Back in bed, Creighton lay staring at the balloon bobbing now on the nightstand. Why couldn't it have really been a UFO? He could have sold tickets. *See the Aliens! Adults $20.00, Children $12.50.* Set up a concession stand. Sell T-shirts at twenty bucks each. *Have your picture taken with an alien!* Hell, there were a hundred ways he could have cashed in on extraterrestrials. But a short circuit and a Happy Birthday balloon were not worth a fiddler's fuck.

As a sunless dawn approached, Creighton drifted restlessly in semisleep. Abruptly, his eyes snapped open, and he sat up as though snakebit.

"Sonofabitch!" He leaped out of bed and stumbled

to the typewriter on the other side of the room. He rolled in a sheet of bond and set the keys clattering. An hour later, he paused, read what he had written, and grabbed the telephone.

"Jesus, Matt, it's the middle of the night."

"It's six A.M."

"That's what I said. It is no fucking time to talk about some cockamamie piece of science fiction."

"Leona, will you listen to me? This is not science fiction. It happened. To me. Last night. I've been up until now making notes."

"Let me understand this. A flying saucer landed in your backyard, and little green men took you on board for disgusting sexual experiments. Haven't I read this somewhere before?"

"Damn it, Leona, pay attention. It was not a saucer, the aliens were not green, and what happened to me was anything but disgusting."

"Are you drinking again?"

"I'm sober as the pope."

The sleepy annoyance began to drain from the agent's voice. "And you really think you've got something?"

"Leona, did Shirley MacLaine have something with stories of her past lives?"

"Hmmm."

"What sells today? New Age stuff and soppy romance, am I right?"

"Hmmm."

"What's fifteen percent of a million dollars?"

"Do you have a manuscript?"

"I'll have it polished in a week."

"Don't forget return postage."

"I'll come in and deliver it personally."

"All right, Matthew, I'll look at it. But, sweetheart,

I do not want to hear anymore that it really happened."

"Leona, it really happened."

"Good-bye, Matthew."

For six days, Matthew Creighton labored at the keyboard of his aging Smith-Corona. If all went well, his next work would be on a state-of-the-art computer. For six days, he ate little, drank only well water, slept in fragmentary naps. He rewrote nothing as the words flowed from his fingertips to the paper. The story told itself.

The title was a natural: *Loving Varna.*

It was a short book, 220 manuscript pages. Printed, it would be a slim volume that would not intimidate the slowest of readers. Perfect for the market he was shooting for.

From Chapter 2:

. . . One of my visitors was at best four feet tall, the other a couple of inches shorter. Their bodies were white, soft, and round, their limbs flexible. Their large heads were smoothly ovoid, with small mouths and breathing apertures, dominated by great, dark, liquid eyes. With their lack of facial or body hair, they resembled walking eggs. Alien though they were, I sensed they would not harm me. It somehow seemed natural that in their flutey, musical voices they spoke perfect formal English.

"So who is this Varna you want me to see?" I asked.

"There is no corresponding word in your language to describe her," said the shorter of the eggs. "'Adored Goddess' comes closest."

"Varna is a female?"

The two eggs exchanged a look and made a whuffling sound that might have been laughter. I shrugged. Still dazed from my sudden awakening, I was not eager to meet the queen of the eggs.

Leona Seltzer flipped through the first twenty pages of manuscript impatiently and squinted across her imposing bosom at Creighton. "Matthew, are you sure you don't want to try the *Star* or *Weekend World News?* Forget the *Enquirer,* they don't do space people anymore."

"Read the next chapter, Leona. Please."

"I don't have to. Your hero's confrontation with the egg goddess does not thrill me. I have a lunch date in a few minutes with Jason Beatty, so I'll have to take a pass."

"Jason Beatty of Oaktree Press?"

"Is there another one?"

"Read just one more chapter, Leona. I'm begging."

The agent took a heavy look at her Rolex, ran a hand across her tight red curls, and resumed reading.

From Chapter Three:

Did I call her an egg? I could rip my tongue out. When my eyes adjusted to the muted light of the interior, I saw Varna, and the breath was sucked from my lungs. She lay on her side on a contoured couch of velvety crimson. She wore a gown that could have been made of smoke. It shimmered and drifted, at once cloaking and revealing a spectacular body well beyond my powers of description. Breasts firm and round thrust their challenge toward me, her nipples alert. Her hair fell in soft waves of French vanilla across milky shoulders, silver eyes matched by no earthly woman, lips full and ripe that smiled at some secret pleasure.

Leona Seltzer blinked her tiny blue eyes rapidly as though trying to bring Creighton into focus.

"Alert nipples? Vanilla hair? Silver eyes? Matthew, what are you giving me here?"

"It's the story I was born to tell, Leona. It's truth and beauty and love and loss."

"And sex," added the agent.

"Sure, and sex. Wait till you read what happens to me in Chapter Four."

"You're going to insist that this is autobiography?"

Creighton clapped a hand over his heart. "Every word is true. I swear."

Leona gathered up the manuscript, shoved it into the envelope. "Let's see what we can do with this."

"You like it, right?"

"Maybe. I'll let you know when I get Jason Beatty's reaction."

"You think it could be Oaktree material?"

"Let's find out. Come along."

Carlino's was a small step-down restaurant in the west fifties in current favor with the publishing crowd. It smelled pleasantly of garlic, oregano, tomato sauce, and wine. The booths were more brightly lit than in most such places to facilitate the reading of manuscripts and book jackets.

Matt Creighton and his agent sat across from a balding young man in unpressed khakis, a nubby sport jacket, plaid shirt, and burnt orange tie. Jason Beatty ignored the glass of club soda at his elbow as he read the pages before him.

* * *

From Chapter Three:

When she spoke, Varna's voice was like cool fur passing over my body. "You are smooth of muscle and tense of nerve. Like a panther. Come to me."

I was drawn toward her as a leaf into a whirlpool. My senses spun wildly and burst in phantasmagoric fireworks. Varna swung her magical legs around and rose to her full six feet. The diaphanous gown whispered away from the rounded swell of her hips. My eyes were drawn across her gently rounded belly to the down that shadowed her Venus mound, soft and pale as the underside of a hamster. Her damp labia fluttered pink and moist.

Jason Beatty looked up from the page at Leona Seltzer, then at Creighton. "Jesus. A fluttering snatch? I think I'm getting a hard-on."

Leona smiled and looked to Creighton.

The writer did not smile. "Excuse me, but you're talking about the most intimate, most beautiful experience of my life."

"Sure, right." The editor spoke to the agent. "Leona, do you really want to go with this as nonfiction?"

The agent looked over at the author. "He swears it happened."

"It happened," confirmed the author.

"No politics, no ax to grind, no libel of anybody important?"

"Just the truth about what happened to me one night a little more than a week ago."

"Stick to that story, and I'll buy it," said the editor.

"Great, Jason," said the agent. "I knew you'd love it."

"What kind of an advance are we talking?" said the writer.

The other two stared at him.

The editor addressed his question to the agent. "What were the sales figures on his last one?"

"Let's go, Leona," said the writer. He reached for the manuscript.

Jason Beatty lay a protective hand over the pages. "Wait. Maybe we can work something out."

They worked something out.

From Chapter Four:

Varna's lips, soft as a whisper, warm as a love poem, sweet as a spring morning, traveled down my chest, across my bare stomach, eased into the bristle of my pubic hair. Her tongue, a moist, darting, living thing, found the root of my erect manhood and traveled its length slowly, slowly, caressingly. Then, with a single graceful bob of her glorious head, she took me completely into the wet oven of her mouth and began a pulsing suction that wrenched a scream of pleasure from my throat. All the while, the silver eyes looked into my soul.

The talk-show host faced the camera and held up a copy of *Loving Varna*—a spare 161 printed pages with generous white space—cover price $23.95.

"I don't know about you folks, but once I opened this, I couldn't get it down, I mean put it down, ha ha." He turned to Creighton, seated on the couch to his right. "I guess a lot of folks agree with me. In less than two months, you're already into, what, fourth printing?"

"Fifth, Jay, but, ha ha, who's counting?"

"Beautiful. And you maintain that everything between these covers really happened."

"Everything."

"Was she . . . was Varna really as beautiful and, well, as sexy as you described her?"

"More. More in every way."

"The wild thing is that while there are some really steamy scenes in this book, there's a sensitivity . . . a tenderness here that makes the women bring out the hankies. It even made me choke up a little."

Creighton's voice cracked ever so slightly. "I'm sorry, Jay, it's still not easy for me to talk about it. I wrote the story as I lived it."

From Chapter Twelve:

I stood in the rain and watched Varna through the oval window of their strange vehicle as the others prepared their departure. The hardest thing I ever had to do was to decline her invitation to go with her to . . . to wherever. I knew my decision was right, the only one I could have made, but I swear, if she had asked me one more time, I would have given up all, risked everything, and gone with her. Her lips formed a sweet goodbye. I touched two fingers to my own in farewell. I was thankful for the rain that streamed down my face and washed away the tears.

Dusty palm trees rattled their fronds in the Santa wind outside the sparkling Dreamworks building north of Hollywood. Inside, a bearded man in jeans and a Planet Hollywood T-shirt gestured with a copy of *Loving Varna* as he spoke.

"I see Tom Cruise and Sharon Stone in the leads."

Creighton frowned off at a corner of the ceiling. "I

don't know if they have the depth. I was thinking more Harrison Ford and Michelle Pfeiffer."

"Good thought, Matt, but hell, we can talk casting after the paperwork is all signed and sealed, am I right?"

Leona Seltzer spoke up. "The contract looks good enough, Steven, but I did promise a look to Michael over at Disney."

"Promise me you won't sign with them before you get back to me."

"You got it, dear," Leona said, and swept out of the Dreamworks office with her client.

Back in New York, Creighton leaned back in the burgundy leather chair Leona Seltzer reserved for star clients. Creighton touched the flame of a gold Dunhill lighter to a cigar that cost more than he used to spend on a full dinner.

Leona hurried over with an ashtray. "I can't believe the momentum we're picking up, Matthew. Book-stores can't keep it in stock. A mob of women trashed Barnes and Noble in Seattle when they ran out. Waldenbooks has tripled their order."

"Only tripled?"

"Twice. Letterman is pissed that you did the other guy first, but he still wants you. You'll have the leadoff spot, right after the Top Ten list. Larry King wants to give you his whole show. Barbara Walters sent over a list of questions for your OK."

"Tell them I'll think it over. What do we hear from Disney?"

"They're talking a solid seven figures, plus a percentage of the net."

"Net? No movie in history has ever shown a net profit. Ask the guy that sold them *Forrest Gump*."

"I haven't bounced it off Spielburg yet."

"Well, bounce it. He'll go higher. And I want a piece of the *gross.*"

"I hear you, Matthew. By the way, Jason Beatty is eager to talk sequel. Are you available tomorrow?"

"No. I'm making one last run up to the old Maine house."

"Sentimental journey?"

"Not likely. Just a last check to see if there's anything there I want. Most of it isn't worth dumping in a landfill."

On the flight from LaGuardia to Bangor, Creighton stretched his legs straight out, sipped the complimentary champagne, and savored the new joy of traveling first class. Thanks to his imaginary aliens, life was good and getting better. At the Bangor airport, he rented a Lexus for the fifty-mile drive north to the old farmhouse.

It was still there—peeling paint, sagging porch, crumbling chimney, just like he remembered it. How he had lived in a dump like this without falling into terminal depression Creighton could not imagine. He made a quick tour of the interior, wincing at the gritty feel of the floor under his feet, the stale odor of long departed people, the cobwebby gloom of the corners. He quickly decided all he needed from here was his manuscript file, a few books, and his Steelers sweatshirt. The rest of it he would leave for the crows.

He hummed happily in his former bedroom-office as he piled rejected manuscripts into a Campbell's soup carton. They would find a ready market now.

A knock at the open door startled him. Two men, one short and thin, one tall and thin, stood side by side in the doorway. They were dressed alike in dark suits, muted ties, black wingtip shoes. They wore their hair short, no mustaches, clean fingernails. Creighton's first thought was: FBI.

"Excuse the intrusion, Mr. Creighton," said the taller man. He spoke with a trace of some accent Creighton could not identify.

"What can I do for you?"

"My name is Mathers, this is my associate, Mr. Dow. We represent Universal Satellite Television and would very much appreciate a brief interview." The shorter man stood impassively as his partner spoke.

Creighton relaxed. "Have you talked to my agent?"

"Time limitations precluded that courtesy."

"Who did you say you're with?"

"Universal Satellite Television. UST. Our transmission reaches many millions."

"That so?"

"Translated into forty-four languages. Our broadcast will be timed to coincide with the release of foreign editions of your book, which might well add to your already considerable sales. If is not too great an imposition, we are prepared to tape an interview now."

"You mean here?"

"Our mobile studio is just outside."

"I didn't hear you drive up."

"We arrived and set up early this morning."

"Millions of people will see it, you say."

"Many millions."

"As long as you've gone to this trouble, I guess I can spare you a few minutes."

"You are most generous. Come this way, please."

The three men crossed the dried-out lawn behind the house, Creighton in the middle, the visitors flanking him. Something about their names tickled his memory, but he had no time to dwell on it. As they circled the small stand of aspen, they came upon a silver and blue mobile unit the size of a freight car. The roof sprouted antennae of various sizes and shapes and appeared to be connected directly to the overhead power lines. A logo on the side of the vehicle resembled a whirling nebula with the stylized letters "UST."

Creighton whistled. "Nice rig. Funny I didn't see it when I drove up."

The shorter man spoke for the first time. "Not really. You see what we want you to see." His voice was an unsettling mechanical growl.

Creighton stopped short and looked quickly at the man called Dow. Their names clicked into place.

"You guys weren't in *Leave It to Beaver,* I suppose."

Neither of them responded. Creighton found he could not pull their features into focus. The faces wavered and blurred like reflections in a rippling pond. Their clothing faded to transparency, then vanished. Creighton blinked trying to recapture reality. Between blinks, he was gripped firmly just above the elbows and propelled toward the vehicle.

He found his voice. "Hey, that hurts. What's going on? Who are you guys?"

"I think you know the answer, Mr. Creighton. For weeks, you have been telling the world about your . . . intimate knowledge of extraterrestrials." The voice of the tall one called Mathers had dropped an octave and turned growly.

"Is this a joke?" Even as he said it, Creighton realized with a tightening of his scrotum that there was nothing funny about the situation.

"On our previous visit, Mr. Creighton, you were afforded a singular opportunity to interact with one of our race. Your reactions were most helpful to our studies. Unfortunately, our erasure of your recall was incomplete. Seizing on your retained fragments of memory, you have described in minute detail our lady Varna. You have vividly depicted a number of unnatural acts you ascribe to her and published them widely. I must tell you there are gross inaccuracies in your report that have embarrassed our people, and our lady Varna in particular."

"Wait a minute . . . there really *is* a Varna? Jesus, that dizzy spell . . ."

"You called us eggs," said Dow.

"And you kept our balloon," added Mathers. "What we now offer you is the opportunity to set the record straight."

Creighton forgot the pain in his upper arms. These weirdos were dropping into his lap the mother of all sequels. Dollar figures whirled in his brain. What he had achieved with his fanciful ET story would be dwarfed by his account of the real thing.

He said, "Hey, guys, no need to get rough. Take me to your Varna. I'm eager to meet her. Again, I mean."

"Do not be too sure," said Mathers.

An ominous note in the growling voice loosened Creighton's bowels for a moment, and he made an effort to tighten his sphincter. He swiveled his head from side to side. Gone were the men in suits, ties, polished wingtips. The manicured hands had morphed into scaly things with claws that pierced his suede jacket and pricked his flesh. The creatures were vaguely reptilian, with wide froglike mouths and tiny burning eyes. No friendly walking eggs here. And definitely not FBI.

"Listen, if it's the balloon, we can work something out."

"You have soiled the name of our lady Varna. You have enjoyed her hospitality, then depicted her as the most licentious, immoral, obscene creature your poor mind could conceive."

"Hey I don't think that's—"

"Such calumny cannot be allowed to stand."

The painful grip on his biceps tightened. Any thought of cashing in on this visitation vanished as he was pushed forward.

"I'll rewrite the book any way you want. I'll have unsold copies recalled. I'll do a complete retraction on national TV with Barbara Walters. Just tell me what you want."

"We want you to again experience our lady Varna, this time with full recall of the sensations."

Creighton sucked in his breath as they hoisted him off the ground and thrust him toward the solid wall of the shimmering vehicle. He tensed, eyes squeezed shut, for a face-first impact with the metal. Instead, he felt only a soft rush as though passing though a curtain of air. When he opened his eyes, he was alone in a chamber much larger than the exterior had appeared. Concealed light sources cast strange shadows on the walls. The floor gave beneath his feet like sponge rubber. The only visible piece of furniture was a huge contoured loveseat of velvety crimson. With a start, he recognized it as a larger surreal version of the couch he described in Chapter Two.

A soft, flutelike music in an unfamiliar tonal scale trickled from somewhere in the gloom. A spicy fragrance touched the air. Creighton leaned forward, staring. He saw nothing except the oversize couch and the shifting shadows.

"Anybody here?" His voice was flat and without timbre. For many heartbeats, there was only silence. Then he heard . . .

"Hello, my Panther Man."

It was the voice of Varna, exactly as he had imagined it, or remembered it according to Mathers and Dow—a sensuous contralto, breathy, purring, promising. His fears subsided a bit. Was it possible this might work out after all? He felt the first stirring of an erection.

"Varna? Is it you?"

"Do you not know my voice?"

Of course he knew it. He invented it. Didn't he?

"Where are you? I can't see you."

"I am here. Right here. You will see me, my Panther Man. You will see all of me."

The voice from the darkness was changing to something ragged and feral. The fragrant spice faded, and a stench like rotting flesh invaded his space and made him gag. His erection wilted like last summer's daisy.

"Seriously, if this is about the balloon—"

Speech died in his throat. A single tentacle thick as his arm snaked over the back of the couch, gray-green and wet. On the end grew a hairy bulb the size of a cantaloupe. Centered in the bulb was a glassy protuberance that might have been an eye. It looked at him, cold and unblinking. From the darkness beyond the couch came a low, growling chuckle.

Creighton's breath exploded from his lungs, and he pulled in another, choking on the stink. The spongy floor sucked at his feet and held him fast. Sweat drenched his body.

A second tentacle slithered across the couch and joined the first. They swayed in unison, a grotesque dance, the eyes never leaving him. A third tentacle appeared, this one eyeless, with cruel lobsterlike pincers clacking, clacking as it weaved ever closer to his face.

The stench increased to the limit of his endurance as the body from which the tentacles grew rose from behind the couch. A shapeless lump the size of a refrigerator, covered with boils the size of doorknobs, each leaking a greenish pus.

So transfixed was Creighton by the abomination that he barely noticed when the pincer tentacle swooped forward and stroked his cheek. He never saw the one that slid along the spongy floor and up his pant leg until it reached his flaccid penis.

* * *

Three miles away, Cale McNaughton looked up from his newspaper. He cocked his head and removed the old briar pipe from his mouth.

"Did you hear that, Mother?"

"Hear what?"

"Sounded like something squealing."

"One of the dogs got himself a coon, most likely."

"Mebbe." Cale McNaughton sat for another minute listening. All was still. "Mebbe that was it."

LA MOURANTE

Thomas Tessier

Y ou need something new," Lawrence said.

"Yes, but what?"

Alex had been a member of Feathers for more than a year when Lawrence made the suggestion. They were sitting in the piano bar just off the grotto, wrapped in towels, their hair still damp. A lovely little nymph brought them Sapphire martinis.

Feathers was one of the most exclusive private clubs in the world. You couldn't buy your way in. You had to be nominated by a current member, and membership was limited to four hundred very wealthy individuals who were profoundly devoted to the pursuit of pleasure. In the age of AIDS, the club was both an ark of safety and an Eden of erotic license. It was located in a sedate brick building near Park Lane, London W1, but its members came from all around the globe to check their fears at the door and to unleash their transcendent fantasies.

Alex couldn't believe his good fortune when he learned that his membership had been approved. He and Lawrence had known each other since their school days together at Charterhouse. They were an unlikely pair, Alex the restless Yank from Westchester County and Lawrence the jaded last son in a played-out line of Wiltshire landowners. But they got along well and stayed in touch over the years. Lawrence made a fortune in the City, and Alex did at least as well on the Street. Now in their mid-thirties, they each had the freedom and the means to do whatever they desired—and they suffered no illusions to hold them back.

Alex had just been complaining about the fact that he seemed to be running out of exotic places and females to try. Last year, he'd done the hill tribes of India and Southeast Asia, and it was for the most part a disappointment. As he'd found so many times, reality can't compete with the imagination.

Which, of course, was why retreats like Feathers existed for those of privilege. But the urge to travel and explore and the need to test himself against raw experience were powerful forces in the composition of Alex's character. Thus, the constant weighing of new possibilities, however dubious.

"Do you know about a place called Fado?"

"Fado." Alex shook his head. "Never heard of it."

"Aha." Lawrence smiled. "It's an island, some-where off the northern coast of South America. The Caribbean, or perhaps it's out more in the Atlantic, I'm not sure which. Anyhow, it's very private, very hush-hush."

"What's the attraction?" Alex had done island paradises two years ago: the Andamans, Polynesia, East Africa—enough.

"Well." The smile on Lawrence's face had turned into a foxy grin. "Have you ever made love with a dead woman?"

"No. It sounds revolting."

"Yes, it does," Lawrence agreed. "But apparently

it's not. In fact, I'm told by very reliable sources that once you've tried it, nothing else will do."

"I was told that about the Bushman girls in southern Africa. And other women, in other places. It's never true."

Lawrence nodded. "Still, you have to wonder."

"I'll pass."

But the idea wouldn't. Necrophilia. Ugly word, it conjured up grisly images of dead meat splayed on a cold slab, stiff limbs, and pale waxy skin. How could anyone possibly sell that, and who (aside from a few demented souls) would want it?

Lawrence provided a name and an address on a scrap of paper, typical of the kind of highly prized information that passes from one hand to another in a place like Feathers. Alex still had no intention of actually going to Fado, but he was curious enough to visit M. Alain Gaudet in an anonymous office on a pleasant street not far from the center of Lausanne.

M. Gaudet extracted a good deal of information from Alex and provided very little in return. He described Fado as unique, an island resort privately maintained and operated, dedicated to the enjoyment of "individual practices unfettered by national laws or treaties or international conventions."

Fado was located off the coast of Blanca and was protected by the military government (for a price and perks, no doubt). In addition to the staff, it had a small permanent population with a mixed background: English, Dutch, Portuguese, Italian, French, and African. The island was only a few square miles in area but had "features of great natural beauty."

So far, so boring. M. Gaudet promised nothing. He allowed a few questions but answered them evasively. There was something in his expression that seemed to suggest that Alex should use his imagination. Alex was good at that.

Two months later, presumably after he'd been investigated in great detail, Alex was notified that he had been cleared to visit Fado. A local New York resident, a Mr. Worboys, could handle the arrangements. But did Alex want to go? Mr. Worboys proved to be only a bit more forthcoming with information.

"There are several hundred women on Fado, all shapes, sizes, and shades, and they're all available to you at any time, in any number or circumstance you want. Some will be otherwise engaged at any given moment, but you'll have as much variety and choice as you can handle. There's also a wide selection of living quarters to choose from—bungalows, cottages, cabanas, suites—you can change them as often as you like. The facilities operate day and night, you can have dinner at four in the morning . . ."

Alex listened patiently until Mr. Worboys was finished and then asked if it was true that Fado provided for even the rarest and most peculiar tastes, as he'd heard. Mr. Worboys was silent for a moment, gazing evenly at him. He glanced briefly again at the papers on his desk, as if to reassure himself that Alex had indeed been properly cleared.

"Behavioral guidelines will be issued to you on arrival, but you can take my word for it that they're minimal." A tight smile flickered at the corners of his mouth. "None of the clients I've dealt with—and there have been a good many of them—has ever expressed the slightest hint of disappointment."

"Is that a yes?"

"Let me put it to you this way, dear boy. If you don't know why you're going to Fado, you shouldn't go."

Alex took that as a yes.

As the helicopter rose and quickly swung back toward Blanca, Alex sat in the lounge and studied the glossy arrivals kit he had just been given. How to get about. Living quarters. A detailed map of the island and its many delights. Restaurants, bars, some intriguing theme houses, woodland trails, jungle paths, caves and ornate gardens, a crater lake, waterfalls, and black sand beaches. All of which was fine, and predictable.

Alex then came across the behavioral guidelines Mr. Worboys had mentioned. There were only two of them, printed on a plastic card attached to a small round keyholder.

Respect your fellow guests. Do not violate their privacy or interfere with their activities unless specifically invited to participate. Disputes to be settled by staff.

Respect those who serve you. Mutilation, decapitation, and dismemberment are prohibited, and will result in severe financial penalties and expulsion.

Alex smiled faintly. He rode a jitney from the heliport to an Iberian-style village square. Along the way, he saw only a few guests and staff members, but plenty of women. Most of them were young, though some were a little older. Most of them were pretty and attractive, though some had average or even plain looks. All were nicely dressed in a variety of styles and outfits.

They didn't stand around, vacantly posturing. There were no lewd gestures, but most of them did seem to notice the jitney and its handful of passengers—with a glance and an innocent smile. *Welcome, stranger. Yours for the taking,* Alex thought.

They all looked very much alive.

Alex chose a simple three-room bungalow nestled in a wooded pocket just off a hillside trail. He sipped a drink and nibbled some fruit while he unpacked, then he took a shower and dozed for a couple of hours. It was late afternoon when he opened his eyes at the sound of someone singing softly nearby.

There was a small garden at the rear of the bungalow. Alex saw a young woman with long dark hair and golden skin. She sang to herself and occasionally clipped a flower, which she put in a wicker basket. She was dressed in a flimsy sleeveless top and a short pleated skirt, both white. Her back was to Alex, who stood at the window and watched her for a moment.

The young woman glanced briefly in his direction and smiled when he stepped outside. She continued to sing, though her voice was so muted and indistinct that it amounted to little more than a light melodious humming, a lilting murmur—but Alex was quite enchanted; he'd never heard anything quite like it before.

He crossed the patch of thick lawn and placed his hands on her shoulders. The woman leaned back against him, eyes shutting, her face half-turned toward him. She put the pruning shears into the basket and let her hand fall to her side, brushing his thigh. The air was full of a delicious scent, a subtle perfume from this lovely creature mingling with the smell of the flowers.

Alex kissed her hair and neck. He stroked her breasts, felt her nipples responding through the thin fabric. He put his other hand beneath her skirt, encountering silky flesh, sleek and firm, and baby-fine hair. When he kissed her open mouth, he didn't want to stop, because she tasted so sweet and felt wonderfully cool and moist.

There was a cushioned wooden bench tucked beneath a wall of arcing shrubs, and Alex took her to it. He put the basket on the grass under the bench as they sat down. Her eyes were deep brown and had delicate hints of amber. She sat patiently, waiting for him to say or do something, but there was a lively brightness in her eyes that suggested playful anticipation.

Alex put his fingers to her lips and pushed gently, and she gave him a wide smile—he saw that her teeth were very white, but not perfect; they were her own, unstraightened.

He held her hand in both of his for several moments, but he could find no pulse. He slid the thin straps off her shoulders and admired her breasts—they were round and neither too large nor too flat, but they weren't flawless. Alex moved closer and rested his head on her chest. She held him there, stroking his hair, and he concentrated—but heard no heartbeat.

Alex sat up again and looked at her. "What is your name?" But she merely gave a slight shrug and a wordless rolling murmur of sound. "You do understand me," he said. She nodded once with a quick smile. "But you don't speak." Again, the faint murmur, and this time Alex noticed that her throat and mouth barely moved as she made it.

He wasn't sure what to think. He knew that there were some languages, Thai among them, that consisted largely of vowels used in extraordinary combinations and tones. These languages sounded like flashing water, and were very difficult to master unless you learned them from childhood.

Perhaps that was it, but Alex didn't think so. The strange sounds this woman made seemed almost older than language itself. Besides, if she could understand what Alex was saying, then surely she could manage a few words of English in response. But if she were not breathing, if there were no significant passage of air to cause and convey voice—

Alex took her hand and pinched the fleshy spot between her thumb and first finger. The skin didn't turn pale, nor did color rush back into it when he let go. It stayed the same.

Alex was vaguely aware of his own heartbeat, increasing at a rapid pace now. His hand shook as he reached down to the basket of flowers and found a rose. He turned it carefully, located one thorn that looked large and strong enough, and jabbed it into the soft pad of the woman's thumb. She sat patiently, watching him. She didn't flinch or show any trace of pain. When Alex withdrew the thorn, the small wound it left was clearly visible, but there was no spot of blood. No blood at all.

The surge of desire within him was deeper and richer than he had experienced in a long time, blinding in its sudden intensity. He took the woman in his arms and pulled her to the ground. They rolled over once, to the edge of the grass, and Alex dimly sensed the nodding ferns and shrubs touching his back as he wriggled out of his pants and pushed into her. He hadn't known such youthful eagerness in years. It was almost a new experience for him. His orgasm was so powerful and hallucinatory that Alex felt as if he were driving into the earth itself. Dazed, barely conscious, he rested in her comforting arms, his head between her breasts. The barest whisper of a happy sound emanated from her—but her body didn't rise or fall with a single breath, there was no heartbeat. She seemed perfectly still, at peace.

At first, he tried to explain it to himself, to make sense of it in a way that seemed plausible. Alex was certain that she was not some kind of robot or android. The technology involved would be too advanced and sophisticated, in several different areas, to keep secret. From his work on Wall Street, he knew about robotics and artificial body parts, he knew what the best companies could do at present—and not do. They made advances all the time, but they were still light-years from constructing a mouth that could kiss like this woman's mouth did. Alex had no doubt that she was entirely human—in body, at least.

Nor did he believe for an instant that a microprocessor had been implanted in her brain, somehow controlling everything that she did. The necessary hardware and software might be possible, but not the incalculable linkage to brain and body.

A much simpler and more plausible answer came to mind. The explanation had to be pharmacological. Alex knew that drug firms spent a good deal of time and money seeking useful new compounds in the unique plant life of the world's rapidly diminishing rain forests. There was a theory that the zombies of Haitian legend, people who were dead but still ambulatory and who could carry out certain basic functions, were in fact the product of a drug that had its origins in ancient African medical lore.

That was possible. The necessary refinements were possible. With the right resources, one lab with a small staff could do the job. Thus, the knowledge could be controlled and protected, even as it was put to use in a pet project as large as Fado. This was a line of thought with extraordinary implications, but Alex had no particular interest in pursuing them.

He didn't care. It didn't matter *how* a woman could be dead but somehow still living. It was enough that *she was.*

He had sex with her twice more that evening, before travel fatigue caught up with him and he fell asleep in her arms in bed. She was awake when he opened his eyes the next morning, ready and available, still sweet. She sang to him as his body sang inside her. The sound she made was so tiny and elusive it almost seemed like a ghost in his mind.

Two days later, they were still together. They had gone out only to take short walks, to make love in a mossy clearing in the woods and later in a stream-fed rock pool. Alex was satisfied to remain with her at the bungalow most of the time. The world fell away, and he didn't miss it.

When his meals were delivered, she sat patiently with him. She dipped large raw prawns in a fiery sauce and fed them to him, but she neither ate nor drank anything herself.

Enough time had gone by, and Alex had to face the new facts of his life. He loved having sex with this woman, and his desire seemed to increase every day. This was a complete turnabout from his usual experience. For years, he'd been quick to lose interest and move on in search of something, someone new. Now Alex wanted to keep this woman to himself. He felt no urge to sample any of the others on Fado. Besides, if he went off alone, she might hook up with another guest, and then he might never get her back. She was sufficient, she was everything Alex wanted and needed—that was the other huge change in him.

It astonished him that the sex was never the same. The best experiences in his long sexual history now seemed like the merest biological asides. Compared to what he enjoyed with this woman, they vanished in significance. It was as if a previously unknown part of him was suddenly revealed, a primordial dimension of vast power and richness.

"Gina," he said to her. "I want to call you Gina."

She cocked her head and smiled. He was ready again.

He seemed to be flying into her, into the earth and beyond, into space and glittering dust. It was as if he were witnessing the birth of stars and galaxies, the universe itself, a million universes—through the window of his body and Gina. Then Alex would swirl together again within his body. There was something sweet and wonderfully sad about it. His whole being felt blurred and hazy. He would find himself in her arms again, tears in his eyes, his face nestled on her breasts. And he thought—if God had sex, it would be like this.

The world continued to fall away, and he didn't miss it. He had a lot of money back there, somewhere. He had done so much on the Street, and could do so much more—but it meant little. It was numbers flickering on a screen, it was nothing.

There were people in his life. A lot of them, in fact. But how many of them did he care about? They were acquaintances, not true friends. Colleagues, mostly. Women? He went through them on a regular basis, but none had ever tempted him into what might be termed a relationship. His life for the most part was made up of glancing encounters, by his own choice.

Until now. How could he continue—after Fado? Was there anything left worth doing? Was there any place on the planet worth seeing that he hadn't already visited? Alex thought of his splendid apartment on Manhattan's East Side, and he was not happy at the prospect of returning to it. His adult life could be seen as one long, restless search for the new and the exotic, but Alex was tired of that now. Tired of always being driven by pointless expectation to ever-diminishing returns.

He didn't travel to visit museums or stare at scenery. Alex went places to have women. Where next? Who next? But now there was no itinerary, no next stop in the quest—because the quest was over. No other women beckoned in his mind. The awful hunger was gone, replaced by a need to keep what he now had, regardless of what the cost might be.

There was only Gina. Sex with Gina took him right into the secret heart of this world, and beyond, and Alex couldn't bear to think of losing it.

* * *

He tried to get Gina to write, but she apparently had never learned how. He gave her a blank pad and a pen, and asked her to show him where she was from. She drew a crooked circle, and Alex assumed that was meant to be Fado. He kept at it, but she had no skill and very little understanding of what he expected from her, so he soon abandoned the attempt.

It didn't matter. He seldom spoke to her because it seemed as if he had nothing truly worth saying. Besides, they had found their own special language—eye contact, facial movements, the subtle varieties of touch and gesture—which served them better than words ever could. And it wasn't long before Alex started to answer the occasional burbles of sound that Gina made with little clicks and murmurs of his own.

Time was running him down. He could stay on Fado until his funds were exhausted, and then go back to the world, rebuild his fortune, and hope one day to return to Gina. But would she still be there for him? The magic might be lost forever in the long interlude. It might be just as good with any woman on Fado, but he was almost afraid to find out. And the work, the need to make money and do business, would be so much drudgery—assuming that Alex could still concentrate on the task, which was by no means a sure thing anymore.

Or he could stay on Fado permanently, by becoming like Gina. That would force their hand. They could hardly risk letting him wander around back in the regular world if he'd been *transformed.* No doubt they'd be unhappy, no doubt they'd find work for him to do. But Alex would still be on Fado; he'd still have Gina.

The funny part was, it seemed more like choosing life than a form of death. He thought that Gina, in her own way, was so much more alive than he'd ever been. The years spent making money he never cared about, *that* was a zombielike existence. The dreary hours spent hanging out with people like Lawrence in places like Feathers, how vacant and pathetic it all seemed. His quest, that sad and lonely search from Mexico to north Africa to Taiwan and a hundred other forlorn outposts, looking for the next thrill, the next "ultimate" erotic experience—pointless, all of it.

He'd had everything that world could offer. It would not be hard to give it up; he no longer had any use for it, anyway. The real thing—the true *ultimate*—was right in front of him. In a way, his whole adult life had been a rehearsal for this moment. If Alex could make the leap. The decision was easy.

"Gina, would you like me to stay here with you always?" Her face lit up, and she snuggled closer in his arms. "You must help me become like you." She looked up at him, uncertain, perplexed. "It's the only way," Alex said. "You must."

She was gone when he awoke the following day. He stayed in, had brunch and a couple of drinks, and waited for a member of the staff to come along and explain to him that his request was quite out of line, impossible.

But Gina returned alone, late in the afternoon. Alex was so desperate for her by then that he felt like a cloud of fire as he flew across the room to take her in the doorway.

A while later, Gina reached into the pocket of her discarded skirt and came up with a vial of oily brown liquid.

Dear Lawrence, he would write if he could be bothered to sit down and write. *It's true. What I've found on Fado is far better than words can tell. To live forever—abandon life! It isn't hard to do, and the next level is the last—is GOD. And YOU are that GOD. Believe me. And God is sex, and the sex is fantastic! Of course, it takes loads of infrastructure, but that's all laid on here—no bother at all.* Alex started laughing, and he couldn't stop for several moments. Gina didn't know what it was all about, but she joined in his mirth. She smiled so strenuously that she ended up burying her face in his lap. *Tell the crowd at Feathers I said: Get a death! Adieu and adios, Lawrence, old chum. It was fun. Or so it seemed for a while. But the next world is not the hereafter, it's the HERE and NOW. Honest!*

Alex drained the vial. Butterscotchy. He looked at Gina and smiled, but she had her hands clapped over her eyes.

Seventy-four paces to the corner.
Seventy-three the last time.
He would get it right one of these days.
Hey, no big deal!
Alex turned the corner and walked the next lane.
A breeze and a blue sky and always the sun.
But, no, sometimes there was a sudden downpour.
Nice shade trees down this way.
Always something new to notice, very nice, too.
Let the breeze whistle through your teeth.
And sometimes it will, for fun.
Nod hello, why don't you?
A nod and a smile, hello.
Well done, very nice, too.
Eighty-seven paces.
A different matter, this lane.
Hullo hullo, what's this?
Coming his way—Gina?
A nod, a smile, hello.
They pass by each other.
Used to know her, didn't you?

Around another corner, the road.
Aha! Aha! Aha!
A jitney, women getting off.
When you've had a live woman, nothing else will
do.
But they like the younger ones.
Smile and nod, hello in hope.
A breeze and blue sky and always the sun.
But, no, the night, too, the dark.
A nod to the live women.
A smile to the live women.
Me! Me! Me! he sang in the breeze.

EROTOPHOBIA

O'Neil De Noux

She shook out her long brown hair, turned her cobalt-blue eyes toward me, and winked as the slim Negro named Sammy began to unbutton her blouse. She was trying her best not to act nervous. Sammy's fingers shook as he moved from the top button of her green silk blouse to the second button.

I leaned my left shoulder against the brick wall of the makeshift photo studio and watched. The second floor of a defunct shoe factory, the studio was little more than an open room with a hardwood floor, worn brick walls lined with windows overlooking Claiborne Avenue and two large glass skylights above. It smelled musty and faintly of varnish.

The photographer, Sammy's older cousin Joe Cairo, snapped a picture with his Leica. Joe was thin and light-skinned and about twenty-five. Shirtless, he wore blue jeans and no shoes. His skin was already shiny with sweat.

Sammy was also shirtless and shoeless, wearing only a pair of baggy white shorts. His skin was so black it looked like varnished mahogany against Brigid's pale neck.

Yeah, her name was Brigid. Brigid de Loup, white female, twenty-seven, five feet three inches with pouty lips and a gorgeous face. Gorgeous. With her green blouse, she wore a tight black skirt and a pair of open-toe black high heels.

She bit her lower lip as Sammy's fingers moved to the third button, the one between her breasts. She looked at him and raised her arms and put her hands behind her head. Sammy let out a high-pitched noise and moved his fingers down to the fourth button.

My name? Lucien Caye, white male, thirty, six feet even, with brown eyes and wavy brown hair in need of a haircut. I stood there with my arms folded and watched, my snub-nosed .38 Smith and Wesson in a leather holster on my right hip. I'm a private eye.

"You're going to have to pull my blouse out," Brigid told Sammy.

Sammy nodded, his gaze focused on her chest as he pulled her blouse out of her skirt and unbuttoned the final two buttons. He pushed the blouse off her shoulders and dropped it to the floor.

I loosened my black and gold tie and unbuttoned the top button of my dress white shirt, then stuck my hands in the pockets of my pleated black suit pants to straighten out my rising dick.

Brigid looked at me as she turned her back to Sammy, who fumbled with the button at the back of her skirt. Her white bra was lacy and low-cut. Jesus, her breasts looked nice.

I moved over to one of the windows and opened it and flapped my shirt as the air came in through the high branches of the oaks lining Claiborne. The spring of '48 was already a scorcher, yet the air was surprisingly cool and smelled of rain. A typical afternoon New Orleans rainstorm was coming. I could feel it.

Brigid came to me two weeks earlier, in a Cadillac, with diamonds on her fingers and pearls around her neck, and told me she needed a bodyguard.

Yeah. Right.

"I suffer from erotophobia," she said, crossing her legs as she sat in the soft-back chair next to my desk.

"What?"

"It's the fear of erotic experiences."

Yeah. Right.

If someone had told me back when I was a cop that a luscious dish would tell me *that* one day, I'd have looked at them as if they were retarded.

She told me her doctor prescribed "shock therapy," and she needed a bodyguard.

"I want to feel erotic. But I also want to be safe."

She told me she was married and her husband approved of what she had in mind.

"What's that?" I asked.

"Sexy pictures."

Sammy finally got the button undone and unzipped her skirt.

"Go down on your knees," Joe the photographer told Sammy, repositioning himself to their side. I kept behind Joe, to keep out of the pictures.

"Now," Joe said, "pull her skirt down."

Brigid looked back at Sammy and wiggled her ass. Sammy's hands grabbed the sides of the skirt and pulled it down over her hips, his face about four inches from the white panties covering her ass. Brigid turned, put her left hand on his shoulder, and stepped out of her skirt.

"Take her stockings off next," Joe said.

Brigid lifted her left leg and told Sammy he'd need to take her shoes off first. He did, then reached up to unsnap her stockings from her lacy garter belt.

He rolled each stocking down, his sinewy fingers roaming down her legs. Brigid put her arms behind her head again and spread her feet wide for him. She bit her lower lip again.

Sammy, on his haunches now, wiped sweat from his forehead and looked back at his cousin, who told him the bra was next. I felt perspiration working its way down my back. My temples were already damp with sweat.

Brigid started to turn, and Joe told her to do it face-to-face. He switched to his second Leica. Brigid gave Joe a look, a knowing look, and something passed between them. I was sure.

"If you don't mind," Joe added in a shaky voice. "It'll be sexier."

Brigid smiled shyly. "That's what I want." Her voice was husky.

Her chest rose as she took in a deep breath. Sammy stood up and reached around her. It only took him a second to unhook the bra and pull it off, freeing Brigid's nice round breasts.

Oh, God!

Her small nipples were pointed. Her breasts rose with her breathing. Sammy stared at them from less than a foot away. He blinked and said, "Wow."

Brigid looked at me and smiled, and I could see a nervous tic in her cheek. She took in another deep breath, her breasts rising again.

Joe stepped up and tapped Sammy on the shoulder and told him to go down on his knees again. "Now," Joe said, "take her panties off."

Joe hurriedly set up for more shots.

Sammy tucked his fingers into the top of her panties. Brigid leaned her head back to face the skylights and closed her eyes. Joe snapped away, and my dick was a diamond cutter now.

Sammy pulled her panties down, his nose right in front of her bush. She stepped out of them, and he leaned back and stared at her thick pubic hair, a shade darker than the long hair on her pretty head. Brigid turned slowly and pointed her ass at Sammy, who reached up and unhooked her garter belt and pulled it away.

"OK. Stop," Joe said, sitting on the floor. He pulled his camera bag to him and unloaded both Leicas before loading them again.

Brigid slowly turned to face me. Her face was serious now and flushed. I moved my gaze down her body and almost came just looking at her. She winked at me when I looked back at her face and rolled her shoulders slightly, her breasts swaying with her movement.

Joe told Sammy to stand up when the cameras were loaded. He took several pictures of them standing face-to-face, looking at each other, and then asked them to stand side-by-side.

"No touching," Brigid said, reminding Joe of the ground rules. He nodded and had them sit next, side-by-side with their legs straight out. Brigid leaned back on her hands, and Sammy leered at her bush.

Then Joe had them sit cross-legged facing each other. I felt my dick stir again when she leaned back and shook out her hair, and the light from the skylight seemed to illuminate her body. God, she looked so sexy with her breasts pointing and her legs open and all her bush exposed.

Joe asked Brigid to stand and put her hands on her hips and move her feet apart as Sammy remained sitting and stared at her pussy, which was at eye level now.

Brigid looked at Joe when he moved her, his hand on her hip. They exchanged brief warm smiles as he moved her.

Sammy let out a deep breath, and Brigid laughed. I was breathing pretty heavy myself, too. Jesus, what a scene. Joe moved them around in different positions and snapped furiously and switched cameras again.

He had them sit again and entwined their legs. Sammy's dark skin was in stark contrast with Brigid's fair skin. Joe moved in for close-ups of Brigid's chest and moved down to snap her bush. She looked at him and moved her knees apart as she sat.

"Yeah. Yeah," Joe said, snapping away. "Don't stop."

Joe pulled Brigid up by the hand and had her stand over Sammy, straddling his outstretched legs as he sat. Then Joe had her sit on Sammy's legs, her legs open as she faced Sammy.

"Now lean back on your hands," Joe said.

Brigid leaned back, her legs open, her pussy wide open to Sammy, and Joe behind him snapping away, and me peeking at her pink slit. She was hairy. I like that in a woman. I especially liked the delicate hairs just outside her pussy.

Jesus. What a sight!

She looked at Joe for a long second, staring at him the way a woman does when she's getting screwed. She wasn't looking at the camera, and Sammy was just a prop. She looked at Joe. The look on her face was for him. It was a subtle move, but I caught it.

Joe snapped at a furious pace.

Brigid finally climbed off Sammy, turned and walked to the bathroom, and closed the door behind her. She walked purposefully, as if she had trouble moving her legs.

Sammy lay all the way down and panted, his chest slick with sweat now. Joe picked up his cameras and hurriedly reloaded both. I opened another window. The air was misty now and felt damp and cool on my face. I looked down on the avenue at the tops of the passing cars and then looked straight out at the dark branches and green leaves of the oaks.

I wondered what the passersby would think if they knew what was going on up here.

The bathroom door opened, and Brigid came out, walking more steadily. She stepped over to her purse and took out her compact, touching up her face with powder, reapplying dark red lipstick.

She smiled at Joe and said, "No pictures right now, OK?"

He nodded.

Brigid moved over to Sammy and said, "Stand up and put your hands on your head."

"Huh?"

She bent over and grabbed his right hand and pulled him up. Then she lifted his hands and put them on his head, the way we did to the Krauts we took prisoner outside Rome.

She yanked Sammy's shorts down, pulled them off his feet, and tossed them aside. He wore no underwear. His long, thin dick stood straight up like a flag pole. Brigid smiled and looked Sammy in the eyes.

She reached down and grabbed Sammy's dick. He jumped. Slowly, she worked her hand up and down his long dick. Sammy moaned.

Brigid looked at me and said, "I don't want y'all to think I'm just a tease."

Jesus, a white woman giving a Negro a hand job. Unbefuckinlievable. I figured she knew it wouldn't bother me in the way it would bother most white boys. She had me pegged from day one, I guess, from the way I treated Joe and the Negroes we'd come across during her posing sessions.

Brigid looked at Joe, and it was there again, that come-hither sexy look, but only for a moment. She bent over, her legs stiff, her ass straight up, and leaned over and kissed the tip of Sammy's cock. He rocked on his feet, and she increased her jerking motion until he came. She caught it with her free hand and wiped Sammy's cum on his chest when he finished. Then she turned to Joe and asked if he wanted a hand job. He shook his head.

She looked at me and said, "Need some help with those blue balls?"

I shook my head slowly and watched her go back into the bathroom. She left the door open this time and washed her hands. She toweled off, left the towel, and walked straight back to me. She put her hands on my chest, leaned up, and gave me a fluttery kiss across my lips.

Then she went over to Joe and gave him the same fluttery kiss. I could see him squirm and then close his eyes. He smiled warmly at her when she pulled away.

"Come on," she said. "Let's finish these rolls."

Joe told Sammy to go wash off. When he returned, Joe posed them together naked. The climax of the shooting had Brigid straddling Sammy's legs again as they sat, her pussy wide open and Sammy's dick up and hard again.

When Joe ran out of film again, Brigid got up and told me, "Time to get the film, big boy. I hope you counted the rolls."

I had.

Joe unloaded both cameras and gave me the six rolls of film. We watched Brigid dress. Sammy went into the bathroom. Brigid and I left before he came out.

Sitting in my prewar 1940 DeSoto, her legs crossed and her skirt riding high on her naked thighs, Brigid smiled at me and said, "Next time we'll shoot in a cemetery."

"Yeah?" I could smell her perfume again in the confines of the car.

"Joe knows some gravediggers at Cypress Grove. Posing naked among the crypts, in front of a captive audience . . . alive and dead, will be so delicious."

It didn't take a fuckin' genius to figure the one thing this woman didn't have was erotophobia. I still hadn't figured her angle.

"When did Joe tell you about the gravediggers?"

She winked at me. "When I called him yesterday. That was when he told me he had his cousin lined up for today's session.

The rain came down hard now, and the windshield was fogging as I tooled the DeSoto up Claiborne, away from the Negro section called Treme toward uptown, where the rich lily-whites lived in their Victorian and neoclassical and Greek Revival homes. I cracked my window and felt the rain flutter my hair.

Brigid leaned against the passenger door and watched me. Her dress was so high I could almost see her ass the way she rolled her hips. She eye-fucked me all the way home, ogling me every time I looked her way.

Jesus, she was so fuckin' pretty and so fuckin' sexy and so fuckin' nasty. She hired me to make sure no one raped her. That was the last thing a man would do with a woman like her. At least, that was the last thing I'd do. I'd want her to come to me, wrap those legs around me, and fuck me back.

"Want to come in and meet my husband?" she asked when I pulled up in front of her white Greek Revival home on Audubon Boulevard.

"No, that's OK."

"He's waiting for me to tell him what it was like." She raised her purse and added, "And to develop the film." Her husband had a built-in darkroom.

She pulled a white envelope from her purse and handed it to me. Cash. She always paid me in small bills. I actually got paid to watch her get naked and pose with her legs open. Tell me America isn't a great country.

Brigid opened the door, stopped, moved across the seat, and kissed me. I felt her tongue as she French-kissed me in front of her big house, and I thought I would come right there.

I watched her hips as she walked away, barefoot up her front walk to the large front gallery with its nine white columns. Her high heels dangling from her left hand, she turned back and waved at me and went in the front cut-glass door of her big house.

The rain came down in torrents that evening. Standing inside the French doors of my apartment balcony, I watched it move in sheets across Cabrini Playground on Barracks Street. The oak branches waved in the torrent. The wind shook the thick rubbery leaves and white petals of the large magnolias. I looked beyond the playground at the slick, tilted roofs and red brick chimneys of the French Quarter. The old part of town always looked older in the rain.

I leaned against the glass door and looked down at my DeSoto parked against the curb. The glass felt cool against my cheek. The street wasn't flooded yet, at least. I took a sip of scotch, felt it burn its way down to my empty belly, and closed the drapes.

I sat back on my sofa, in front of the revolving fan, and closed my eyes and remembered the first time we went out to shoot pictures. It was in Cabrini Playground. It was a real turn-on watching Brigid sit in a tight red skirt, sit so Joe could see up her dress and take pictures of her white panties.

The second time was in City Park, where she stripped down to her bra and panties to pose beneath an umbrella of oak branches. Two workers came across us, and Brigid liked that. She liked an audience. Joe moved us to the back lagoon for some topless pictures, only some fishermen saw us and got pissed at the half-naked white girl with the black boy, so we had to bail out.

My dick was a diamond cutter again as I sat on my sofa. I finished my scotch, readjusted my hard-on, knowing the only relief I could feel would be in a hot washrag.

I closed my eyes and remembered the two whores we came across just outside Rome, the day before I was wounded. The girls were brunettes, about twenty, a little on the plump side with pale white skin. They fucked the entire platoon and got up to wave good-bye to us early the next morning, when we moved out.

My doorbell rang.

I stood slowly and walked down the stairs to the door. Through the transom above the louvered front door, I saw the top of a yellow cab. I peeked out the door, and Brigid was there, her hair dripping in the rain.

I opened the door, and she turned and waved to the cabby, who drove off up Barracks.

Brigid stepped past me and stood dripping in the foyer. Wearing the same clothes she had for the photo session, she shivered and cupped her hands against her chest, her head bent forward. I closed the door.

I put my hand under her chin and lifted her face, and she blinked those cobalt eyes at me. They were red now, with a blue semicircle bruise under her left eye.

"Pipi hit me," she said, her lower lip quivering. "Can I come up?"

I took her right hand and brought her up and straight into my bathroom. I grabbed the box of kitchen matches from the medicine cabinet and lit the gas wall heater. Standing, I turned as Brigid dropped her bra.

"Don't leave," she said, bending over to run a bath. "You've seen it all."

I put the lid down on the commode and sat and watched her take her clothes off. She smiled weakly at me, her lips still shaking as she climbed into the tub. The water continued running as she sank back.

"How about some coffee?"

"You have any Scotch?"

I stood and looked down at her. Her eyes were closed, and the water moved dreamily over her naked body, and she looked so damn sexy.

I poured us each a double Johnnie Walker Red and went back in.

A silent hour and two drinks later, as well as two hard-ons, she stood up in the tub and asked me to pass her a towel. In the bright light of the bathroom, her skin looked white-pink. She dried herself and wrapped a fresh towel around her chest just above her breasts. She took my hand and led me out to the sofa.

She poured us both another Scotch, left hers on the coffee table next to the bottle, and turned her back to me to lie across my lap as I sat straight up. I had to adjust my dick again, and she knew and smiled at me.

"I'll take care of that," she said softly, and closed her eyes.

With no makeup, with her hair still damp and getting frizzy, with the mouse under her eye—she was still gorgeous. Some women are like that, plain-knockdown-gorgeous.

After a while, she told me that Pipi, that's her husband, couldn't get it up when she came in and told him about what she'd done. She even dug out the previous pictures and went down on him, but he was as limp as a Republican's brain.

Then he hit her, punched her actually, and kicked her out, shoved her out into the rain.

"At least he called a cab for me." She opened her cobalt-blues and blinked up at me. "Guess you figured he's the one with erotophobia. Pipi's the one afraid of erotic experiences."

No shit.

She leaned up, reached over and grabbed her drink, and downed it with one gulp. I got up a second later and moved to the balcony doors. I didn't hear the rain anymore, so I cracked them. It was still drizzling, so I left them open and went back to the sofa. I felt the coolness immediately. It was nice.

She settled her head back in my lap and closed her eyes again. The towel had risen, and I could see a hint of her bush now. I reached over and picked up my drink and finished it, then put the glass back on the coffee table.

A while later, she sighed and turned her face toward me, and I could see by her even breathing she was asleep. The towel opened when she turned, and I looked at her body again.

I wanted to fuck her so badly. I climbed out from under her head, stood, and stretched. I reached down and scooped Brigid into my arms. I took her into my bedroom and laid her on the bed. She sighed again, and I leaned over and kissed her lips gently.

I grabbed the second pillow and went back out to the sofa and poured myself another stiff one. I was feeling kinda woozy by then, anyway, so I lay back on the sofa and tried some deep breathing with my eyes closed.

There was a movie I saw where a private eye turned Veronica Lake down because it ain't good business to sleep with clients. Fuck that shit. Brigid won't have to ask me again.

I pulled off my socks and gulped down the rest of my drink and lay back on the pillow and closed my eyes. I tried deep breathing and letting my mind float.

And just as I was drifting, I realized it wasn't Veronica Lake. It was Ann Sheridan. Or was it Barbara Stanwyck in a blond wig?

The banging of the French doors woke me. I sat up too quickly and felt dizzy and had to lean back on the sofa. It was pitch outside and nearly as dark inside. Lightning flashed, and the rainy wind raised the drapes like floating ghosts. A roll of thunder made the old building shiver.

The wind felt cool on my face. I started to rise and saw her standing next to the sofa. I sank back as lightning flashed again, illuminating her naked body in white light. I felt her move up to me and felt her arms on my shoulders as she climbed on me. She said something, but the thunder drowned it.

I felt the weight of her body on my lap as she ripped at my shirt. I tried to help, but she tore it, and we both pulled it off. She grabbed my belt and slapped my hand when I tried to help. Rising, she shoved my pants and underwear down and then sank back on me.

I felt her bush up against my dick, her mouth searching my face for my lips. Our tongues worked against each other as I raised my hands for those breasts.

She moved her hips up and down slowly as we kissed. I felt the wetness between her legs. She rose high and reached down with her hand to guide my dick into her. She sank down on it and shivered and then fucked me like I've never been fucked before.

And she talked nasty.

"Oh, fuck me. Come on. Fuck me. Oh, God, I love your dick. I love it. Fuck me. Yes. Yes. Oh, God."

I like it when women call me God, even if it's just for a little while.

She bounced on me. "More," she said. "More!"

Hell, there was no more. She had it all.

She screamed, and I came in her in long spurts, and she cried out and held on to my neck. Then she collapsed on me, and it took a while for our breathing to return to normal.

I looked over her shoulder as lightning flashed again and saw the wet floor next to the open balcony doors. The wind whipped up again and felt so damn good on our hot bodies. The thunder rolled once more and sounded farther away.

When I could gather enough strength, I kicked off my pants and shorts. I lifted her and carried her back into the bedroom. I climbed on her and fucked her nice and long the way second fucks should be, deep and time-consuming.

She wrapped her legs around my waist and her arms around my neck and kissed me and kissed me. She was one great, loving kisser. She made noises, sexy noises, but didn't talk nasty. She just fucked me back in long, hip-grinding pumps.

After I came, I stayed in her until her gyrating hips slipped my dick out. I rolled on my back and pulled her to me, and she snuggled her face in the crook of my neck, her hot body pressed against me.

Every once in a while, I felt the breeze come in and try to cool us.

She was still pressed against me when the daylight woke me. I slipped out of bed, relieved myself, and pulled on a fresh pair of boxers before brushing my teeth. She lay on her stomach, the sheet wrapped around her right leg, her long hair covering her face.

I went to the kitchen and started up a pot of coffee-and-chicory, bacon and eggs. She came in just as I was putting the bacon next to the eggs on the two plates on my small white Formica table.

Naked, she walked up and planted a wet one on my

lips. She leaned back and brushed her hair out of her face and said, "I used your toothbrush."

"Sit down."

I went back and put the bacon pan in the sink and poured us two cups of strong coffee.

"You don't have a barrette, do you?" She moved around the table and sat.

"Huh?"

"Left over from a previous fuck?"

"Yeah. Right." I put her coffee in front of her and sat across the table and ate my bacon and eggs and watched her breasts as she lifted her fork to eat.

OK, I looked at her face, too, and stared into those turquoise eyes that glittered back at me as she ate. But mostly I looked at her tits. Round and perfectly symmetrical, they were so fuckin' pretty.

I can't explain it. Tits have a power over men we can't explain. Women will never understand. We have no fuckin' idea ourselves.

The eggs and bacon weren't bad. The coffee was nice and strong. After, we took a bath together. Soaping each other and rinsing off, we stayed in the tub until the water cooled, and that felt even better than the warm water.

"Will you take me home? I don't want to go alone."

Brigid stood in the bathroom, her belly against the sink as she applied makeup to her face. In her bra and panties, she had her butt out.

I told her I'd bring her home.

"I want to pick up some things. Will you take me to my mother's after?"

"Sure."

I finished my coffee, put the cup on the nightstand, and then dressed myself.

She came out and ran her hand across my shoulders as she passed behind me to pick up her skirt.

I finished tying my sky-blue tie, the one with the palm tree on it, and ran my fingers down the crease of my pleated blue suit pants.

"Nice shoes," she said when I slipped on my two-tone black-and-white wingtips. Women always noticed shoes.

I finished in time to watch Brigid finish. I liked watching women dress, nearly as much as watching them undress.

I grabbed my suit coat and black hat on the way out.

"You're not bringing a gun?"

"You gonna get naked in front of any strange men on the way home?"

"No."

"Then I don't need to shoot anybody, do I?"

Pipi's black Packard was in the driveway. I parked behind it and followed Brigid in. I waited in the marble-floored foyer, my hat in hand, and watched Brigid's hips as she moved up the large spiral staircase.

I figured I was about to meet old Pipi, the fuckin' wife beater himself. I hate men that hit women. Hate 'em.

Just as I peeked in at the Audubon prints on the walls of the study, Brigid screamed upstairs. I took the stairs three at a time and followed the screams up to a large bedroom with giant flamingo lamps, blond furniture, and a huge round bed with the body of a man on it. The man's head lay in a pool of blood.

Brigid had her back pressed up against a large chifforobe in the right corner of the room, next to the drapes. She covered her face with her hands and screamed again.

The man lay on his side. I leaned over to look at his face. I recognized Pipi de Loup from the society page, even with the unmistakable dull look of death on his waxen face and his eyes blackened from the concussion of the bullet. The back of his head was a mass of dyed black hair and brain tissue.

Brigid turned around and started crying.

I looked at the mirror above the long dresser, looked into my own eyes, and felt my stomach bottom out. I saw the word "sap" written across my face.

I moved over and grabbed Brigid's hand and led her out of the bedroom and down the stairs and out to my car. I opened the passenger door and told her to sit. Then I went next door and called the police.

Brigid was still crying when I got back to the DeSoto. I leaned against the rear fender and waited. Two patrolmen arrived first. I knew neither. I pointed at the house. The taller went in, the other took out his notebook and asked me my name.

A half hour and fifty questions later, Lieutenant Frenchy Capdeville pulled his black prowl car behind my car. He stepped out and shook his head at me, took off his brown suit coat, and tossed it back in the prowl car.

Short and wiry, with curly black hair and a pencil-thin mustache, Capdeville looked like Zorro—with a flat Cajun nose. He waltzed past me and stood next to the open door of my car and looked at Brigid's crossed legs. He pulled the ever-present cigarette from his mouth, flicked ashes on the driveway, and looked at me.

"You stay put."

He reached his hand in and asked Brigid to step into the house with him. He left a rookie patrolman with an Irish name to guard me while other detectives arrived, one with a camera case, and went into the mansion.

I looked up at the magnolia tree and tried counting the white blossoms but lost count after twenty. At least the big tree, along with the two even larger oaks, kept the sun off me as I waited. I looked around at the neighbors who came out periodically to sneak a peek at the side show.

A detective arrived and waved at me on the way in. He was in my class at the academy. He was the only white boy I ever knew named Spade.

Willie Spade came out of the house an hour later and offered me a cigarette.

"I don't smoke."

"I forgot." He shrugged and lit up with his Zippo. About an inch smaller than me, with short carrot-red hair and too many freckles to count, Spade had deep-set brown eyes.

"I need to search your car, OK?"

He meant, *do I have your consent?* I told him sure, go ahead, but didn't expect him to pat me down first.

No offense, he said. No problem, I said.

While he was digging in my backseat, he said we needed to go to the office for my statement.

"I'd like to drive," I said. "I'd rather not leave my car here."

Spade turned and wiped sweat from his brow. "You can drive us both."

"No," I said. "I didn't touch a fuckin' thing in the house. She opened the door, and I didn't touch the railing on the way up the stairs. The only thing I touched was her arm, when I dragged her out."

Spade narrowed his deep-set eyes. "You touched more of her than her arm."

I nodded and leaned back in the hardwood folding chair in the small interview room. I looked out the lone window at the old wooden buildings across South White Street from the Detective Bureau Office on the second floor of the concrete Criminal Courts

Building at Tulane and Broad. A gray pigeon landed on the window ledge and blinked at me.

"We found the murder weapon on the floor next to the bed."

"Yeah?"

"A Colt .38. The missus says it's Pipi's gun. He kept it in the nightstand next to the bed. The drawer was open."

"I didn't notice." I picked up the cup of coffee on the small table and took a sip. Cold.

"The doors and windows were all locked," Spade said, watching me carefully for a reaction.

"What time did the doctor say he died?"

"Between two and four A.M. Give or take an hour." I nodded.

Spade leaned back in his chair and put his arms behind his head, and I saw perspiration marks on his yellow dress shirt. His brown tie was loosened.

"So you're her alibi, and she's yours," he said.

I nodded again and felt that hollow kick in my stomach.

There was a knock on the door, and a hand reached in and waved Spade out. A couple minutes later, Spade returned with a fresh cup of java, along with my wingtips. He dropped my shoes on the floor and put the coffee in front of me. He pulled my keys out and put them on the table before sitting himself.

"Find anything?" I said as I leaned down and pulled my shoes on.

"Nope." Spade didn't sound disappointed. He sounded a little relieved. He put his elbows up on the table and told me how they knew the killer came in the kitchen door. It rained last night. The killer came in through the back with muddy shoes, wiped them on the kitchen mat, and still tracked mud all the way up to the bedroom, then tracked mud right back out.

"That's why we had to search your pad and office."
He explained the obvious. They had to check out all
my shoes, and everything else in my fuckin' life.

"Let himself in with a key?" I asked when I sat up.

"Or." Spade shrugged. "The door was unlocked,
and the killer flipped the latch on his way out, locking
it. We have some prints, but smudges mostly."

I nodded.

Spade let out a tired sigh and said, "You know the
score. Whoever finds the body is automatically the
first suspect."

"Until you prove they didn't do it. I know."

I didn't say—especially when it's the wife and the
man who's fuckin' the wife.

"I'll be right back," Spade said, and left me with my
fresh coffee and my view of South White Street.

A while later, just as I was thinking how an interview room would be better for the police without a
window, the door opened, and Frenchy Capdeville
walked in with Spade. Capdeville took the chair.
Spade leaned against the wall.

Capdeville smiled at me and asked if I knew
anything about the pictures they found in Mr. de
Loup's darkroom. I told them everything. Fuck, they
knew it anyway.

I ended with a question. "Did your men sniff my
sheets?"

Capdeville smiled again. "Who found the photographer?"

I waited.

"You come up with a nigger photographer for her,
or did she?"

"She told me Pipi found him."

Capdeville blew smoke in my face and gave me a
speech, the usual one. I could leave for now, but they
weren't finished with me yet. They'd be back with
more questions, he said, flicking ashes on the dirty

floor. He made a point to tell me they weren't finished with Mrs. de Loup by a long shot. Her lawyer was on his way, and they expected a long interview.

"One more thing," Capdeville said, looking me in the eyes. "You have any idea who did it?"

"Nope," I lied, looking back at him with no expression in my eyes.

They let me go.

I drove around until dark, checking to see if I was followed so many times I got a neck ache. I meandered through the narrow streets of the Quarter, through the twisting streets of the Faubourg Marigny and over to Treme, where I parked the DeSoto on Dumaine Street.

I jumped a fence and moved through backyards, jumping two more fences to come up on Joe Cairo's studio from the rear. As I moved up the back stairs, I thought how much this reminded me of a bad detective movie. Easy to figure and hard to forget.

I knocked on the back door. A yellow light came on, and Joe's face appeared behind the glass top of the wooden door. His jaw dropped. It actually dropped.

"Come on, open up," I told him. "You don't have much time."

He opened the door and gave me a real innocent look, and I knew for sure he did it. I breezed past him, telling him to lock the door. I followed the lights to a backroom bed with a suitcase and camera case on it.

"Going somewhere?" I sat in the only seat in the room, a worn green sofa.

Joe stood in the doorway. He looked around the room but not at me.

I put my hands behind my head and watched him carefully as I said, "She's gonna roll over on you."

Joe looked around the room again, his fingers twitching.

"If I figured it out, you know Homicide will. They're a lot better at this."

Joe started bouncing on his toes, his hands at his sides.

"They found the pictures. She'll bat those big blue eyes at them, roll a tear down those pretty cheeks, and tell them, 'Look at the evil things my husband made me do . . . with a nigger.'"

Joe stopped bouncing and glared at me.

"Don't be a sap," I told him. "She'll tie you up in a neat package. Cops like neat packages, cases tied up in a bow. Get out now. Leave. Go to California or Mexico. Just leave, or you'll be in the electric chair before you know it."

Joe leaned his left shoulder against the door frame. "There's nothing for her to tell."

"OK." I stood up. "Wait here. They'll be here soon." I looked at the half-packed suitcase and said, "Don't tell me you thought she was gonna run off with you."

Joe puffed out his cheeks.

"Look around. Look how you live. You saw how she lived." I stepped up to his face. "She used you, just like she used me."

Joe squinted at me. "What you mean, she used you?"

"She came over last night."

Joe shook his head. "She went to her mama's."

"Come on, wise up. She fucked us both. Only you're gonna take the hot squat."

Joe balled his hands into fists.

I looked him hard in the eyes. "What's the matter with you? You killed a fuckin' white man. You're history."

He blinked.

"Forget her, man."

I could see the wheels turning behind his eyes. He

opened his mouth, shut it, then said, "He beat his wife."

"I know." That was the thing that tipped the scales, that brought me to Treme, instead of just going home. I hate wife beaters.

I lowered my voice. "You killed a white man. You're in a world of shit, man."

"How . . . how did you . . . know?"

How? It was a gut feeling. It was the way Brigid looked at him, the way he looked back. It was that look of intimacy. Joe was the obvious killer, so obvious it was obscene.

"It had to be you," I told him, "because it wasn't me."

Joe blinked, and I could see his eyes were wet.

"You willing to turn her in? You willing to tell the cops she was in on it?"

He looked at me and shook his head. "I'd never do that."

"Then you better beat feet. Go to California. Change your name. But get out now."

Joe looked hesitatingly at his suitcase.

"Forget her," I said forcefully.

"Forget her?"

"Like a bad dream."

I stepped past him. I knew if I was caught here, I'd be in a world of shit, too.

Joe grabbed my arm but let go as soon as I turned. He looked down at my feet and said, "Why you helpin' me?"

"Because I'm more like you than I'm like them."

I'm not sure it registered, not completely.

"You're not getting rid of me to keep her for yourself," he said in a voice that told me he didn't believe that.

"She's done with both of us, man."

I went out the way I came, my heart pounding in

my chest as I jumped the fences. I slipped behind the wheel of the DeSoto and looked around before starting it.

I took the long way home.

It's night again. The French doors of my balcony are open, but there is no breeze. I'm on my fourth Scotch, or is it my fifth? I'm waiting for Capdeville and Spade.

They'll be here soon, asking about Joe Cairo, wondering where the fuck he went.

I'll tell them I drove around and went to Cairo's on a hunch. Figuring someone must have seen a white man jumping fences, I'll tell them I tried to sneak up on Cairo, but he was gone.

They'll do a lot of yelling, a lot of guessing, but won't be able to pin anything on me. After all, I didn't do it. I was too busy fucking the wife at the time of the murder.

I close my eyes for a moment, and the Scotch has me thinking that maybe, just maybe, she'll come. But I know better.

Rising from the sofa, I take my drink into the bedroom and look at the messed-up bed.

God, she was so fuckin' beautiful it hurt.

I sit on the edge of my bed. It still smells like sex. I'm sure, if I look hard, I'll find some of her pubic hair scattered in the sheets. That's all I have left—the debris of sex, the memories, and the fuckin' heartache.

BONUS NOTCHES

Nancy Holder

So this is how it would go with us, I mean the honesty level we had and depth of camaraderie we actually felt for each other in those early, innocent days. For example, Tutu would come over in these ludicrous clothes, you know, those spangly bra things, tight pants and heels, slut clothes, and do a hokey-pokey circle, va-voom, va-voom, and I would say, "No, honest, Tooter, it does not make you look fat. Really."

Or she would buy one of those incredibly tacky figurines you get in magazines. You know, like, the limited edition of "The Little Beggar Girl," complete with a real fabric scarf and some miniature bread crusts? I mean, it's to gag, but I would smile and say, "Oh, how *adorable!*"

Girlfriends will lie through their teeth to each other sometimes just to be nice, and sometimes because, frankly, it makes you feel superior to say, "You look great," when in fact they look like hell but don't have the sense to know it.

But Tutu—we all called her that because she used

to take ballet lessons, and they wear those skirt things?—Tutu actually looked pretty good in almost everything she bought, and never like some old hag chasing after her youth even though officially the things she bought were years—decades, centuries— too young for her.

Bitch.

Men do not understand women at all. I know that, and I can accept it. I have run with it and worked with it, and now, oh, well, that's the way it plays. We run with the wolves because we are wolves. Underneath all the big sad-eyed velvet paintings, we're just as fierce as and probably more competitive than men. Which has got to be why Tutu and I started the Game, even though we blamed it on our husbands.

It began one Friday night when they were working late. They worked late a lot, and when they weren't working, they were playing poker or bowling or jawing in some crowded, smoky bar about hunting season. So, like we always did, we went to a movie. I cannot tell you how many movies I saw with Tutu.

I can't remember what this one was, but it had some hunky guy in it without his shirt on, and we both sighed, "Yum," as we chomped our popcorn. I got a little depressed. I knew it was all fantasy and that even if Bobby worked half the hours he worked and stopped playing poker and bowling altogether, he was still not going to float through the door in slow motion and *take* me on a bearskin rug. I had no notion at all where you even bought a bearskin rug; it was probably illegal now, just like ivory.

After the movie, rather than facing our empty houses, we decided to have a drink. I was in one of those stylish baggy outfits Bobby called "mom dresses," even though we didn't have any children, and Tooter had on one of her regulation boob-crushing, fanny-molding enchantress uniforms. In the same strip mall as the fourplex was a new place called the Stampede, took over the lease on the Yum City ice cream place. It looked to be country-western, and we looked at each other and shrugged. What the hell.

So in we swung, Thelma and Louise, me regretting it instantly, because you know what you find in a cowboy bar—women dressed like the Toot, tight, tight, tight—and I felt like I should take a corner table, order a glass of milk, and start grading English papers or something.

A waitress in a frilly blouse and short, tasseled denim skirt gave us a nod and told us'all to sit anyol'whar. We both giggled under our breath at her accent, and Tutu led the way to a sort of side-pocket table near the dance floor. Four or five couples were doing country-western dance steps in a circle, kind of like folk dancers on Valium, lightly bouncing, moving forward, twirling raht slow and easy.

"Longnecks," Tutu said to another waitress, and I perked up a little, because, after all, we were there to have medium fun, not big fun, and it would be pretty easy to have medium fun here. When you're married, you don't cruise, you just paddle.

We were starting our beers when a tall and rather good-looking man in a black cowboy hat and tight jeans sidled over to our table and smiled at us both. He said, "Evenin', ladies," like we were in Dallas, Texas, and not Byrd, Kansas. He asked Tutu to dance.

She was startled. I don't think it occurred to either one of us that men might hit on us, which is a pathetic statement, to be sure, but true. We hadn't discussed any ground rules. She threw me a look, and I shrugged, "I don't mind," although I did. I hated being the one not asked. As I watched them go off, I remembered the wallflower days of my youth and felt a flash of anger. He might have asked *me* if I'd been dressed like a hooker, too.

So I sat there and drank my beer and decided I would go home and vacuum after all.

But halfway through the song, a tall guy in a brown cowboy hat and tight jeans sidled up to the table and asked me to two-step. I said, "I don't know how," standing as I said it so he would be forced to reply, "That's OK, I'll teach you," even if he didn't want to.

Tutu looked happy to see me out there, and I gave her a little ho-hum wave like I did this kind of thing all the time. Then her guy dropped her back off at the table, and my guy said, "We really didn't have that long to dance," so we went through another. I don't know if we two-stepped or what, but whatever it was was fun. He smelled good, and his body was tight, tight, tight, and I enjoyed myself thoroughly, from the tips of my boobs to the crotch of my panties, though of course I didn't show it.

Then I ended up back at the table just as Tutu got asked again.

Then *I* ended up on the dance floor as Tutu got escorted back to the table.

We started keeping score on our paper beer coasters (which we each had a couple of), a notch per cowboy.

"Whoever gets the most, the other one pays for our beers," Tutu announced, and I agreed because I was one notch ahead at the time.

So it became a game: trying to snag one more dance, one more guy, until we were flirting and laughing and, finally, asking guys to dance.

We were out there bouncing with the rest of the hey-howdies in their Midwest cowboy getups, and then the music slowed way, way down, and Tutu's dance partner held out his arms. He was a little blitzed, and she was blitzed, and with a strange, wild smile at me she slid into his arms. He bent her slightly backward—he was as tall as a Marlboro Man billboard—and their crotches rolled against each other.

"That looks like a good idea," my partner drawled, and before I could react (I think, or at least, I keep telling myself it was before), I was in his arms, against his chest, his tight stomach, and his hard-on.

Oh, God. Oh, Bobby. I tried to think of him, but the man dipped me backward, smiling, and his white teeth blinded me. Nervously, I said, "Oh, you're a good dancer."

He pulled me back up. "I'm good at a lot of things," he said, and I know it sounds corny or sleazy or what, but at the time my knees buckled. "Whoah-ho." He laughed. "You OK?"

"Haven't had any complaints," I shot back, and his smile grew.

I looked over at Tutu, who was watching me and looking a little miffed. Then she turned to her guy, raised up her face, and he kissed her. She opened her mouth. There was tongue action. It grew more intense. I thought she was going to swallow the damn thing. She slid her glance at me as if to say, *I win.*

"Want another beer?" my guy asked, and I thought about saying, "That ain't the longneck I hanker for, sheriff," but I nodded. My face was hot. Tutu was going too far.

But a beer (or maybe two) later, I was in the parking lot with Dwayne (that was his name), and my mom dress was unbuttoned, my bra unhooked, and he was cupping my breasts and grinding his hard-on against my wet-on.

"Come on, honey, please," he whispered. "I'll make you happy."

I had not been that turned-on since the drive-in in high school, with Bobby, of course, and not going all the way, ever. We would steam up the windows and crush together on the backseat, our underwear pulled down around our thighs so he could rub against me and save himself from blue balls without compromising my virginity. What I got out of this was intense excitement but no climax, and hadn't even known until two years after we were married that women actually did that.

Now I was excited beyond belief, panting, oblivious, reckless, and when he opened the door of his truck, I murmured something about too much beer, which he ignored, and then he was on his knees in the gravel, my jeans and panties were around my ankles, and he was giving me the best oral sex I had ever had in my entire life.

I wondered how Tutu was doing, and *what* she was doing. She wouldn't go this far, I thought smugly, even though I was scared to death and wracked with guilt, even as Dwayne climbed on top of me and, with one strong thrust, destroyed my wedding vows.

"But it was worth it," Tutu insisted as we sat in my kitchen over coffee the next day. Our husbands were at work. As usual. Afterward they had a poker night at Sam's. "At least, it was for me." She stretched like a trampy little cat.

"I can't believe I did it," I said miserably.

"Well, I can believe *I* did." She shifted meaningfully in the chair and grinned. "I'm so sore. We did it three times."

"What? You didn't tell me that last night." I frowned and poured myself more coffee.

"Three times," she crowed. "He just wouldn't quit." She stirred her cream in lazily. "Damn, girl, if you're going to commit adultery, you might as well get a complete sin workout."

"We did it twice," I said, even though we hadn't.

Tutu raised her cup and drank. "Then I win," she said. "You owe me ten bucks."

"No way!"

"That includes tax and tip." She held out her hand. "We made a bet. The most notches wins. That was me. I won."

I narrowed my eyes at her. "This round, anyway."

She blinked, and then she laughed. "OK, this round."

So that night we went to a bar farther out of town and picked up two more guys. It's easy when you're a little older. God, I wish I'd known how simple most men are when I was in high school. I probably wouldn't have married Bobby, would've waited to snag someone else. Oh, well.

I won that round. Yes.

Then we moved on to Round Three of the Game: not just how many times but how many positions. Then Round Four: how many different places. Then Round Five: how many different guys.

Round Six: how many men at the same time.

Round Seven: how many women at one time.

Round Eight: how many of *everybody* at one time.

And how can I describe the mind-blasting combination of shame and power that zinged through me with each round and each notch? Some man thrusting into me, some woman with her tongue, her fingers, her privates, some of each, so many that I couldn't tell where one tongue ended and one beautiful pink (or black or brown) sharpshooter began. I was a writhing mass of nerve endings and, what's the word, euphoria. Once I shed my inhibitions, I couldn't get enough. I was addicted. I couldn't wait for the next round of the Game, the next danger, the next thrill, and all those beautiful notches.

Round Thirteen: kink. Leather corsets and gags and

hip boots and all manner of rings. We bought them in mail-order catalogs, in stores, from other people.

Round Fourteen: advanced kink. Clamps and needles and things that made you bleed just a little. (Bobby never even noticed.) Bondage.

Discipline.

Whipping, being whipped. Hanky-spanky. I got the essence: freedom beyond humiliation, beyond obedience and being obeyed. One pure climax of mind, spirit and body.

Round Twenty: prostitution in a bordello.

Round Twenty-one: streetwalking. Alleys and cheap motels and once in a ditch with the john's coat under me. Once on a pile of garbage. I don't know what that guy was thinking. Or if he was even thinking at all.

Round Thirty: Tutu seriously upped the stakes.

She deliberately got herself arrested. She was with some john when a police car crept by, and she flashed the officer and gave him the finger. Her husband cried for three days and three nights, smashed all her porcelain figurines, and moved to another state.

So I tried to bribe a policeman out of a speeding ticket with some "personal attention," as he said at my trial. He blushed when asked by the prosecutor to be more specific. I was afraid his gentlemanly ways would make me lose.

Still, Tutu insisted she had won that round because while we both had been arrested, she had done time while I had gotten probation. I sulked but finally admitted she was right. Fair was fair.

My husband left me. Now we had both been abandoned, but Tutu and I didn't care. The Game was all we wanted. We were jackals on the hunt, sex princesses, addicts of the competition, two little trick-or-treaters ringing every doorbell we could think of. Winning through ecstasy. We could have run seminars. We ran every night, prowling, one-upping each other, high-fiving and shouting, "Bonus notches!" which you could get when you upped the stakes in a significant way. An extra point, two if it was really, really special. See, it's a play on words: *Buenas noches* means "Good evening" in Spanish. We used to say it in high school, thought we were so funny: "Bonus notches, Tutita." "Bonus notches, Boobita." (It took me a while to develop.)

Now we were at Round Thirty-six, convicted sex criminals moving into the depraved, the patently illegal. The really good and gross stuff that made you think, *What the hell am I doing?* And then you felt like shouting, *But it's me who's doing it! Who would have imagined I could get this far?*

I would pull ahead, then Tutu, and then we would be even.

It was glorious.

And then she thought to beat me once and for all. At the time, I thought it was cheating. Now I feel more generous.

When they found the guy all trussed up in leather with a mask and strangled, and her sobbing unconvincingly (on purpose, of course) that she hadn't meant to kill him, it was this erotic thing he loved to do, I was so furious with her I was almost declared a hostile witness at her trial. Not that it mattered much: she was convicted and sentenced to years and years of jail.

She was led out of the courtroom in shackles, triumphant. "I win," she mouthed at me as the reporters and cameras and onlookers swarmed around her. "I definitely win."

But she was wrong. She had to be wrong. I had to win.

And that's why I have come to you. You with your sneaky ways and secret glances and all that work to cover your tracks that was so unnecessary. I followed you. I *wanted* you.

I wanted *this.*

Oh, I'll scream and fight and I'll beg, but inside I will be soaring. Maybe I will even manage to laugh, though with this gag on, it will only sound like a muffled whimper. I've taken a lot of pain in my day, although I suspect you really know how to dish it out.

You know what you're doing.

And somehow, as I watch you take out your instruments, I doubt I will laugh. In fact, I'm starting to panic a little, which I guess is understandable. But I'm committed. I have to hold on to that. There's no turning back, clearly. This is the big one.

You're smiling at me. Your teeth are big and ugly and yellow. You look so nuts, I'm panicking even more. God *damn,* this is going to really hurt. You are going to really do me.

You're coming closer. I see the scalpel. You're about to bust your buttons, aren't you? You think you ensnared me. It took me months, but I figured out your route, your habits. I even watched you pick up someone else. You were so obvious, I thought she might be a police decoy. I saw the headlines the next day, imagined the picture the paper refused to print because it was too graphic.

Of all the murderous lunatics in this great nation of ours, I picked you because you're savage, and because you use razors, and scalpels, and knives that can cut through car bumpers.

You make notches.

So come on. Do it. Do it hard and vicious and merciless and agonizing. Never mind my struggling. Never mind the pleading in my eyes. Put me in headlines so big they'll talk about it at her jail for weeks.

Oh, God, just do it. Don't make me wait. Don't

make me suffer. But that's what it's about, isn't it? Making me suffer.

Making me win.

Take *that*, Tutu.

Oh, God, God, I'm winning. I'm winning so *bad*. I'm winning.

I'm

THE CONTRIBUTORS

Gary Brandner

Californian Brandner has written twenty-seven novels, 100-odd short stories, six screenplays sold, and two produced. His latest work is 1995's *The Boiling Pool.* Of "Close Encounters," he reported, "Maybe it's just because I've been waiting for years, since Publishers Weekly credited *The Howling* to Whit Streiber, to say hi there."

Terry Campbell

Texan Campbell's fiction has appeared in the anthologies *100 Wicked Little Witch Stories* and *Blood Muse,* as well as several small press magazines. He remarked about his story "The Healing Touch," "The seed . . . was a brief conversation with an elderly man whose hand was deformed much like the young man described in the story. As much as I tried to resist, my stare kept returning to his hand, and I started thinking: How many times in this man's life has he had to endure the stares of others? What if someone wanted only to heal the pain of the afflicted, rather than draw attention to it? And what if this person became so obsessed with his or her desire to nurture that normalcy was shunned?"

Max Allan Collins

Max Allan Collins has earned an unprecedented seven Private Eye Writers of America "Shamus" nominations for his Nathan Heller thrillers. Iowan Collins also wrote, directed, and executive-produced "Mommy," based on a short story from *Fear Itself.* "Interstate 666" is based on Collins's own fascination with urban legends, and is set to become a future film-directing project for him. Collins noted, "Thanks to Phil Dingeldein, who has worked with me on a prospective screen version of this story. This novella is dedicated to Brinke Stevens."

Deidra Cox

More than one hundred thirty pieces of short fiction by Cox have appeared since 1989 in such publications as *The Year's Best Horror, Desire Burn,* and *Crossroads.* Of "Players," she said, "We received some bad news that some friends were in the midst of an ugly divorce. Once the shock wore off, I looked at my husband and wondered exactly how far would a person go to keep someone faithful."

O'Neil De Noux

A former homicide detective, Louisiana's De Noux has written four mystery novels: *Grim Reaper, The Big Kiss, Blue Orleans,* and *Crescent City Kills,* with a fifth awaiting publication. His short fiction has appeared in dozens of magazines and anthologies throughout the world. He also teaches mystery writing at Tulane University.

Michael Garrett

Native Alabamian Garrett is coeditor of the *Hot Blood* series, author of the movie-optioned suspense thriller *Keeper* and numerous short stories, but he was first published in the proliferation of comics fanzines in the mid-1960s. He is an instructor for the Writer's Digest School, teaches writing workshops across the nation, and is a frequent speaker at writing conferences. He and coeditor Jeff Gelb have been best friends for more than thirty years.

Ray Garton

California's Garton is the author of *Seductions, Live Girls, Dark Channel, Lot Lizards,* and a dozen other books and numerous short stories. His most recent books are *Pieces of Hate, Shackled Innocents,* and *Biofire.* His next novel is a romantic thriller called *Loveless.*

Jeff Gelb

As coeditor and cocreator of the *Hot Blood* series, Gelb is thrilled to see it reach its eighth volume and advises *Hot Blood* fans to watch for future volumes. When the California resident is not editing or writing horror fiction, he usually can be found reading horror comic books (especially ECs, Harveys, and Jack Kirby monster comics) from his extensive collection.

Brian Hodge

Hodge has written for books, films, and comics. His most recent novels include *Prototype* and *Miles to Go before I Weep*. He has also published close to sixty short stories and novelettes. Of "121st Day of Sodom," he admitted, "I've long had a fascination with the issue of sexual control, both in philosophy and practice. Who wields it, who surrenders it, and why; and the way the undercurrents of power can be very contrary to the way they appear on the surface. Plus, I'm always fascinated by anything that gets carried to an extreme . . . because on the far frontiers of experience can lie distinct revelations, if you're ready to face them. Or maybe the whole story was just fantasy fulfillment."

Nancy Holder

Holder has written eighteen novels and more than one hundred short stories, articles, and columns. She has also written comic books, game fiction, and television commercials. A four-time winner of the Bram Stoker Award, she has been translated into more than twenty languages. The Californian's most recent novel, *Witchlight,* written with Melanie Tem, was a 1996 release. Holder has new stories in *Mother, Gothic Ghosts,* and *A Horror a Day.*

Graham Masterton

Masterton has just seen published the last of his Manitou trilogy, *Burial.* Forthcoming titles include *The House That Jack Built* and *Wednesday's Child.* "Heroine" was inspired by the recent discovery of a crashed B-17 buried in the Downs close to his home in Epsom, England.

Rex Miller and Lynne Gauger

A decade ago, Jeff Gelb bought Miller's first short story, "The Voice," for *Hot Blood*. Since then, Miller has written thirteen books, two teleplays, and more than fifty short works. This collaborative story is Lynne Gauger's first published fiction.

Thomas S. Roche

Roche is a California-based writer whose works have appeared in *Blood Muse, Dark Angels, Splatterpunks 2,* and others. He recently edited *Noirotica.* "Razor-blade Valentines," he reported, "is part of a series of stories I wrote about the cyclical repetition of suicide rituals by ghosts. It has to do with the inevitability of the past and how our choices define us."

John B. Rosenman

Two books of Rosenman's horror/fantasy/SF short stories are due for publication by 1997, while short fiction is due to appear in *Lore, Fantastic Worlds, The Cosmic Unicorn,* and elsewhere. Of "Trophies," the Virginia resident said, "perhaps it's sexist, but I've often felt the female of the species is deadlier than the male, and therefore a prime source of horror."

T. Diane Slatton

Illinois resident Slatton has sold stories to *100 Wicked Little Witch Stories, Desire Burn,* and others, with nonfiction appearing in *Spin, Reader's Digest,* and others. She mentioned, "I've thankfully never met a person like Harrison Jenko. Any police officer who's ever pulled me over to hit me with a bogus traffic citation has been every inch a gentleman."

Thomas Tessier

Tessier's short stories have appeared in numerous anthologies, and he is the author of several novels, including *The Nightwalker, Phantom, Finishing Touches,* and *Rapture.* He lives in Connecticut, where he is working on a new novel. "La Mourante," Tessier reported, "is a title that Henry James meant to use for one of his novels but never did. I took it, since it seems somehow appropriate."

Graham Watkins

Watkins is the author of four novels: *Dark Winds, The Fire Within, Kaleidoscope Eyes,* and *Virus,* with a fifth in progress. Watkins has turned "Hillbettys," his story from *Hotter Blood,* into a screenplay for Roger Corman's Concord/New Horizons Films. Watkins reported that "Comeback" was inspired by the TV show "Married . . . with Children," "where there is an ongoing joke about Bud Bundy's use of inflatable love dolls."

Pocket Books presents
its collection of
EROTIC HORROR

HOT BLOOD 66424-7/$5.99
HOTTER BLOOD 70149-5/$5.99
HOTTEST BLOOD 75367-3/$5.99

THE HOT BLOOD SERIES:

DEADLY AFTER DARK 87087-4/$5.50
SEEDS OF FEAR 89846-9/$5.50
STRANGER BY NIGHT 53754-7/$5.99
FEAR THE FEVER 53765-2/$5.99
KISS AND KILL 53766-0/$5.99

EDITED BY JEFF GELB AND
MICHAEL GARRETT